THE TRUTH AND OTHER LIES

SASCHA ARANGO

Translated by Imogen Taylor

SIMON & SCHUSTER

London · New York · Sydney · Toronto · New Delhi

A CBS COMPANY

First published in Germany by C. Bertelsmann, 2014
First published in Great Britain by Simon & Schuster UK Ltd, 2015
This paperback edition published by Simon & Schuster UK Ltd, 2016
A CBS company

5 7 9 10 8 6 4

Simon & Schuster UK Ltd
1st Floor
222 Gray's Inn Road
London WC1X 8HB

www.simonandschuster.co.uk

Simon & Schuster Australia, Sydney
Simon & Schuster India, New Delhi

A CIP catalogue record for this book is available from the British Library

Paperback ISBN: 978-1-4711-3972-7
eBook ISBN: 978-1-4711-3973-4

Typeset in the UK by Hewer Text UK Ltd, Edinburgh
Printed and bound in Great Britain by CPI Group (UK) Ltd, Croydon, CR0 4YY

For Kadee

'Perhaps deep down all horror is helplessness that wants help from us'
Rainer Maria Rilke, *Letters to a Young Poet*

1

No getting away from it. A quick glance at the image was enough to give shape to the dim suspicions of the past months. The embryo lay curled up like an amphibian, one eye looking straight at him. Was that a leg or a tentacle above the dragon's tail?

Moments of absolute certainty in life are few and far between. But in this instant, Henry saw into the future. The amphibian would grow into a person. It would have rights and claims, it would ask questions, and at some point it would experience everything it takes to become a human being.

The ultrasound image was about the size of a postcard. On it, to the right of the embryo, a spectrum of grey could be made out; to the left were letters; at the top were the date, the mother's name and the doctor's name. There wasn't the slightest doubt in Henry's mind that it was real.

Betty sat beside him at the steering wheel, smoking, and saw tears in his eyes. She laid her hand on his cheek; she thought they were tears of joy. But he was thinking of his wife, Martha. Why couldn't she have a child with him? Why did he have to be sitting here in the car with this other woman?

He despised himself, he felt shame, he was genuinely sorry. His motto had always been that life gives you everything—but never everything at once.

It was afternoon. The monotonous rumble of the surf rose from the cliffs; the wind flattened the grasses and pressed against the side windows of the green Subaru. Henry only had to start the engine and put his foot on the accelerator and the car would shoot over the cliffs and plunge into the surf. In five seconds it would all be over; the impact would kill all three of them. But first he'd have to get out of the passenger seat to change places with Betty. Much too complicated.

'Say something, Henry!'

What should he say? The whole business was bad enough as it was; this thing in her womb was no doubt already moving, and if Henry had learnt anything, it was to reveal nothing that's best left unsaid.

Betty had only ever seen him cry once—when he was awarded an honorary doctorate at Smith College in Massachusetts. Until then she had thought he never cried. Henry had sat quietly in the front row, thinking of his wife.

Betty leaned over the gearstick and hugged him. They listened in silence to one another's breathing, then Henry opened the passenger door and threw up in the grass. He saw the lasagne he'd made Martha for lunch. It looked like an embryo compote of flesh-coloured lumps of dough. At the sight of it, he choked and began to cough uncontrollably.

Betty slipped off her shoes, jumped out of the car, pulled Henry up from his seat, locked her arms round his ribcage and squeezed energetically until lasagne streamed from his nostrils. Phenomenal, the way she did the right thing without thinking about it. The two of them stood there in the grass next to the Subaru, while sea spray whipped about them in the wind.

'Tell me. What should we do?'

The right answer would have been: *My love, this is not going to end well.* But that kind of answer has consequences. It changes things or makes them disappear altogether. Regrets are no more use then. And who wants to change anything that's good and convenient?

'I'll drive home and tell my wife everything.'

'Really?'

Henry saw the astonishment on Betty's face; he was surprised himself. Why had he said that? Henry wasn't given to exaggeration; it hadn't been necessary to say he'd tell Martha everything.

'What do you mean, *everything*?'

'Everything. I shall quite simply tell her everything. No more lies.'

'And what if she forgives you?'

'How could she?'

'And the baby?'

'I hope it's a girl.'

Betty hugged Henry and kissed him on the mouth. 'Henry, you can be a great man.'

Yes, he could be a great man. He would drive home and put truth in place of falsehood. Reveal everything at last, all the nasty details—well, maybe not quite all, but the essentials. It would mean cutting deep into healthy flesh. Tears would flow and it would hurt dreadfully, himself included. It would be the end of all trust and harmony between Martha and him—but it would also be an act of liberation. He would no longer be an unprincipled bastard, no longer have to be so ashamed of himself. It had to be done. Truth before beauty—the rest would sort itself out.

He put his arms around Betty's slender waist. A stone was lying in the grass, big enough and heavy enough to inflict a lethal blow. He had only to bend down to pick it up.

'Come on, get in.'

He sat behind the steering wheel and started the engine. Instead of shooting forwards over the cliffs, he put the car into reverse and let the Subaru roll backwards. A great mistake, he would later decide.

Barely visible, the narrow road of perforated concrete slabs wound its way through a dense pine grove from the cliffs to the forest track where his car was parked, concealed by low-hanging branches. Betty lowered the window, lit herself another menthol cigarette and inhaled deeply.

'She won't do herself any harm, will she?'

'I certainly hope not.'

'How will she react? Will you tell her it's me?'

That *what* is you? Henry wanted to ask.

Instead, he said, 'I'll tell her if she asks me.'

Of course Martha would ask. Anyone who discovers they've been systematically cheated on wants to know why and for how long and with whom. It's normal. Betrayal is a riddle we want to solve.

Betty laid her hand with the lighted cigarette on Henry's thigh. 'Darling, we were careful. I mean, neither of us wanted a child, did we?'

Henry could not have agreed more wholeheartedly. No, he had not wanted a child, least of all with Betty. She was his lover, she'd never make a good mother; she was far too hard-hearted, too wrapped up in herself for that. Having his child would give her power over him; she would destroy his cover and put pressure on him, until everything reached its logical conclusion. For a time he had toyed with the idea of a vasectomy, but some vague impulse had held him back—maybe his desire to have a child with Martha after all.

'It looks as if it wants to exist,' he said.

Betty smiled; her lips were trembling. Henry had pitched it just right.

'I think it'll be a girl.'

They got out, swapped places again. Betty sat behind the steering wheel and pulled on a shoe. Without thinking, she put her foot down on the clutch and moved the gearstick back and forth.

He's not pleased, she thought. But wasn't that asking a bit much of a man who had just decided to change his life and end his marriage? Although their affair had been going on for years, Betty knew very little about Henry, but this much she did know: Henry was not a family man.

She can't wait, he thought. She can't wait for me to give everything up for her. He did not, however, intend to exchange his quiet, carefree existence for a family life he wasn't cut out for. After the grand confession to his wife, he'd have to see about a new identity. It would be hard work, thinking up another Henry, a Henry just for Betty. The mere thought made him feel tired.

'Can I do anything?'

Henry nodded. 'Stop smoking.'

Betty took a drag on her cigarette, then flicked it away. 'It'll be awful.'

'Yes, it'll be awful. I'll give you a ring when it's over.'

She put the car in gear. 'How are you getting on with the novel?'

'Not much more to go.'

He bent down to her through the open door. 'Have you told anybody about us?'

'Not a soul,' she replied.

'It is my child, isn't it? I mean, it really is there, it is going to happen?'

'Yes, it's yours. It's going to happen.'

She offered him her slightly parted lips for a kiss. Reluctantly, he stooped to her; her tongue penetrated his mouth like a fat, threadless screw. Henry closed the driver's door of the Subaru. She drove down the forest track in the direction of the main road. He watched her until she had disappeared. Then he stamped out her half-smoked cigarette that lay smouldering in the grass. He believed her. Betty wouldn't lie to him; she had far too little imagination for that. She was young and sporty, and much more elegant than Martha. She was beautiful and not as bright, but extremely practical. And now she was pregnant with his child—a paternity test was hardly necessary.

* * *

Betty's cool pragmatism had impressed Henry from the first time they'd met. If she liked something, she took it. She had wit, she had slender feet, she had freckled breasts as round as oranges, green eyes and curly blonde hair. The first time he saw her she was wearing a dress with a print of endangered species.

Their affair had begun the moment they met. Henry hadn't had to make an effort or put on an act or court her. As so often, he hadn't had to do anything, because she thought he was a genius. For that reason it didn't bother her in the slightest that he was married and didn't want children. On the contrary, it was all a question of time. She had waited a long time for a man like him—she was quite frank about that. In her opinion most men lacked greatness. What she meant by that, she didn't say.

Now, Betty was editor-in-chief at Moreany Publishing House. She'd started out as a temp in the marketing department, although she considered herself overqualified because she already had a degree in literature. Most of the seminars had been boring and she regretted not having taken her parents' advice and studied law. In spite of her qualifications, the prospects of promotion at the publishing house were limited. In her lunchbreak she would sneak into the editors' offices to browse. One day, out of sheer boredom, she pulled Henry's typewritten text out of the slush pile and took it with her to read in the staff kitchen. Henry had sent the typescript without an accompanying note, so as to save on postage. Until then he'd always been strapped for cash.

Betty read about thirty pages, leaving her food untouched. Then she rushed up to the third floor, into the office of Claus Moreany, the founder of the publishing house, and put an abrupt end to his afternoon nap. Four hours later the man himself was on the phone to Henry.

'Good afternoon, this is Claus Moreany.'

'Really? Gosh!'

'You have written something marvellous. Something truly marvellous. Have you sold the rights yet?'

He hadn't. *Frank Ellis* sold ten million copies worldwide. A thriller, as they're so wonderfully called, with a great deal of violence and little of a cheering nature. It was the story of an autistic man who becomes a police officer in order to find his sister's killer. The first hundred thousand copies sold out in only a month and were no doubt read cover to cover. The profits saved Moreany Publishing House from bankruptcy. Today, eight years on, Henry was a bestselling author, translated into twenty languages around the world, a winner of countless prizes and God knows what else. Five bestselling novels had now been published by Moreany; all of them had been made into films and adapted for the stage, and

Frank Ellis was already being used as a set text in schools. Almost a classic. And Henry was still married to Martha.

Apart from Henry, only Martha knew that he hadn't written a single word of the novels himself.

2

Henry had often wondered what course his life would have taken if he hadn't met Martha. The answer he gave himself never varied—the same as before. He would not have become a significant author; would not, as a result, have been able to live a free and prosperous life; certainly wouldn't drive an Italian sports car—and no one would know his name. Henry was quite straight with himself on the matter. He would have remained invisible—an art in itself. Of course, the struggle for survival is exciting. It is, after all, only scarcity that gives things their value; money loses all meaning as soon as there's plenty of it. No denying any of that. But aren't apathy and indifference a reasonable price to pay for a life of wealth and luxury, and better than hunger and suffering and bad teeth any day? You don't have to be famous to be happy, especially as popularity is all too often confused with significance. But ever since Henry had stepped out of the shadows of anonymity into the light of a particular existence, his life had been incomparably more comfortable. And so for years now his sole concern had been to preserve the status quo. There was no more for him to achieve. In that, he remained a realist. Even if it was boring.

The manuscript of *Frank Ellis* was his discovery. It was lying wrapped in greaseproof paper under a stranger's bed. Henry found it, his head throbbing with pain, as he hunted for his left sock so that he could steal out of the stranger's room as he'd stolen out of so many others. He couldn't remember the woman lying next to him in bed, and he felt no desire to get to know her now. He could only see her foot and the feminine silhouette running from the dip of her pelvis up to her fine, chestnut-brown hair, and he investigated no further. The stove was cold; the room was dark. It smelt of dust and bad breath. Time to make himself scarce.

Henry was hideously thirsty because he'd drunk a particularly large amount of alcohol the night before. It had been the eve of his thirty-sixth birthday. Nobody had wished him any happy returns. How could they? Nobody knew. Who could possibly know? Drifters don't form close friendships, and his parents had been dead for a long time.

He had no flat of his own, no fixed income and no idea what he was to do next in life. Why should he? The future is uncertain. Anyone who says they know what the future holds is a liar. The past is nothing but memory and thus pure fabrication—the present alone is certain, gives us space to evolve, and is over again in an instant. What tormented Henry far more than uncertainty was the thought of certainty. Knowing what lay in store for him was tantamount to the pendulum over the pit. What was there left to hope for except remorse, death and decay? In keeping with this entirely clear-eyed outlook, Henry defined his life as a cumulative process, to be judged by historians only after his death. And happy is he who leaves nothing behind; he need fear no judgment.

Keeping silent goes against human nature. Thus, the opening sentence of the manuscript. It might easily, Henry thought, be something he would say. Absolutely to the point and so simple. He read the next sentence, and then on and on. His left sock stayed off; he didn't creep out of the little flat. Nor did he, as was his wont, walk off with whatever cash or items of value happened to be lying around in order to buy himself something to eat.

From the first paragraph he had the impression that the story was not unlike his own. He read the whole manuscript in a sitting, turning the pages as quietly as he could, so as not to wake up the unknown woman gently snoring beside him. There were no corrections on the densely typed pages as far as he could make out, and no typos either—not a comma out of place. Every now and then, Henry stopped reading for a moment to take a closer look at the sleeping woman. Was it possible they'd met before? Had he told her about himself and then forgotten they'd ever met? What was her name again? Had she even mentioned it? She hadn't talked much, that was for sure. She was unprepossessing, delicate, with long eyelashes that now shielded her closed eyes.

* * *

When Martha awoke in the early afternoon, Henry had already lit the stove, solved the mystery of the dripping tap, fixed the shower curtain, cleared up the kitchen and made fried eggs. He had oiled the small typewriter that stood on the kitchen table and straightened out a jammed key over the gas flame. Martha's manuscript was lying wrapped up under the bed again. She sat down at the table and devoured the fried eggs.

He suggested they live together and she said nothing, which he took for a yes.

They spent the entire day together. She told him how he had carried on the night before, declaring that he was insignificant in every way. Henry agreed with this, but could no longer remember anything.

Later, they ate ice cream and sauntered through the botanical garden, where Henry told her a bit more about his past. He spoke of his childhood, which had ended with his mother walking out and his father falling down the stairs. He didn't mention the years he'd spent in hiding.

Martha didn't interrupt him once, nor did she ask any questions. She held his arm tight as they walked through the tropical hothouse, and at some point she laid her head on his shoulder. Until that day, Henry had never told anyone so much about himself, and most of what he said was actually true. He left out nothing important, didn't gloss over anything, and made almost none of it up. It was a happy afternoon in the botanical garden, the first of many happy afternoons with Martha.

The next night too they slept in Martha's bed near the stove. He was tender and sober this time, gentle and almost shy. And she was completely silent, her breath hot and quick. Later, when he was fast asleep, Martha got up and sat down at the typewriter in the kitchen. Henry was woken by the clatter of the keys. Steady, with short breaks, a full stop. Then the ringing of the little bell at the end of the line. Full stop, new line, full stop, paragraph. A high-pitched rasping sound as she pulled the typed paper out of the typewriter, and several short rasping sounds as she put in the new sheet. So that's how literature is born, he thought. The clatter went on all night until morning.

The next thing Henry did was to mend the bed. Then he got hold of a rubber mat for the typewriter to stand on, procured two new kitchen chairs, and bored open the electricity meter to save on heating costs. While he was getting all that done, he reflected on the possibilities of creating a home without any capital and wondered to what extent he was cut out for it.

He tidied and cleaned. Martha didn't comment on his domestic activities. She didn't ever comment on anything; Henry admired that. He didn't, however, have the feeling that she was indifferent or devoid of opinion—no, she was quite simply contented and could find no fault with him. It was as if she had foreseen everything.

It struck Henry that Martha never read her stories herself. She never talked about them; she wasn't proud of them. When she'd finished one, she started on the next, like a tree shedding its leaves in the autumn. The story must have taken shape in her mind even as she was working on the previous one, for there was no pause for inspiration. For a long time it remained unclear to Henry what she lived off. She had studied, but did not reveal what. She must have had some savings, but only rarely went to the bank. If there was nothing to eat, she ate nothing. In the afternoon she regularly left the flat to go swimming in the municipal baths. Henry followed her once; she really did just go swimming.

In the cellar, Henry found a suitcase filled with rotting manuscripts, hastily buried like children's corpses beneath mouldy rat droppings. The pages had clumped together into a pulp; only the odd phrase was still legible. Lost stories. The manuscript of *Frank Ellis* would have rotted too, or been turned into a brief blast of heat in the stove on a cold day, if Henry hadn't hidden it. He was to thank for that. As he would later tell his conscience, even if he hadn't created *Frank Ellis*, he had at least rescued it. That had to count for something.

'I'm not interested in literature,' Martha said on the subject. 'I just want to write.'

Henry made a mental note of the sentence for later. Where Martha in her hermetically sealed world got hold of the ideas for creating such illustrious characters remained a mystery to him. She wasn't well travelled, and yet she knew the whole world. He cooked for her; they talked, were silent, made love. At night she got up to write; in the early afternoon he made them something to eat, and then read what she'd written. He kept every single page of her writing safe; she never asked about it. In this way their love grew quietly, as a matter of course. They took pleasure in doing things together and profited from one another. Henry could not imagine ever being happier. It was just up to him not to destroy the harmony.

Henry sent the manuscript of *Frank Ellis* in his own name to four publishers he'd looked up in the Yellow Pages. First, he had had to make a solemn vow to Martha that he would under no circumstances reveal who had written it. It was to remain a lifelong secret, and if anything actually got published, then it could *only* be under *his* name. Henry thought that was all right and swore not to tell. In his own way, he kept his word.

* * *

For a long time, there was no reply. Henry forgot he'd sent it off, and if he'd known how infinitesimal the chances of an unsolicited manuscript are, he wouldn't have invested in the postage. But ignorance often proves to be a true blessing.

Meanwhile, Henry worked at the fruit market. He got up at two in the morning and came home towards midday, dead tired and reeking of vegetables, to set to and cook something for Martha.

Martha introduced Henry to her parents. She had hesitated for a long time, and Henry understood why when he met her father. Throughout their first meeting, Martha's father, a fireman who'd taken early retirement, eyed Henry with smouldering ill will from his velour armchair. Rheumatism was gnawing away at his joints and had already claimed his thumb. Martha's mother was a cashier at a supermarket checkout, a cheerful woman, warm and sensitive, just the way a mother ought to be.

They drank coffee with cardamom in the upholstered landscape of the living room and chatted about trivialities. Henry saw yellow birds in a cage on the sideboard, waiting for death. The father's pride and joy was his collection of historic firemen's helmets, which he kept in an illuminated glass-fronted cabinet. He told Henry all about every one of them, specifying date, place of origin and function, while his eyes scrutinised Henry's face for signs of weariness or indifference. But Henry endured the ordeal with unflagging stoicism and even interrupted him to ask interested questions.

There was a cold winter. Henry got hold of a new door and two fabulous electric blankets, and insulated the windows. He had spotted the door in a skip full of scrap timber. He climbed into the skip in thick, driving snow to salvage the heavy door, which he shouldered and lugged home on his back like a leaf-cutter ant. He took the plane to it here and there, added a piece at the bottom and hung it. Now there was no longer a cold draught coming in.

Martha was delighted. Henry's handyman skills had always turned women on. DIY and hobbies drive away the demons of boredom and negative thoughts. Henry simply liked mending things—not in order to impress, but because it was fun and because there was nothing better to do.

The following spring, Henry killed his father-in-law. He bought him an historic helmet once worn in the Vienna fire brigade, which is, as it happens, the oldest professional fire brigade in the world. The ageing collector's surprise and pleasure were so great that his aneurysm ruptured and he fell down dead. Henry had carried off the perfect tyrannicide without either knowing what he was doing or meaning to do it. As a result he had no guilty conscience, because, as Henry said to himself, the insidious blood vessel in the old man's brain could have burst when he was taking a shit. Everyone was pleased and no one suspected anything.

The entire helmet collection disappeared into the earth along with the dead fireman. Martha's mother blossomed; she gave away the yellow birds and emigrated a year later with an American businessman to Wisconsin, where she was struck by lightning. From then on she wrote long (now only ever left-handed) letters about her new life in America.

Then Moreany's call came. Henry cycled to the publisher's. If he had had any idea what a fateful course the whole affair would take, he might perhaps not have gone.

* * *

Betty was waiting for him in the lobby. They got into the lift together and went up to the sixth floor. Her lily-of-the-valley perfume filled the lift. She saw that he had handyman's hands; he spotted a small hole in her earlobe and the constellation of the Plough mapped out on her throat in ravishing freckles. On the regrettably short journey up, he could intuit her sizing up his DNA. When the lift doors opened, the essentials between them had been settled.

Moreany came round the side of his publisher's desk and touched Henry with both hands, as you might greet a long-lost friend. His desk was laden with books and manuscripts. Right on top was the manuscript of *Frank Ellis*. This was pretty much what Henry had imagined a publisher would look like.

Henry kept his promise to Martha and introduced himself as the author. This turned out to be quite straightforward. He didn't have to say or prove anything special, because everyone knows an author can't do anything except write, and anyone can write. You don't need any particular knowledge or skill, or have to say anything particular about yourself. Apart from a modicum of life experience, you don't require any education to speak of; there's no need to produce a diploma, only a manuscript. You leave the final judgment to your critics and readers, because the less you speak about your work the more radiant your aura. He wasn't interested in literature, Henry explained. He just wanted to write. That hit the spot.

The novel sold fantastically well. When the first royalty cheque arrived, he and Martha moved into a larger, warmer flat and got married. The money kept on pouring in, heaps of it. Money didn't trigger any kind of buying reflex or wasteful impulses in Martha. She carried on writing undeterred, while Henry went on shopping sprees. He bought himself costly suits, expensive moments with beautiful women, and an Italian car. Moreany gave Henry a share in the profits that were now raining down on Moreany Publishing House. Henry felt like a gangster who has pulled off the perfect crime, and drove Martha all the way across Europe to Portugal in the Maserati. They stayed in good hotels; otherwise nothing much changed. Martha continued to write at night; Henry played tennis and saw to everything else. He did the shopping, wrote shopping lists and learnt to cook Asian food.

Every afternoon he would read the new pages. No one except him got to see a single line before the book was finished. He only ever said whether he liked it or not. Mostly he did like it. Finally, he would take the finished manuscript in person to Moreany. Betty and Moreany would read it simultaneously in Moreany's wood-panelled office, while Henry lay on the sofa in the adjoining room and read the *Adventures of the Grand Vizier Iznogoud*, which are, as it happens, the best comics in the world.

For hours, absolute silence would reign in the publishing house, until Betty and Moreany had finished reading. Then Moreany would summon the sales manager. 'We have a book!' he would shout. Eight weeks later the press campaign would be launched. Only selected journalists were allowed a look at a proof copy in Moreany's office. They had to sign confidentiality agreements, because although they were expected to hype up the novel in the media they were also to torment the public by withholding information.

Martha never accompanied Henry to public appearances. When he went to writers festivals or public readings it was Betty who went with him. A lot of people took her for his wife, which to all appearances made complete sense, because they looked like the perfect couple.

Wherever he went, Henry was greeted with applause, smiled at, shown around and congratulated. He didn't look particularly happy on such occasions, because he didn't enjoy the walkabout. This, however, strengthened the general delight at his modesty, especially among the women. Henry's shy, understated manner was purely precautionary, for he never forgot that he wasn't a writer but a mere fraud, a frog in a snake's territory.

Besides, he had trouble remembering all the friendly faces and new names. Whenever he stood still, knots of people formed. Cameras flashed, greedy eyes drank him in without let-up, and he was always being shown something he wasn't interested in or having something explained to him he didn't really understand. He gave short interviews, but refused to discuss his working methods. The feeling of unreality intensified; reality began to blur like a watercolour in the rain— first at the edges, then altogether. Martha had warned him that success was a mere shadow that shifts with the moving sun. The day will come, Henry thought, when the sun will set and they'll realise I don't exist.

It was from his critics that Henry learnt how his work was to be interpreted. He knew himself that the novels were good—after all, he was the one who'd discovered them. But just *how* good they were, and why exactly, came as a surprise to him. He felt sorry for all those poor artists who aren't discovered until after they've perished from nutritional oedema. He would have liked to have read Martha some of the most flattering reviews, but she didn't want to know anything about them. She was already at work on the next novel. Fame meant nothing to her. She read no reviews on principle, while he read every single one, underlining the most flattering passages with a ruler, cutting them out and sticking them in a scrapbook. *Every sentence a stronghold.* He particularly liked that phrase. It was in bold type in the blurb and had been penned by a certain Peffenkofer, who wrote for the literary supplement of one of the big dailies. It was so wonderfully pithy, Henry thought, it might have been something he would say. But it wasn't. Nothing was his.

3

Death of an author on a wet road. A lurch, one's entire life flashing past, then eternity. Such were Henry's thoughts as he drove home from the cliffs past luminous yellow rape fields. Could any death be more tragic and at the same time more unjust than that inflicted by the cold hand of chance? And so fitting for him. Camus had died such a death, and Randall Jarrell and Ödön von Horváth—no, not him, poor thing. He was killed by a branch falling from a tree on the Champs-Elysées.

Henry was now forty-four. The sun of success was beating down on him; death would immortalise him, and the secret was safe with Martha. She would carry on writing after his death and leave all the manuscripts to rot in the cellar. Henry found that very reassuring, even if he didn't intend to die before his wife. In this instant, however, he wished he could.

Anything was easier than to confess to her that he was to father a child with another woman. And with Betty, of all people.

Henry saw the two women standing at his grave. Martha, the hidden source of his fame, so delicate and unfathomable, side-by-side with Betty, the freckled Venus, the mother of his child. He hoped the two of them would get along and not wage war on one another; they were after all so very different. And between them his child. Martha would spot the child's resemblance to Henry straight away. Would she ever be able to forgive him? Did Betty have what it took to make a good mother? Not really. But what did it matter to him now? A lot of people would weep at his grave, some indeed would suffer, others would be jolly pleased. But the best thing was that he wouldn't be available for anyone; he'd no longer have to be ashamed of himself, or put on an act, or be afraid of anything. Terrific.

Unfortunately, the road was dry and there wasn't a tree in sight. Henry's dark blue Maserati had every conceivable safety gimmick: ABS and EPS, and all the rest of it. The airbag would cushion his head, the explosive charge would tighten his seatbelt. The car wouldn't let him die—and Henry saw himself joining the undead, dwindling on a heart-lung-machine. A ghastly thought. Henry cranked up the speed. At two hundred kilometres an hour, even the best safety system would be no use if a tree came along now.

His phone rang. It was Moreany. Henry took his foot off the accelerator.

'Henry, where are you?'

'On page three hundred.'

'Oh, how splendid. How splendid!' Moreany liked to say anything gratifying twice over. Quite unnecessarily, in Henry's opinion. 'Can I read some?'

'Soon. I'm still twenty pages short, I reckon.'

'Twenty? That's fantastic, fantastic. How much longer do you need?'

'Twenty minutes.'

Moreany laughed.

'Then I'll be home and can get back down to it.'

'Listen, Henry, I've decided we'll come out with two hundred and fifty thousand copies.'

Henry knew that Moreany didn't borrow any money from the bank. He didn't want to. Moreany liked to deploy his entire personal wealth in financing the printing and marketing of Henry's books.

'Don't you want to read it first, before you mortgage your house again?'

'I'll mortgage my house when it suits me, old boy, and never more willingly than today. Just imagine— Peffenkofer is asking for an advance proof copy. He *begged* me. What do you think of that?'

Peffenkofer, the man behind *Every sentence a*

stronghold, was a magnet among the critics. In this capacity he drew everything bad out of literary production and left only the good things. There was little that impressed him, nothing that surprised him, and nothing original he didn't already know about. But, whatever one might think of him, he had an eye for what mattered and he revealed beauty, making it shine. He worked out of the public eye; no one knew what he looked like and whether he didn't perhaps still live with his mother.

'Let him wait till you've read it.'

'Of course! Do you have a title?'

'Not yet.'

'We'll think of one. Tell me, when can I read it?'

Henry saw a deer standing in the rape field. He reduced his speed some more. 'You've gone and done it again, Claus. You weren't going to put pressure on me. You might be disappointed.'

'Let me worry about that.'

Henry stopped the car at the side of the road. 'Claus, I still haven't decided how the story's going to end.'

'You've always made the right decision so far.'

'This time it's going to be hard.'

'Have you discussed it with Betty?'

'No.'

'Talk to her. Give her a ring. Arrange to meet her.'

'All in good time, Claus.'

'Only twenty pages to go. I'm thrilled, thrilled. Shall we say ... mid August?'

'Mid August sounds good.'

* * *

Martha and Henry's property stood on a hill, surrounded by thirty hectares of fields and meadows that they leased to farmers. It was a classic half-timbered manor house, with barns built on fieldstone foundations, and its own chapel. Symmetrically planted poplars ran in a straight line to the house. There was no fence enclosing the overgrown garden with its old trees, no sign to keep trespassers out, no name at the door. And yet all the locals knew who lived here.

The black hovawart came bounding towards Henry, twisting energetically in the air. Poncho's joy, untroubled by any knowledge of human nature, never failed to touch Henry. The Maserati rolled on its gently grinding wheels up to the house. Martha hadn't yet returned from her daily swim in the sea, otherwise her folding bicycle would have been propped up next to the front door, which was, as always, open. For almost a year the flyscreen door had been hanging in shreds, because Poncho had simply run through it. Henry had often mended Martha's folding bicycle, and was always patching up the tyres. Her Saab was parked in the barn, but she almost never used it. She could have had a plane or a yacht, but she was content with a folding bike.

Henry stroked the cashmere-like coat of the dog, and let it give the back of his hand a good lick. Then he took a stone and threw it far out into the meadow. He watched Poncho vanish into the long grass to look for it, as if released from a catapult. Fortunate dog—only needs a stone.

As soon as Martha's back from her swim, Henry decided, I shall tell her everything.

Six typed pages lay on the oak surface of the kitchen island, neatly arranged one beside the other. The third part of Chapter Fifty-four. Martha had finished it the night before; Henry had heard the typewriter tapping away into the early hours of the morning. He flung the car key onto the counter, took a carrot out of a wooden dish, bit into it and began to read. Clear and in quick succession, Martha's words followed one upon the other; no word could be added, no word removed without wrecking her trademark style. The chapter fell seamlessly into line with the previous one; the story flowed towards its climax with such assurance that it was as if, instead of having been thought up, it had emerged from itself, like a plant from a seed. Incomprehensible, Henry thought. Just where did this knowledge come from? What was this voice that spoke to her and was so inaudible to him?

When he'd finished reading, Henry opened the selection of fan mail that was forwarded to him by his publisher every day. He signed a few copies of *Frank Ellis*, most of them sent by women. Some of the copies he signed turned up later on eBay at prices which were, in Henry's opinion, completely ridiculous. Some women enclosed photographs of themselves, or pressed flowers, and quite often kiss prints. Henry regularly found locks of hair too, and there were even proposals of marriage, although all the media broadcast the fact that he was already married.

Where should he begin? Start with the worst, the thing about the baby? Or better to leave that out— not everything at once? It wasn't love he felt for Betty; it was more like a cyclical urge such as comes over every man, regardless of the object of his desire. How long had it been going on with her now? Should he count their first meeting or only the exchange of bodily fluids in the Sea Breeze beach motel? When had that been, anyway? Martha would ask. The correct answer called for meticulous checks—Henry owed that to his wife. He took the post with him into his study to look through his papers and find out how long he'd been cheating on his wife. If it had to be the truth, then make it the whole truth.

But first he sat down in his wing armchair and leafed through the *Forensic Journal*—an extraordinarily informative periodical about evil. Anyone planning a crime or in the process of committing one should read specialist literature. It provides information on the risks of discovery consequent upon developments in forensic technology. At the same time it makes clear the futility of battling against human evil, for no science or punishment can contend with the bloodthirstiness innate in us all. From an historico-cultural point of view, greed, vengefulness and stupidity are all natural causes of death, just one facet of the human condition.

Henry awoke when the automatic blinds went up at the picture windows. It must already be early evening. He had told Martha everything. Unsparingly and comprehensively, just as he had planned. He had gone for the hard-hearted version, to make the break easier for his wife.

Listen, my love, he had begun, I'm going to leave you, because I desire another woman and no longer desire you. I can't stand this woman, but that's beside the point just now. I love you, but you're not a stranger to me any more, and for that reason our love is only friendship. It always was. I never could despise you enough to desire you—there's no thrill between us any more, never really was, in fact. Besides, the other woman's younger and more beautiful than you. We've known each other for a while, this woman and I. You know her—it's Betty. Yes, Betty, of all people. She is my trophy, my muse, my slave—and I despise her. We are accomplices. My base instincts arouse her, I idolise her feet, and I'm to tell you from her that she's sorry. I'm really sorry too. Please don't get me wrong, I have the fondest of feelings for you. I worship you as if you were a saint. I've always wanted to protect you, and I have protected you, as best I could, but now matters have become somewhat complicated. Betty's expecting my child. You didn't want one. I don't want one either. Bringing up a child's the last thing I want to do—you know how much screaming babies get on my nerves, and it's bound to scream all the time—but that's just the way things are. Thank you for all you've done—I'm going to feel bad for the rest of my life, I can promise you.

Martha had quietly cried out his name when he'd mentioned the baby. Then the sea had poured into the house and swept her away.

Henry got up from the leather sofa, his right foot still asleep. He massaged it until the blood returned to his toes, and looked dazedly through the glass out onto the fields. The sea had vanished.

He hobbled into the kitchen to make himself a ristretto. The damned sea should have carried *him* away, not her. He was really sorry about what he'd said to Martha, and it was all so completely wrong! Why hadn't he spoken of respect and gratitude, of admiration and of love, which he felt for her like no other man could? But no, he had torn out her heart like a weed. She'd never get over the pain, that was for certain.

He stood on one leg next to the coffee machine, waiting for the water to get hot. It was clear that the whole thing had to be broken to her more gently; it would be better if he didn't mention the baby at all; it might drive her clean out of her senses. But if he kept that quiet, why confess to anything at all? Wasn't everything in fact fine just as it was? The longer Henry pondered, the clearer it became to him that he must spare his wife and tell Betty the whole truth instead. Betty was tough; she'd come to terms with it more easily than Martha. She could start a new life, find a new man for the baby; she was made for survival.

With an elegant creak of the cherrywood floorboards, Martha came down the stairs. She was wearing her silk pyjama suit and Japanese straw sandals; her dark hair was pinned up with an ebony hair slide. As always, she beamed at Henry when she saw him. Martha hardly made a sound when she walked; she was still as petite and light-footed as ever. In the past years she hadn't put on a single ounce. For a long time now they had been sleeping and working separately, Martha upstairs, Henry downstairs. She still only ever wrote at night, and slept, as she had always done, until the afternoon. He saw to everything else. They could have had servants, chauffeurs and gardeners, but Martha wouldn't tolerate anyone except Henry around her.

While he watched the late-night news or sat up until dawn working on his enormous matchstick drilling rig, he would hear her walking round in circles upstairs. Then he would go into the kitchen and make camomile tea. He would carry the teapot up and put it down outside her door. Sometimes he listened at the door without touching it. Then he went quietly back down again. At some point the typewriter would begin to clatter. The demon inside her had started its dictation.

Henry had never seen his wife writing. Quite possible that her loins turned to marble as she wrote and that snakes flickered their tongues in her hair. He'd never dared look.

'Henry, we've got a marten in the roof.'

'A what?'

'A marten. It's making grey lines.'

'Grey lines?'

'Grey stripes that turn into long lines.'

'Like squirrels?'

'Longer and parallel.'

That did indeed suggest a marten. If Martha saw short, grey stripes, it normally meant a small rodent;

if the stripes were longer and parallel, it was bound to be a larger animal.

Martha was a synaesthete from birth. Every smell and every noise had her seeing colours and patterns. Even in school, when she was learning to form her first letters, she saw photisms colouring the words, usually the same shade as the initial letter.

She thought it was normal. It wasn't until she was nine that she realised that not everyone saw these wondrous emanations, which was really rather a shame. She told her mother, and was taken straight to the doctor. The doctor was old school and colour-blind. He prescribed drugs whose sole effect was to make her fat and sluggish. Martha retched up the tablets and never mentioned the colourful apparitions again. It remained her secret until she met Henry.

'Can you come upstairs, please, and have a look?'

Oh, darling, I'm afraid I'm a worthless wretch, Henry wanted to say, not worthy of you at all. I deserve to die—why can't you release me from my suffering? Take pity on me and see me for who I am at last.

'What do you say to fish for supper tonight?'

'Henry, this animal gives me the creeps.'

'Come here, darling.' He hugged her, kissed her hair. Martha laid her head on his chest, drinking in the scent of his skin.

'You smell a little bit orange today,' she said. 'Is it anything serious?'

'I have to tell you something.'

'What?'

He couldn't bring himself to say it. He mumbled something, incomprehensible even to himself, and laughed nervously. When he laughed, Martha saw deep blue spirals leap out of his mouth. No other man in the world laughed pure ultramarine with dancing, star-shaped splashes.

Martha kissed Henry on the lips.

'If it's a woman, keep it to yourself. And now let's go and look for the marten, shall we?'

She took his hand and pulled him up the stairs behind her. Henry followed her, pleased. So she already knew and wasn't cross. The way she understood his failings was something he particularly valued in her, and so whenever Henry saw other women he did it discreetly and tactfully. He was often ashamed of himself; he frequently made up his mind to reform. But every time he came home after an affair, he was wreathed in telltale patterns; Martha could read the X-ray images of his guilty conscience. Only in Betty did Martha see a serious threat, not entirely without reason, as we know. And yet the two women had only met once, at a cocktail party in Moreany's garden.

It had been a remarkably mild evening; the night-flowering plants in the garden had opened their calyces, luring the moths to pollinate. Betty stood at the buffet, her low-cut, backless dress exposing her dimples of Venus; she was poking around with a fork in a bowl of strawberries. 'Not *her*, Henry,' Martha had said quietly, as she caught the gaze of her husband swinging towards Betty's magnetic dimples like a compass needle. Henry knew at once who Martha was talking about, and that he'd never give Betty up. He promised he'd never see her again. From then on he only ever saw Betty in out-of-the-way places. He bought himself a mobile phone with a prepaid card, and paid for motels and candlelit dinners in cash. All the same it remained a liaison of hasty fondlings, accompanied by a constant sense of sad foreboding.

* * *

Martha's room was not big, and was done out in creamy white. She didn't like rooms with high ceilings; they reminded her of her time in the psychiatric clinic. Her small desk and swivel stool stood under the sloping roof at the dormer window; her bed, with its white covers, was positioned between the dormer and the bathroom door. Henry had really wanted to buy a French château with the first million from *Frank Ellis*, but Martha thought castles were too big and cold, and insisted on something more modest.

While she was working on the next novel, Henry discovered the old manor house on the coast, fucked the estate agent and set about restoring the property straight away.

Henry looked round Martha's study, listening. There was a blank sheet of paper in the typewriter. There were no crumpled-up pages lying around; the small wastepaper basket was empty; there were no notes, nothing that suggested rough drafts or corrections. The cataract of words poured out of her brain and straight through the machine onto the paper; not a single word got spilt.

'Can you hear it?'

'I can't hear anything.'

'Maybe it's asleep.'

They both listened in silence. Now was the moment, he thought. Now he had to tell her. But his thoughts didn't turn into words.

'It was a stork on the roof.'

'There aren't storks at night, Henry.'

'True. Where did you hear it?'

Martha indicated a point on the ceiling. 'There. Over the bed.'

Henry pulled off his shoes, climbed onto the bed and pressed his ear against the sloping ceiling. A narrow crawling space ran along the length of the roof between the lining and the rafters. The air it contained provided first-rate insulation. For the space of a few breaths Henry didn't move. Then he heard it. There was indeed something gnawing in the rafters directly overhead. He could hear the rasp of sharp teeth. Then it stopped; the animal seemed to be aware of him.

Henry got down off the bed with the expression of a concerned expert.

'There's something there.'

'How big?'

'It's not moving any more.'

'A marten?'

'Possibly.'

'Bigger or smaller than a cat?'

'Smaller. Don't worry yourself. I'll catch it.'

'But you won't kill it.'

He put his shoes on. 'Of course not. And now I'll go and buy some fish.'

4

The small town fronted on to a bay. Low houses, a natural harbour, little shops and pointless flower beds. No monument, but a small bookshop, where a framed picture of Henry hung on the wall—for the tourists who came here on pilgrimage to meet the famous author.

Obradin Basarić, the local Serbian fishmonger, put aside his knife and washed his hands when he heard Henry's Maserati. As he'd plastered the shop window with photographs of fish, he could only guess at what went on in the street. For Obradin, Henry was—since the death of Ivo Andrić—*the* greatest living writer. The fact that Henry had chosen to settle in this nondescript coastal town couldn't be a coincidence, because coincidences only happen to atheists. At least once a week, Henry came to him to buy fish, smoke unfiltered Bosnian cigarettes with him and philosophise about life. This most congenial and at the same time most brilliant of all people was a lover of fish—and he, Obradin Basarić, sold fish. Where did coincidence come into that?

Henry had asked Obradin not to tell anyone where he lived and Obradin had promised. But the secret knowledge weighed on him. When the tourists—most of them women—came into the fishmonger's to enquire shyly or with shameless directness about Henry, he would lie to their faces, telling them that no one of that name lived there, when all the time he would have given anything to tell them that he was a particular friend of his. At night his wife Helga often heard him yelling in his sleep: *I know him! He's my friend!*

'You can't imagine how awful it is to have a secret,' he confessed to Henry when they were out fly fishing one day. 'A secret like this,' he continued, 'is a parasite. It feeds on you and grows bigger and bigger. It wants to get out of you, it gnaws its way through your heart, it wants to get out of your mouth, it crawls through your eyes!'

Henry listened in silence. 'Do what I do,' he suggested. 'Dig a hole and shit your secret into the hole. Then you'll be rid of it and not full of shit any more.'

Obradin considered this remark unworthy of a serious writer. But Henry just laughed and was pleased with himself for the rest of the day.

Today, Henry entered the fishmonger's looking gloomy. 'My friend,' he said to Obradin, 'we have a problem in our roof. It's a marten.'

Obradin kissed Henry on both cheeks in greeting. 'I'll kill it for you.'

'No, best not. Martha wouldn't like that. How do we go about catching the brute?'

'With a trap. But what will you do with it when you've caught it?'

'I'll set it free somewhere.'

'It'll come back, because it'll know you're not going to kill it.'

'OK. When I've caught it, I'll bring it to you and *you* can kill it.'

Henry didn't ask how business was going, because he knew it was going badly. Obradin's sky-blue fishing cutter, *Drina*, was forty years old and beginning to give up the ghost. More and more often, Obradin was having to buy frozen fish from the wholesaler, because her diesel engine had packed up again. Henry had already made him several offers of an interest-free loan for a new cutter, but Obradin had rejected the offers out of hand. He didn't even want Henry to act as guarantor for him. Friendship should be debt-free, was all he said. And so Henry had started to slip cash to Obradin's wife Helga on the sly, so that she could settle the most urgent bills. Without Henry's discreet support, Obradin would long since have gone bust. It would no doubt have been the end of their friendship if Obradin had found out.

The men lit two Bosnian cigarettes and talked about the weather, and the sea and about literature. Sometimes Obradin talked about the war, the mass shootings in Bratunac and his time in the internment camp at Trnopolje. When he started on the subject, his eyes would grow dark and his voice would harden and he would switch into the present tense, as if everything was happening right now. Listening, Henry was never quite sure whether Obradin was a victim or a perpetrator. After Chetniks had raped and impaled his daughter, Obradin had driven back to his homeland every weekend to gun down a few of them in the mountains around Sarajevo. Henry couldn't swear that he wasn't still doing it on the sly.

'How are you getting on with your novel?'

'Not much to go. Maybe twenty pages.'

'We have to celebrate that. I have a monkfish for you.'

'I'm going to pay for it, though.'

'That's up to you,' Obradin replied. 'I saw they want to film *Frank Ellis*.'

'Yes, awful,' Henry said. 'I'm against it.'

'Then why have you allowed it to happen? My Helga says you can't film literature. I say it's wrong

46

to film it. Film, do you know what film means?' Obradin rubbed his finger through the fish blood on the chopping board, drew out a transparent thread and held it under Henry's nose. 'Here, *that's* film— gunk, slime, filth.'

'How right you are,' Henry said. 'That's just what Martha always says. But I'm so bad at saying no. Do you understand?'

Obradin swung his hairy index finger to and fro like a pendulum. 'I don't like the way you're talking today. What's happened?'

'Nothing. Nothing's happened.'

'Then don't be so hard on yourself, Henry. What does fame matter to you any more? You don't enjoy it! You hide from it, because you're a good person. You're always talking yourself down. Why do you do that?'

'That's the way I am, Obradin. I'm a thoroughly bad, utterly insignificant person, believe me.'

Obradin narrowed his eyes to slits. 'You know what the Jews say: "Thoughts become words and words become deeds." I know bad people. I have some in my family. I've lived with them, slept with them, eaten with them. You're not one of them; you're a good person. That's why we all love you.'

'You love me because I contribute to the community coffers.'

Henry inhaled the tarry smoke of the tobacco and

suppressed a cough, drawing one foot up to his knee like a wading bird.

'Bloody hell, that's strong. Do you know what the Japanese say, Obradin?'

'Who cares what the Japanese say?'

'They say that being loved is a curse.'

'Maybe they do, Henry. But how do *they* know that?' Obradin spat on his tiled floor. 'You don't just become a writer, Henry. I know that—you're destined to it. I can't do it, my Helga can't do it, and we thank God for it. It must be a real burden.'

'There's something in that,' Henry replied and pointed to two silhouettes on the other side of the papered-up windowpane. 'I see customers.'

Obradin glanced up. 'Tourists,' he declared disparagingly.

'Are you sure?'

'Who looks at my fish pictures? Who does a thing like that?'

'Only tourists.'

'There you are then. They've come because of you. You just watch.'

Obradin went and waited behind the fish counter, setting down his cigarette on the bloody chopping board. The bell over the door rang. Two skittle-shaped women with red cheeks came into the shop. They stood at the counter, contemplating the dead fish without interest. No, it wasn't the fish they were after.

The cigarette smoke bothered them. The older one looked from the fish to Obradin, closed her eyelids and set them vibrating, as Anglo-Saxon women often do—no one knows why.

'Do you speak English?'

Obradin shook his head. Both women were in white trainers and carrying Gore-Tex rucksacks. Their hair was close-cropped, their lips were thin, their skin rosy; the older one's chin wobbled underneath when she whispered to the younger one.

Henry cleared his throat. 'Can *I* help?'

The younger one smiled shyly at Henry. Her teeth were white as alabaster and perfectly regular. 'Perhaps you know Henry Hayden?'

Before Henry could reply, Obradin had answered for him.

'*No.*' The Serb leaned his hairy arms on the fish counter. 'No here. Here only fish.'

The women looked at one another helplessly. The younger one turned round and bent forwards slightly, and the older one took a well-thumbed book out of the rucksack on her back. It was an English edition of *Frank Ellis*. She held it out to Obradin. With an immaculately clean fingernail she pointed at Henry's photograph.

'Henry Hayden. Does he live here?'

'No.'

Henry stamped out his cigarette and strode

across to the women. 'Allow me.' He held out his hand. Taken aback, the woman put the book in his hand.

'Have you got a pen, Obradin?'

Obradin handed him a pencil smeared with fish gut.

'What's your name, ma'am?'

The older woman put her slender hand to her mouth with a start. She had recognised him. 'Oh, my God . . .'

'Just Henry, ma'am.'

Henry loved moments like this. Doing good and feeling good at the same time. Can there be any act more worthwhile and at the same time more delightful? After all, they'd travelled from God knows where just to see him. Such a lot of trouble for a moment's beneficence.

Henry wrote two brief dedications, Obradin took a photo of the two of them with Henry in the middle, and the women floated out of the fishmonger's on air. Obradin snarled as he watched them go.

'I've been tearing hairs out of my arse so as not to give you away and you come along and say: *Here I am.*'

'They'll come back and buy your fish, now they know you're not going to kill them.'

* * *

For dinner, Henry grilled Obradin's monkfish medallions *a la plancha*. He and Martha ate on the veranda in the cool night air that was fragrant with the scent of cut grass, and drank Pouilly-Fumé.

'Should I be worried?' Martha asked, in that inimitably terse way of hers that made any further questions superfluous. Henry knew his wife well enough to know that the unspoken context of this question was: Spare me the details, I don't want any explanations, and, above all, *don't play dumb*.

Henry speared a piece of fish with his fork and spread a little riesling froth over it with his knife. 'Not in the least,' he replied truthfully. 'Don't worry, I'll take care of things.'

With that, the essentials had been said. The telepathic contact that comes with years of marriage is often misinterpreted by outsiders as silence. Before getting married, Henry too had assumed that couples who sit at restaurant tables and eat in silence have nothing to say to one another; he now knew that they make eloquent conversation without exchanging a word, sometimes even telling each other jokes.

Martha went upstairs to work on the final part of the fifty-fourth chapter. At the veranda door she turned to Henry again.

'Do you really want a change, Henry? Aren't things all right the way they are?' She didn't wait for a reply.

Henry did the washing up and fed the dog. Then he withdrew into his studio to watch the sports round-up and stick some more matchsticks onto his drilling rig.

High shelves of unread books stood alongside filing cabinets full of newspaper articles. Everything ever published about him was filed here by date, language and author. The most important prizes and awards hung on the walls or were displayed in glass-fronted cabinets. Even in early childhood, Henry realised he had a bent for copying and archiving. With every novel that came out, his collection grew by an entire bookcase. He'd stopped showing it to Martha; the very thought made him blush to his ears in shame.

At the window was his desk. It was here he answered letters, sorted his expenses for the accountant and constructed all manner of drilling rigs out of matchsticks. Once finished, these were banished to the cellar and later burnt on the barbe-cue when they grilled sausages at their midsummer parties. He'd already stuck over forty thousand matches on the true-to-scale model of the Norwegian Troll A platform—which is, as it happens, the largest Condeep production platform for crude oil in the world. Henry wound up by watching two episodes of *Bonanza* and went to sleep feeling inspired. He had no dreams that night, but slept peacefully and soundly like Hoss Cartwright from the Ponderosa, for he now knew what was to be done.

* * *

He was woken by the whirr of the automatic blinds. Sunlight penetrated the room and he flung the duvet aside; the sundial pointer of his morning erection showed a quarter past seven. Poncho was asleep next to the bed.

Henry drank coffee, had a long shower and got his hiking boots out of the cupboard. As soon as Poncho saw the boots he began to twist and turn, prancing up and down at the front door, wagging his tail. He ran ahead of Henry to the car and leapt onto the passenger seat. It was the hour of their daily ramble.

To avoid being recognised by the locals on his outings with the dog, Henry always chose remote places within a hundred-kilometre radius; after all, a novelist is not a rambler. Thanks to a military map on which even the smallest woodland paths were marked, he had, over the last two years, discovered large tracts of meadowland and forest, roamed over picturesque moors and through secluded coastal regions, seen all kinds of rare birds and wild animals, and even lost some weight. There was hardly any danger of getting lost, because the two hundred and twenty million scent-detecting cells in Poncho's nose always found their way back to the car.

This time, Henry picked a tract of forest forty kilo-metres west of the small town, where he'd roamed with the dog a few times before. He got out at a glori-ously shady picnic area. Not far away a cascade was burbling in the bracken. The scent of fresh pine resin hung in the air and sunlight fell through the treetops, showering radiance on thousands of leaves.

From his jacket pocket he pulled out his red tele-phone and put in the battery. He never rang Betty twice from the same place; it was one of the cautionary habits he'd acquired during the years he'd spent lying low in an overpopulated world. He typed in the code and then waited. He never even got bills for this tiny thing, because it was prepaid. You could top it up at any petrol station, conveniently, cheaply and anonymously. Henry loved going incognito.

Betty answered at the first ring. Her voice was husky; she'd been smoking. 'Have you told her?'

'I'll tell you everything this evening. Are you in your office?'

'I'm staying at home today. How did she react?'

Henry paused for effect. This always did the trick in a phone call, whereas face to face it was the myste-rious smile that carried the day. You simply couldn't go wrong with it. 'Martha's incredibly brave.'

He heard the metallic snap of Betty's lighter. She inhaled menthol smoke. 'Moreany will fire me when he finds out about us.'

'He won't find out anything from Martha.'

'Are you sure?'

'Positive.'

'But she must be incredibly angry with me, right?'

'Yes, she is. Are you worried about your job, Betty?'

'Me? No. I just feel sorry for her. To be honest, I'm a little bit ashamed.'

'Why only now?'

She drew on her cigarette. Henry could positively feel the tip glow. 'What are you getting at, Henry? Do you think I don't care?'

'You haven't cared so far.'

'I've *always* cared. Now you're being so cold again. Don't take it out on me. I understand you—it's difficult for you, but please don't blame me.'

'It's the truth—that's all.'

'Yup—that's all. I don't want to know what's going on in your head at the moment.'

That, in Henry's opinion, was for the best. He saw that the dog had picked up a scent and was zigzagging across the dewy, glistening meadow.

'You don't think I got pregnant on purpose, do you, Henry? Be honest.'

'I'm always honest with you, darling. Always.'

The idea hadn't crossed his mind. But now that she mentioned it, he thought it was a definite possibility. Betty was almost thirty-five, she'd been waiting a long time, he hadn't been careful—and now it had happened.

'We're breaking up, Betty.'

'What do you mean?'

'I'm serious. My credit's running out—I've got thirty seconds left. We'll talk this evening.'

'You gave me a bit of a fright, Henry. Is that what you wanted?'

'Just a bit. You know me. Wait for me—I'll be there at eight. And stop smoking. Think of our baby.'

'I will, my darling. Henry . . .'

'Yes?'

'I love you.'

'You're wrong.'

'You always say that. Accept it, don't fight it. I love you, I love you, I love you. Big kiss!'

Henry pulled the battery out of the phone, making himself invisible once again. Betty was afraid Martha might grass on her to Moreany. She feared with good reason that she would lose her job as editor-in-chief, a job that she didn't know she owed solely to Martha. Moreany would fire her, because she was no longer able to do her work objectively. But that was the good thing about Betty—she thought only of herself, and he was part of her plan. Henry liked that. Betty was eccentric; she wanted success and intimacy all at once—wanted, as it were, an adventure in the wilds with central heating. Deep down she was as spoilt and unconscionable as he was. That made everything easier.

Henry whistled to the dog. He could see him about a hundred paces away. Poncho had got his teeth into something. It looked big. Henry walked across the clearing, his boots sinking into the sandy ground. The hovawart was too slow and heavy to chase hares, and whatever was lying there was bigger than a hare. The nearer he got, the more resolutely Poncho tore at his prey. About twenty yards away, Henry could see it was a deer. Poncho was pulling a big piece of flesh out of its haunch; its hind leg was waggling in the air.

The deer was still alive. Maybe it had been shot at, maybe it was ill. The creature looked at Henry uncomprehendingly as the dog's teeth sank into its flesh. Trembling, it raised its head, its blue tongue hanging out, breath steaming from its mouth.

'Let go, Poncho, drop it!'

With blood-red muzzle, the hovawart tore another piece off the deer, and then lay down a few metres away to chew its hand-sized piece of prey. Henry knelt beside the dying animal. The white fur on its belly was torn right open and its guts were hanging out. Everything in this open body wanted to carry on living. Henry patted his pockets. Apart from his phone he had nothing on him. The deer let out a moaning sound. Henry ran his hand over its warm, wildly throbbing neck. Far and wide there was no stone with which to put the deer out of its misery.

Henry put both hands round the creature's neck and squeezed. The deer started to twitch; Henry didn't let go until it was dead. Then he ran his hand over its warm cadaver. Life had already fled from the animal; decomposition was setting in. Henry sat down next to the corpse and thought about a parting gift for Betty. She would be angry and disappointed. But doesn't all deception end in disappointment? It was forecast to rain that night. In ten hours he would tell Betty everything.

5

The long corridor of the courthouse was deserted. Sitting on the wooden bench under the window, Gisbert Fasch clutched his brown briefcase in both hands, with no further thought for his toothache. People passed him, some hurriedly, some hesitantly, and then vanished behind grey doors. In a dim recess of the court archives, he had found two grey files in a box labelled with question marks. A bureaucrat had scrawled on the files 'Please destroy'; after that they had lain forgotten in this box of delights. A real find—thank goodness for administrative sloth.

The court files on the Hayden case were meagre and at first glance not particularly revealing. The disappearance of Henry's mother, Charlotte Hayden, née Buntknopf, on the second of December 1979, was related in matter-of-fact terms. Since no one had reported her missing, there had been no attempt to find her.

In the next paragraph—the death of the tax collector, Martin E. Hayden, the same day, late evening, due to a fall downstairs under the influence of alcohol. No connection was implied between the two events; there was no mention of murder. A tragedy, no doubt about it, mysterious and terrible enough to break a nine-year-old boy, make a genius or a criminal out of him, or silence him forever.

The whereabouts of Henry Hayden were only noted in passing; his fate was to be settled in a separate lawsuit. Since it was obvious that no one reckoned with the reappearance of his missing mother, Henry was granted the status of an orphan and it was arranged that he be sent to an orphanage.

A year after the disappearance of Charlotte Hayden, the care and education of little Henry was settled by the family court.

* * *

So Henry had been lying back then. His father had never been a big-game hunter: he'd been a tax collector in the dog-licence department. And little Henry hadn't been the sole survivor of a shipwreck, fished out of the icy cold Norwegian Sea. He had simply been left behind. A bed-wetter, that's what he was—a bed-wetter, a liar and an unpredictable psychopath.

Fasch remembered meeting Henry over thirty years ago in the Catholic orphanage of Saint Renata. Henry had been about eleven years old at the time and not a nice boy. It's quite possible that the career of every psychopath begins with a tragic event, but often that event is birth itself. Evil is born innocently. It grows up, seeks shape and form, and begins its work playfully. At that time, Henry already had a pretty long history of children's homes behind him: he'd been kicked out of all of them or he'd scarpered. But he never breathed a word on the subject. It was as if each day that passed was left behind him like a frozen stone.

When Henry came to Saint Renata, he was a precocious, sturdy lad with a shadow of down on his upper lip. He was sporty and cheerful; there was something cat-like about him. He was always up for a bit of fun, often at other people's expense, but never without a certain charm. Henry had more experience with the girls than most of the other boys—and in dealing with the authorities and fighting over the largest helping. That's why he always ended up with the most. He radiated an almost adult indifference, which made him seem invulnerable and terrifyingly strong. Whether in class or in the children's home, he never failed to keep an eye out for himself, but he did it so subtly that few actually realised they'd been conned.

He was especially talented at claiming as his own what was best in others, and wangled himself praise and privileges in this way. Conscience presupposes respect, and he had neither. He must have felt pain, but it didn't bother him, and punishment only frightens the weak. Henry was armoured with something that couldn't be seen.

In class he always sat next to the top students so he could crib better, but he was sloppy at cribbing and made mistakes. This arrogance could only mean that it was the theft alone he was interested in; the booty bored him as soon as he had it in his hands. On the odd occasion when he was caught, he put the blame on others. No one dared rat on him, for Henry could issue fatwas of limitless effect against anyone at any time. *You never know when*—that was Henry's pledge of vengeance. The real threat was unspoken; it stuck fast like a poisoned arrow.

Back then Gisbert was reading *Beowulf*, the saga of Grendel, that disturbing mythic creature who comes out at night to abduct sleeping men and feast off them in its lair under the swamp. Henry was a replica of that monster. You never knew when he would strike, but you could be sure it would turn out badly.

His guest performance at the orphanage of Saint Renata lasted a year and three months. Then, one winter's day, Henry disappeared and with him the director's cash box. No one knew where or why he'd gone. And no one asked. It was a red-letter day. The echo of the long corridors was as cheerful as fairground music to Gisbert's ears—even the nuns were relieved. According to the caretaker's reports, Henry had smashed a small window in the boiler room and crawled out. Blood on the shards of glass indicated nasty gashes. Gisbert suspected him of abducting one of the other boys from the home, but no one was missing. Everyone waited for him to come back, but nobody went to look for him.

As far as Gisbert could remember, the police weren't called in, nor were the authorities informed. First, the nuns wanted to wait and see whether he really wasn't going to come back. As the night lengthened, the boys in the dormitory lay awake listening for a long time. Henry did not return. Grendel had climbed back down to his ugly mother in the abyssal well.

* * *

To stick to the facts, Travis Forster was a pseudonym. Everyone has the right to assume a more melodious name than Gisbert Fasch, but nobody has the right to steal other people's lives and call himself a writer if he isn't one. Gisbert Fasch had created his nom de plume out of the names of two idols and had it entered in his passport. He chose the first name because of the fictional figure Travis Bickle, whose struggle for recognition and respect he had greatly admired ever since watching Scorsese's *Taxi Driver*.

He chose the surname because of the adventurer Georg Forster, a figure who has received too little attention in world history.

Gisbert Fasch, as we shall call him for the sake of simplicity, looked back from the wooden bench of the criminal court at the stuffy dormitory of Saint Renata, which in those days was studded with small portholes like the bowels of a ship. Saint Renata was a gulag; the most brutal individuals held sway over the weak, and Henry was the worst of them all. On his first day, he'd knocked out two of Gisbert's front teeth, because he'd wanted the upper bunk. He was not entitled to the upper bunk—as a new boy, Henry had to sleep on the bottom. Two dozen boys listened to the goings-on in the dark. After lights out, Henry came climbing into Gisbert's bed like the terrible Grendel and set on him without warning. He laid hold of him and dragged him onto the lower bunk. Nobody laughed; they were all terrified. Gisbert never forgot that night. He lay awake with his mouth full of blood, while the psychopath in the bunk above him screamed in his sleep and wet the bed.

When, decades later, Fasch saw the name Henry Hayden in a literary supplement, he thought it must be just a coincidence. The review spoke of his great success, then delivered a paean to his style and vigour— there was no way it could be referring to Henry. But there was a photograph portraying the author. It was him. The same grey-green eyes, the same malicious winner's smile. Grendel was back. The gap in Gisbert's teeth had long since been closed with two post crowns, but the memory still hurt. He bought the novel shrink-wrapped in the bookshop on the corner, ripped it open and began to read, walking along.

Frank Ellis was indeed a no-nonsense thriller, really well written, spare and precise down to the smallest detail—by no means the novel of the century, but that's of no relevance here. *Every sentence a stronghold*, read the critic's praise on the cover. Millions had bought and read it. Fasch felt his teeth ache. He couldn't work out how that unfeeling monster had managed to write a bestseller on his own. But if *he* hadn't written the novel, then who had? And what had he done in all those years between the children's gulag and getting published? He'd left no clues. No school leavers' certificate, not a single publication, not so much as a minor contribution to an anthology. One would assume that a psychopath would at least have a criminal record, but nothing like that was to be found. Hayden hadn't studied—no trace of him as a budding author anywhere, no sign of friends or fellow writers. Had he perhaps published under a pseudonym? And if so, what? Don't even the most secretive writers reveal themselves through their lives? Aren't they always in search of a readership? Not Henry

Hayden. After escaping from the children's home he'd gone straight underground, only to burst into prominence decades later, a comet in the literary sky.

Gisbert began his investigations secretly, like everything he did—at least in the realm of art. His dream of becoming a writer was beginning to fade. He'd long since stopped sending off manuscripts. The white nights of stapling paper in copy shops were a thing of the past, as were all those pointless readings to audiences of literary pedants, their index fingers yellow from smoking, crumbs of tobacco between their teeth.

Fasch spent eleven years working on his novel about Stone Age nomads. In the end, after receiving nothing but pro forma letters of rejection, he published his life's work himself under the pseudonym Travis Forster. That plunged him straight into bankruptcy. For another six years he led a miserable existence under the heel of the official receiver. Copies of the book stood piled up unread in his small flat; in the end he had them made into insulating fibre. After this purge of his literary self he stopped writing. His short stories, plays and radio dramas stayed in the drawer. He went back to calling himself Gisbert Fasch and had his pseudonym removed from his passport. *Basta*.

Now Fasch was teaching German as a second language, mostly to Africans. He helped them create a new existence. These people cross the Atlantic in rowing boats, fleeing drought and war and poverty, and then find they have no right to residence in the land of Cockaigne without a language certificate. Gisbert's work was right and good, and he enjoyed it. A decent job. As a hobby he wrote book reviews on Amazon. Only positive ones, mind you: he thought negative reviews were about as unproductive as the black stuff under his toenails. He wrote them under his old pseudonym, Travis Forster. For old time's sake. But he wasn't satisfied with himself.

Fasch followed Henry through all the European capitals, listening to him at various festivals, studying his rather skimpy interviews, analysing all his quotations. Several times they came face to face but, even when their eyes met, Henry didn't recognise Fasch. For such a discerning connoisseur of human nature, he had an incredibly bad memory for faces.

Henry could have filled huge halls, but he always chose bookshops for his readings. Fasch attended every one of them. The front rows were filled almost entirely with women, most of them at that alluring age between thirty and fifty. Fasch could see them positively hanging on Henry's lips, listening until their thighs grew wet, letting his words enter them, all the time pretending they'd only come for the culture. Those readings were nothing but a secret lubrication fest.

True, it was powerful stuff. What Henry read was gripping, without a single superfluous word. Nonchalant in his custom-made shoes and his tweed jacket, he always read with a degree of indifference in his voice, such as the Roman emperors must have felt at the sight of the laurel wreath. He didn't read expressively, but with an unobtrusive and down-to-earth detachment, as if he couldn't wait to catch the train home and return at last to the solitude of his writer's dungeon. Poor old Henry, Fasch thought. You can't even read.

Henry took his time over the book-signing. He chatted charmingly and had his photo taken with his swooning women readers. He could captivate them all, but he never took any of them home. At some point, Fasch decided to carry out the litmus test and queued up along with the others. He handed Henry a copy of *Aggravating Circumstances* to sign.

'For Gisbert Fasch, please.'

Henry glanced up and looked him in the eye. It was the gaze of a lion that has eaten its fill and watches the gazelles passing by. He gave a friendly nod and wrote: *For Gisbert Fasch from Henry Hayden*. That was all. Not so much as the flicker of an eyelid. He really had forgotten him, just as he'd forgotten the teeth he'd knocked out of his mouth and the essays he'd cribbed off him. Just as well.

From then on, Fasch avoided any more personal encounters, so as not to alert his enemy. Instead, he began to piece together all the available fragments of Henry Hayden's lost biography. It was a task that fulfilled him in every way. He stopped smoking—but that was nothing. He came off anti-depressants, whose side effect is to make you so terribly fat, and slept through the night again. Even his perfectly round bald patch stopped spreading. Find an enemy for life and you've no more need of a doctor.

* * *

Henry drove into town for lunch, parked in an underground car park at the station, and threw the red mobile phone in a bin near the ticket machine. In the lift he wondered whether he should give Betty a flat of her own as a parting gift, but dismissed the idea and ate a meatball at a stand right next to the car park, where the rent boys warmed themselves in the winter. Henry liked the district around the station and he liked meatballs with hot mustard. No one recognised him here; there was an atmosphere of mild despair. Anything discarded here lay around for a while.

There was no question of suggesting abortion to Betty. Maybe she'd think of it herself, in which case he would of course agree to pay for it. 'We'll still be friends' made equally inappropriate parting words; after all, they never had been friends. On the contrary, he'd always desired her more than he'd liked her. She must have sensed it because, whenever he penetrated her, her immune system was turned on. Instead of receiving him, she resisted, which aroused him all the more, adding as it did a hint of rape to every act of intercourse. How this could have resulted in a child remained a mystery to Henry. In a somewhat throwaway remark, Betty had once summed up the sexual component of their relationship: 'It may not be a match made in heaven, Henry, but we can improvise.'

But now it was over. The break-up had to be quick and conclusive; there should be no room left for hope. It was time to cleanse his conscience and start on something new. And, yes, he would miss her. He'd miss her a lot. But not until after they'd split up.

Opposite the fast-food stand, Henry discovered a pawnshop. 'Instant cash' was etched in the bullet-proof glass door. He liked the empty promise. Henry finished the meatball, licked his fingers clean and crossed the road with a spring in his step.

The locked door opened with a buzz. Two bespectacled men sat behind panes of armoured glass, fingering pieces of jewellery. They could smell at once that he had money. Henry asked to see a diamond necklace, but it struck him as too showy; after all, splitting up is not a cause for celebration. A brooch was far too old-fashioned, and as for earrings—they were completely off-target!

He was just about to leave the shop when his eye was caught by a Patek Philippe. He liked its tasteful shape; it was elegant and practical, and Betty loved practical things. What is more, like everything in a pawnshop, the watch was tied up with a tragedy. Who sells a watch if they don't have to? Maybe the previous owner had been driven by need or hatred or a dark secret. Whatever had brought this watch here, its history lent it patina. Henry bought it. If Betty threw it in his face, he could always give it to Martha on their wedding anniversary.

Afternoon, four o'clock. The best time of the day, when it's too late to catch up on whatever you've failed to do, when the light grows softer and the ice cubes glint in your glass. You treat yourself to a long drink instead of an afternoon nap, forget your vices, write imaginary letters and escort yourself out of this squandered, pointlessly spent day.

Henry sauntered through the pedestrian precinct with its shops and cafés. He'd donned a baseball cap and large dark glasses so as to look like a celebrity who doesn't want to be recognised. But nobody recognised him. Just like every day, Henry had the feeling that he'd achieved nothing, and so couldn't decide whether or not he deserved a short visit to a bookshop. People were pouring out of the surrounding buildings now, most of them after a hardworking nine-to-five day. They'd been slogging away for a ridiculously paltry sum of money, thoroughly and conscientiously doing their bit for family, nation and pension. Sometimes, Henry wished he could be like them, leading a normal life, and knowing what it's like to knock off after a day's work, at peace with oneself.

He went into a bookshop. On the table right next to the entrance he saw two of his novels, nicely displayed on a small plinth. He signed a copy surreptitiously and left the shop. He still had three hours. In an empty hardware store he found a wooden trap that was over a metre long and had flaps at either end. It was surprisingly cheap.

The salesman pulled the trap down from the enormous shelves and explained how it worked. 'This is our marten hotel,' he said, not without modest pride. He snapped the flaps open and shut. 'The little brutes check in, but they never check out.' Henry could smell the micro-organisms inhabiting his yellowish salesman's tongue. How, for heaven's sake, did the poor bloke put up with the monotony of his existence in amongst all this brand-new junk? To avoid having to inhale any more explanations, Henry fled to the checkout. Still two hours to go.

In an arcade cinema he watched a Korean film in which a man was locked in a room for fifteen years without finding out why. Henry was surprised it hadn't ever happened to him. He had bought two cinema tickets, one for him, one for the marten trap. It lay there on the seat beside him like a child's coffin. Before the film was over and the lights had gone up, Henry took the wooden box and crept out of the cinema. It was time.

Towards seven in the evening, Henry drove back along the main road in the direction of the coast. It was already growing dark. There were no cars coming the other way and the rain fell in transparent sheets. He passed a defunct bus stop and turned off onto the sandy forest track, rolling slowly with dimmed head-lamps over the concrete slabs to the cliffs.

The rain was steaming on the warm earth, and swathes of mist were rising. A piece of wasteland covered with tall grasses opened out at the edge of the cliffs, shielded from the wind by pines. Crumbling foundations and rusty iron rods still stuck up out of the grass. Maybe an old bunker or a weather station had once stood here. Henry could feel the palms of his hands grow moist; his heart was beating more rapidly. As soon as he saw Betty coming, he would get into her car and tell her everything. He looked at the clock; it wasn't yet eight. It had to be done quickly. His message would be like a sharp butcher's knife— inflicting no pain and wielded by a sure hand. Maybe she would scream and hit him. She was bound to cry.

Betty's green Subaru was already there. Close to the cliffs, as usual. Henry switched off the lights and rolled up to the car from behind. He could see Betty's silhouette behind the steering wheel, illuminated by a little light in the rear-view mirror, the inevitable cigarette in her right hand. She was probably listening to loud music and hadn't noticed him yet. She had to stop that damn smoking, he thought. Maybe she'll stop if I give her the watch.

There was a slight lurch as the bumpers touched. Henry put his foot a little way down on the accelerator and the Maserati effortlessly pushed the Subaru forwards. Henry saw the brake lights flare up, then the car tipped over the edge of the cliff and vanished.

For a while, Henry sat there, motionless; he left the engine running. Hope the airbag didn't go off, he thought, closing his eyes and leaning back on the leather headrest. She must be hitting the windscreen now and trying to open the door. It's dark down there; the cold salt water will help her die. Maybe she died when the car hit the water. The child in her belly won't notice anything; it doesn't know that it was ever alive, poor thing.

After about ten minutes, he opened his eyes again and switched the engine off. He got out to have a look around. The rain soaked his shirt instantly. He went and stood at the edge of the cliffs and looked down. The rock face fell away vertically; the car had fallen straight in without touching it. There was nothing to be seen: the sea had swallowed up the car—the black, indifferent sea. This would have been the right moment to jump in after it. But Henry felt nothing but the cold rain and the certainty that he had done something irreversible. He examined the front of his car. Not so much as a dent on the registration plate. He ran his thumb over it; rainwater fell in his eyes. He was a criminal now, a murderer. Just as he had foreseen.

On the way home he headed for a petrol station and bought a packet of chewing gum to get rid of the nasty taste in his mouth. He paid in cash, giving the money to an obese cashier who looked like an albino rabbit that had managed to escape from the laboratory. As he was paying her, he caught a glimpse of himself in the surveillance mirror over the till. Just look at that, he thought, I look the same as ever. Tomorrow afternoon, at the latest, someone would inform the police. Who would it be? Probably Moreany. The good man was always so easily worried, and everyone knows instinctively when it's bad news. Then the waiting would begin, and the hoping and worrying—and in the end it would all turn out just as he feared, or even worse. The hardest thing, Henry was sure, would be the waiting itself.

It would probably be parents and concerned friends who would start to look first, get hold of a key and go to Betty's flat. There the ultrasound image of his baby would be hanging on the pinboard next to the fridge for all to see. But no, a pregnant woman doesn't hang a scan by the fridge; a thing like that she carries around with her—in her handbag, for example. Maybe Betty had told the gynaecologist who the father was. But why should she? It wasn't relevant, after all. This reminded him that he had always wanted to ask Betty if she kept a diary. Doesn't every woman keep a diary at some point in her life? Presumably Betty had too. He should have asked her.

Henry was almost at the door when he heard a woman's voice.

'Hey . . . you?'

Henry stopped in his tracks and turned round. The giant rabbit at the till was waving the packet of chewing gum at him. He'd forgotten it.

Henry went back, took the chewing gum and returned to his car. She would remember him. Sooner or later the police would be knocking at his door. He was prepared and he would pass every test, because he had nothing to reproach himself for. He had done what had to be done. He drove home to make Martha her camomile tea.

The light was on in Martha's room. That meant she'd already gone upstairs to commune with the nocturnal writing demon. Henry put the marten trap down quietly at the foot of the stairs and crept into the kitchen to boil water for tea, and to feed the dog. The enormous kitchen was neat and tidy as usual; it smelt of grease on metal. Poncho was wagging his tail as usual. It was absolutely silent as usual. Everything was as usual. Then he suddenly thought of the phone. He tried to remember whether or not he'd taken out the little SIM card. He'd been thoughtless.

What if the phone was still working and Betty had rung him up in extremis? Who else would she ring? After all, she couldn't know that *he* had been the dark shadow who'd pushed her over the cliffs from behind—who suspects a thing like that? The phone in the bin next to the car-park ticket machine would have rung; he hadn't turned it off. Maybe someone had heard the ringing and answered it—but no, you don't make phone calls under water. No one can talk under water; the cold sea gets into your mouth and into your nose. You want to live, you flail around, you blow bubbles, you struggle until your hands are battered and bleeding. No sensible person makes a phone call in such a moment. Do they?

Henry supported himself with one hand on the kitchen island benchtop and drank Scotch straight from the bottle. The cigarettes. Betty was forever flicking the burning butts into the countryside. How often had he stamped the damn things out in annoyance, preventing how many forest fires? It's well known that cigarette butts are the first thing the forensic team looks for; every child knows that from the telly. Betty's saliva on them was a major lead. And then there was his puked-up lasagne too, full of murderer's DNA. Half a kilo of it. It was just a question of finding its owner. He might just as well have nailed signs to the trees displaying his photo and phone number. Wouldn't it be better to ring a lawyer straight away? But what was he to say? That he'd killed his mistress by accident? That he'd just forgotten to brake?

No one would believe him. No, if anything, he ought to talk to Martha first and explain everything to her; he'd done it for her, after all. Martha would be bound to understand him and forgive him. Martha was never cross with him. Then again, maybe she would be this time. But she definitely wouldn't go to the police. Poor thing—who was to look after her, if he wasn't there any more?

On a sudden impulse, Henry went to the window. It was still raining. Only I know what I've done, he thought. Who in the world would suspect him? And who would ever think of searching by the cliffs? There was no chance of tyre tracks of any evidential value being found now. That was good. The rain and sea were his allies, not that he'd ever been able to bear either of them.

Henry relaxed. Strictly speaking it could just as well have been an accident—no, it really had been an accident. Because it would all have happened just the same without him; it was entirely Betty's fault. A case of fateful inadvertence. She had stopped at the very edge of the cliffs, hadn't put the car into gear, hadn't even put on the handbrake—thoughtless, the way women are. She had simply rolled a little too far. Who was going to think anything else? Who could prove the contrary? And who would ever find her?

Somewhat reassured, Henry put on his slippers, took the bottle of Scotch and crept softly down to the wine cellar to treat himself to a cigar. Not that there was anything to celebrate, but tobacco is a good antidote to negative thoughts. He sat in the cellar on the wooden stool under the naked light bulb and smoked the entire cigar. Like all those years ago when he'd smoked his first cigar, a factory-reject left by his dead father.

On that fateful night, which from a psychological point of view had marked the end of Henry's childhood, his father had come ranting and raving up the stairs to punish Henry. Henry had hidden under the bed, his urine-soaked pyjamas clinging to his legs. His father came into the room, snorting like an ox, his sour beery breath polluting the air. He didn't even put the light on; he just reached under the bed and pulled him out. Henry could still feel that painful grip, the incredible strength with which the old man grasped him by his pyjama top and then felt his trousers.

'Gone and pissed yourself again, have you, junior?'

Of course he had. It happened every night. His father

dragged him out of the room to the stairs. Henry clutched the banisters and screamed for his mum. That made the old man even more furious, and he tugged at Henry, who was still clinging to the stair post. Then the cloth of his pyjamas ripped and the heavy man crashed down the stairs to the bottom. There he remained, never to get up again. He was carried out of the house in a black plastic bag with all the neighbours looking. What happened afterwards was to prove even worse.

Today, so many years on, Henry came out of the wine cellar completely drunk, tripped over the sleeping dog and fell sideways on his face. He saw gracefully dancing lights.

The doorbell rang. Poncho leapt up and began to bark. Henry looked at the clock; it was almost eleven. The police—could they be that quick? It is well known that modern investigative techniques can perform wonders, but how the devil had they worked it all out that quickly? Maybe it had been Betty's emergency call from the car. She hadn't rung *him*; she'd rung the police. That had been her last act of revenge. Now the house was surrounded, and marksmen were lying in wait in the fields. He'd better not get up until they came into the house.

So Henry stayed lying down a little while longer. He saw the glowing cigar butt burn a small hole in the wooden floor, but it didn't matter any more. He remembered Dostoevsky's superb description of the last moments of a man condemned to death before a firing squad. Never again would one minute be so intense. He didn't like Dostoevsky otherwise, because he was so longwinded and his stories always interlocked in such a complicated way.

The doorbell rang again.

This time urgently, long-long-short, like a Morse-code signal. Once again, Henry saw into the future. Any second now, Martha would come down the stairs. Awful idea, he thought, her watching them handcuff him and read him his rights. I expect she'll pack my toothbrush and a change of clothes. Bound to cry then. Why did you do it? she'll ask. I'll have to come up with a good answer, Henry thought, and got up to open the door on the inevitable.

Outside in the rain stood Betty.

She was alone. She looked pale and serious. Under her raincoat she had on the tailored houndstooth suit she looked so fantastic in. She'd put up her blonde hair, presumably because she knew how much he liked it that way. She looked stunningly healthy and didn't seem the least bit cross with him.

'Henry, your wife knows everything,' she said.

It was a complicated feeling. On the one hand, joy. Yes, he was glad that Martha knew everything and that Betty wasn't hurt. Not a scratch was to be seen on her immaculate skin; she hadn't even caught cold in the icy water, although that could still happen of course. On the other hand, he was more than a little surprised. How had Betty managed to free herself from the sinking Subaru without ruining her hairdo? She must somehow have gone home to get changed. But what was she doing turning up at his house in the best of spirits rather than going to the police? A mystery. Well, there was sure to be a straightforward explanation.

'Have you been drinking, Henry?'

'Me? Yes.'

'Henry, I must have rung you fifty times, but you just didn't answer.'

There was no tone of reproach in her voice, Henry noted. He would have bet on her at least reproaching him for what he'd done—after all, he had tried to kill her. Instead, she stepped out of the rain and kissed him on the mouth. Her kiss tasted of menthol. It was the first time she'd set foot in Henry's house. Henry could smell the lily-of-the-valley perfume he'd given her. She'd even found time for that.

'It's so dark here. Have you hurt yourself, my poor love?'

'I fell over.'

'You're bleeding. Did you understand what I said?'

'No. What did you say?'

'I said: Martha came to see me earlier.'

'Who?'

'Your wife.' Betty spoke to him as if to a child. Henry didn't like that, but now was not the moment for such trifles. 'She already knows everything. Why have you been keeping it from me all this time?'

Henry could hear himself breathing.

'What does Martha know?'

Betty gave a ringing laugh. 'Don't play dumb. She knows about us two. Everything. Has done all along.'

He wondered whether he should go back to the cellar and see whether he'd fallen asleep smoking.

'Did you tell her?' he asked.

'Me? No, *you* told her everything.' Betty poked his chest with her index finger. Another thing he couldn't stand. 'She came to see me. In my flat. It's all a lot easier than we thought.'

'How does she know where you live?'

The conversation was beginning to tire Betty. She took off her raincoat. 'Well, really, she can't know *that* from anyone except you. She was sad, and she was very angry and very worried about you. We drank tea together and she told me about your writing crisis. Really, she understands you and she loves you. Afterwards, she drove to the cliffs.'

Something cold reached into Henry's chest. It broke through his ribs and churned everything up inside him. Betty saw him turn grey.

* * *

Martha's room was neat and tidy as usual. The standard lamp was on, there was a white sheet of paper in the typewriter and the waste-paper basket was empty. Her bed was untouched. A book lay open on the pillow; her swimsuit was next to the bed. She wasn't in the bathroom either.

Henry flung open the window. Martha's white Saab was parked below in the rain. The headlamps were on, the windscreen wipers were moving to and fro. He called out her name, but she did not reply.

As he was going slowly down the stairs he saw Betty's raincoat on the marten trap. Her slim shoes stood beside it. In the visitors' loo it was dark; the door stood ajar. There were no lights on in the kitchen. Henry followed the smell of cigarettes along the wood-panelled corridor to his studio. She came towards him soundlessly out of the dark.

'What's happened, Henry?'

'She's gone. Martha's gone.'

'What do you mean, gone? Just like that?'

'Why did you come here?'

'Martha and I had arranged to swap cars back again. She asked me to. Hasn't she come back?'

Betty wanted to walk past him out of the dark corridor. He held her back.

'What are you doing in my studio?'

'You're hurting me! I was looking for Martha. She's bound to come back soon. Don't worry.'

Henry noticed that she was no longer holding the cigarette.

'What did you talk about?'

'What do you think? About *you*, of course. We must have talked for a whole hour about you. She idolises you. Then I told her where we always meet.'

Henry tightened his grip.

'Why? *Why* did you do that?'

Betty squirmed in his grasp. 'She wanted to go to you. That's why she went to the cliffs.'

He studied her face. 'How could she find her way?'

'Oh, come on, that's why we swapped cars. Because she doesn't have a sat nav. She'd never in her life have found it otherwise, as you know. Don't say you didn't go?'

'Give me a cigarette.'

'You did go, didn't you?'

'Yes, I did. Give me a cigarette.'

Betty took one from the packet and gave Henry a light. His hands were trembling so badly that Betty had to hold them tight. Her gaze fell on the wooden box at the foot of the stairs, but she didn't ask.

No doubt about it, Martha was dead. She'd been sitting in the car when he'd pushed it over the cliffs. He'd destroyed his life and killed the only person who'd ever loved him for his own sake. Martha was gone and with her the full life, the good life. The pictures came back to him. Henry saw her screaming soundlessly as she hit the windscreen, saw her trying to open the door and the horribly cold water entering her lungs. He saw Martha die.

As he was driving Betty home, Henry felt the beginnings of a numbness on the right side of his face. It spread from his eyebrow across his temple to his ear.

'Did you tell her about the baby?'

'No, she doesn't know anything.'

'Don't lie to me, Betty!'

'Why should I lie?'

'Have you rung anyone, talked to anyone?'

'Why are you asking? Won't she *ever* come back?'

Betty sat strangely stiff beside him, her fingers with their painted nails clasped tightly together. She didn't smoke, she didn't look at him and she didn't ask any more questions, at least not audibly. Henry stared at the road ahead. In his mind's eye he was already back home, killing the dog and emptying a canister of petrol all over the house. He'd start with that damn drilling rig, then the books. The flames wouldn't take long. Then the wooden staircase. The fire would spread upstairs quickly, the damn marten in the roof would burn too. That's what comes of creeping into strangers' houses.

'Don't talk to anyone about it, do you hear? Not anyone.'

Then she got out. She could feel Henry's gaze as she walked the fifty paces to her flat.

*　　*　　*

The rain had eased off and all the windows, except Martha's, were dark when Henry got back. Although he knew he wouldn't find her, Henry searched the whole house for his wife. With an excruciating certainty that was already a phantom pain, he flung open doors, called out her name and shone a torch behind bookcases and into cupboards and corners, as if it were a silly game of hide-and-seek. Of course she didn't respond to his calls, because she was lying at the bottom of the sea, but the thought was simply unbearable, so he called out another dozen times.

In his studio he found Betty's burnt-out cigarette. The blinds were down; she couldn't have seen much, not enough to understand. But all the same, she'd crept into his studio in stockinged feet to snoop about.

He drove Martha's Saab into the barn. He searched the car, but only found an old wooden sandal, yellowing maps and empty water bottles. The whole interior of the car smelt of Betty's lily-of-the-valley perfume. The dog panted after him as he came out with a spade and two canisters of petrol and went into the kitchen. He wanted to set fire to the house first, and then hurl himself into the well behind the chapel. He put down the canisters, laid the sharp spade on the counter and drank the remains of the whisky from the bottle. As soon as he was drunk enough he was going to use the spade to chop off Poncho's head. But however much he drank, he remained sober. Stuff tastes like whisky, he thought, but it must be water, otherwise I'd be drunk. He took the rubber gloves out of the sink. OK, let's get it over with. Come here, you filthy cur.

The dog had slunk away. Henry staggered through the house, knocked his shin and made a change of plan.

He grabbed Martha's green parka, took the dirty washing out of the laundry basket and stuffed underwear, sandals, shirt and trousers into a plastic bag. Then he put her folding bicycle carefully into the boot of the Maserati and set off. In the rear-view mirror he could see two shining yellow points. It was the eyes of the dog watching him. The creature knew everything.

Four o'clock in the morning, an hour before sunrise. The narrow road to the bay led through the town. Bright moonlight shone on the roofs as Henry let the car roll along the main street, the headlamps switched off. A cat crossed the road in front of him, carrying the night's prey in its jaws.

Sleepless as usual at full moon, Obradin stood smoking as the Maserati glided along under his window. He heard the familiar rumble of the engine and recognised the curves of the bodywork. Nobody drives towards the harbour at night with the lights off without good reason. Unless Henry was intending to load the car onto a ship in the harbour and sail away, he would at some point have to return the way he'd come.

In the bed up against the wall his Helga turned over without waking and stretched out her fleshy hand to feel for him. He fetched his Russian night-vision device from the cupboard, opened a new packet of cigarettes, and went back to stand at the window and wait.

Beyond the little fishing harbour was the bay. Henry carried the bike over the shingle beach and propped it up against the fissured cliff just as Martha had always done. He hung her parka over the handlebars by its hood and positioned her clothes carefully next to the bike as she herself might have done. Then he looked out at the cold, gleaming sea. Were the fish already eating Martha's corpse, or might her body be washed ashore here? Would she still be wearing clothes? How amateurishly I've acted, he thought. Why did I do it? The eternal metronome of the surf rolled the stones to and fro, slowly grinding them to sand. Martha had always loved the sea. But why?

As Obradin had predicted, the Maserati rolled back along the road under his window half an hour later. The headlamps were still switched off. On the green image of the goggles' residual light amplifier he could see Henry sitting at the wheel. After careful consideration, Obradin reached the conclusion that an author can have many compelling reasons for driving to the harbour at night with his lights off—the quest for the *mot juste*, for instance. The search for the right word had driven Flaubert out of the house at night, Proust into bed, Nietzsche into lunacy—why the hell should Henry Hayden be spared? This elegant conclusion brought Obradin temporary relief. When the sound of the engine had died away, he got into bed beside his wife and instantly fell asleep.

Shortly before sunrise, Henry was home again. The dog was waiting for him in the same spot. He trotted behind him into the house. In the fireplace, Henry put a match to Martha's swimsuit, then sat down in his wing armchair and watched the burning polyester melt into a glowing ball. It had been a bargain, bought on the promenade in outrageously expensive San Remo, and had fitted her so well, accentuating her shapely but not skinny waist. She had spun around in front of the mirror, as pleased as a child. Afterwards, they'd drunk Campari together and written postcards. Happiness can only be experienced with someone else, he had thought at the time. And now that was all over and done with. Charred into little pellets of plastic.

In the warmth of the flames, Henry could feel the numbness on the right side of his face. It had spread across his cheek as far as his nose. He touched his skin with his fingertips. I'm rotting, he decided. I'm rotting from the inside out. Serves me right.

And then he heard a scratch of sharp teeth above him.

6

'Martha?'

Henry came in from the garden. He took off his rubber boots at the bootjack and listened. He looked at the clock. It was getting on for nine. Really she ought to be asleep still, but—how odd—her bicycle wasn't where it usually was, leaning beside the door.

The vegetable stew was already cooking on the stove. Henry had just nipped out into the garden to pull up a few shallots. He put them on the kitchen counter next to the Patek Philippe, which he'd gift-wrapped. The dog sniffed at his trousers.

'Where's Martha, Poncho?'

The dog put his head on one side. What do you want from me? he seemed to ask.

'Then I'll just have to do it myself.'

Henry climbed the stairs to Martha's room and knocked gently.

'Martha?'

He put his hand on the doorknob and carefully opened the door.

'Darling? Are you awake?'

The standard lamp was on, the bed was untouched and a book lay open on the pillow. The dog came into the room behind Henry and sniffed. Martha wasn't in the bathroom either. Henry flung open the window and called out her name, but she didn't reply. That was odd. But not yet cause for concern. Maybe she was in the barn.

He ran a little faster on the way down, put his boots back on and went out of the house. He opened the back door; her Saab was still there. Maybe she'd just got up early, taken her bike and cycled to the sea.

Henry closed the barn door again. He stopped to think. She knows I'm already awake—she wouldn't leave without letting me know? No, she wouldn't. Henry decided to drive to the sea to look for her.

He opened the car door to let Poncho onto the passenger seat; the dog was simply crazy about driving. But he didn't get in; he lay down and pressed his nose to the ground. He normally only did that when Henry got out the garden hose to shower him down after he'd rolled in something foul. Henry took a piece of dried meat out of his pocket and held it up, but the dog didn't move. Henry threw him the treat, got in the car and started the engine. The dog knew everything.

Obradin was just pulling up the shutters in front of the fishmonger's when Henry stopped outside and lowered his window.

'Obradin, have you seen my wife? Has she come past?'

Obradin shook his head. 'I've only seen my own wife. I have cod. Do you want some cod?'

'Later.'

'Have you caught the marten?'

'Not yet.'

Henry drove on slowly. In the rear-view mirror, he saw that Obradin was watching him. Before the harbour he took the westerly fork and reached the bay a minute later. The wind was coming from the sea; the red flag that warned of dangerous currents was fluttering wildly. Henry left the key in the ignition, got out of the car and walked the hundred metres over the shingle beach to the water. Martha's bike was still propped up against the cliff. But her green parka was no longer hanging on the handlebars. The wind had blown her clothes over the beach; some of them were caught between the rocks. He saw one of Martha's green rubber sandals lying on the shingle and bent down to pick it up. Shreds of dried seaweed were dancing over the pebbles. The surf was now ash grey with gleaming white crests.

Right by the water stood Martha in her green parka.

His heart missed a beat when he saw her, his throat fired up, his knees began to tremble. She was standing with her back to him, barefoot, her trousers rolled up. Her hair was concealed beneath her hood. She bent down, picked up a pebble. Henry ran across the shingle to her.

'Martha!'

She turned around in alarm. Henry stood still. No, it wasn't her. This woman was much younger; her face was pink from the wind. She smiled, startled.

'I'm sorry, I thought you were my wife. That's her parka.'

The woman pulled the hood down off her head and Henry saw her short, reddish brown hair. She was young, not yet thirty, and began to undo the parka. If God is another word for nature, Henry thought, then there's no reason to doubt his existence.

'No, leave it.'

With Martha's sandal in his hand, he shaded his eyes and looked out to sea. The woman followed his gaze.

'Are you looking for somebody?'

'My wife. She's about your size and my age.'

Now she too looked around.

'Sorry, I haven't seen anyone here.' An apologetic smile revealed white teeth set in firm, pink gums.

'How long have you been here?'

'Must be an hour or more.'

Henry pointed at the fissured cliff behind him. 'Her bike's over there. She must be somewhere about.'

Henry set off. He ran along the water's edge, looking out to sea. The young woman looked around too, walked towards the bicycle, searched the rocks. Henry could see her out of the corner of his eye, stooping to pick up the clothes and gather them together.

Henry ran from one end of the beach to the other, the water lapping over the tops of his boots. He was out of breath when he finally got back to the bicycle. The young woman was sitting on a rock, clutching the clothes she'd gathered on her lap. She saw Henry fall to his knees and cover his face with his hands.

She was still sitting on the rock when the lifeguards pulled their boats down the slopes and launched them in the water. Two hours later a naval helicopter arrived and began to circle. The local fishermen scoured the area around the bay with dogs.

In spite of the noise in the engine room of his old cutter, Obradin heard the thundering of the rotors. He climbed up through the smoke onto the deck of *Drina* and saw the heavy naval helicopter circling low over the bay. That could only mean that they were looking for someone who'd drowned, or for a ship in distress. Obradin climbed back down into the smoke and switched off the engine. It wouldn't hold out much longer. It had lost compression and had started to spew out oil. Its time had come. Obradin didn't know where he was going to get hold of the money for a new engine. *Drina* was no ocean trawler. Since the herrings no longer came in endless droves, Obradin had been sailing further and further out to sea. Even on rough seas, he'd worked the old diesel mercilessly. Now it was nearing its end.

When Obradin reached the beach and leapt out of the car, he saw Henry standing in the surf up to his hips; two men had him by the arms and were pulling him out of the water. The men supported him on the short walk to the ambulance. His face was white; he was staggering. Half the town had already gathered in the bay. No one spoke a word; everyone was thinking the same. Obradin saw Henry's look; his eyes were as dark as molten quartz that's been burnt into the sand by a bolt of lightning.

Elenor Reens, the mayor, short-haired, petite and dressed in yellow oilskins, handed Obradin her binoculars and summed up the ineluctable. 'There won't be a funeral. She's already a long way out.'

Obradin looked through the binoculars out to sea and made the sign of the cross. There was no more he could do.

Towards evening, the wind got up. Two trawlers with searchlights tacked up and down, and another coastguard ship arrived with divers, even though everyone had long since given up hope. At midnight, the search was called off. One by one, the lights in the town went out. Only in the pub in the harbour did the drinking go on late into the night, as the day's events were discussed. There was no one who wasn't convinced that the silent, unprepossessing writer's wife had been caught by the current while bathing and carried out to sea where she had eventually drowned. Everyone knew her by sight, but nobody knew her; she'd only ever been the writer's wife. She had rarely come into town to do the shopping or go for a walk. In all weathers she had cycled to the bay to swim, always alone. The sympathy of the locals went out to the lonely man who would be spending the night without his wife, without any consolation, or hope of her return.

7

There is no silence like another person's absence. Drained of anything familiar, it is a silence that is hostile and reproachful. The shadowy figures of memory surface noiselessly and begin their picture show. Hallucinations mingle with reality; voices call us and the past returns.

For a long time after he'd closed the door behind him, Henry stood there in the dark and listened. It was no longer the same house. Martha was gone—and he was pitifully alone, locked up with a demon of guilt that was bound to torture him. He'd killed the wrong woman and stripped himself of everything, destroyed it pointlessly in an act of rashness. His punishment had already begun: each day when he awoke, the memory would wake with him and be renewed. *To keep a secret, you should never lose concentration; tell nobody and never forget.* That was how Martha had begun the first chapter of *Aggravating Circumstances*. She must have meant him. Who else could she have meant?

His dramatically staged search on the beach had been convincing. His encounter with the young woman was a gift of serendipity, for what can be more authentic than coincidence? An unsuspecting woman is gathering pebbles on the beach and witnesses a tragedy. She scours the area with the man who is out of his mind with grief; she calls the coast-guards and gathers up Martha's orphaned clothes; she cries with him, suffers with him, sees everything in every detail. *That* is authentic.

The liars among us will know that every lie must contain a certain amount of truth if it's to be convincing. A dash of truth is often enough, but it's indispensable, like the olive in the martini.

The idea of going to look for Martha had come to Henry just as he was about to call the police. Clutching the telephone receiver, he had reflected that anything you want to believe in is best experienced at firsthand. Made-up stories are soon forgotten; lies need remembering, which requires effort. Eventually, every lie becomes an unexploded bomb lurking beneath the surface, rusting away, ready to detonate. You grow careless, inattentive, you forget. But other people don't forget, so that anyone who no longer knows where the forgotten lies are buried should avoid the whole area. Henry's biography was full of these dangerous things; his past was a minefield, which is why he never set foot in it. But anything you've experienced is stored in your memory for a long time.

Trusting to this wisdom, Henry had set out in search of his dead wife, in order to recreate the growing distress that any self-respecting husband would surely have felt. And so it came about that he really was in a bad way when he broke down on the beach. He felt real despair; he wept bitterly and from the bottom of his heart. And the young woman saw it all. So far, so good.

Still very touched by himself, Henry sat down on the marten trap and pulled off his sand-filled boots. His wet socks dripped on the wood. He glanced up the stairs. The bottom steps were visible in the faint moonlight, but higher up they disappeared into the darkness. No one lived up there any more, except the marten; that was something he'd have to deal with soon enough. From now on he would live with his memories. There would be no more novels.

Henry leapt up from the box. The novel! He had promised Moreany the finished manuscript in August. Where was the manuscript? Had he overlooked it in all the excitement?

Henry took the stairs two at a time. Outside Martha's closed door lay the dog, its nose pressed to the wooden floor. The manuscript wasn't on the little table next to the typewriter as it usually was. The waste-paper basket was as empty as ever. Henry threw himself to the floor and looked under the bed; he rummaged through the cupboard and the bed and the bathroom—the manuscript wasn't there. He opened the window, unbuttoned his shirt—he was unbearably hot—and sat down on Martha's bed. Poncho trotted into the room and began to groom himself at Henry's feet.

Martha had known everything. Before driving to Betty's yesterday she had burnt the novel in the fireplace—or no, worse still, she'd sent it to Moreany. Registered, with a little postcard message in her lovely, curvy, feminine hand. Something like this:

Have fun reading, Claus. Henry didn't write a line of this. He's never written anything. He can't even write a school essay. This isn't a joke; I'm deadly serious. The only thing my husband has produced in the years of our marriage is a bastard. If you of all people, Betty, should happen to edit my last novel, you can be sure that the child in your belly will turn out like its father—a creature of no significance, worthless from the moment it's born. By the way, Henry killed his father. And ask him where his mother's buried when you get the chance. Do me a favour, Claus—if I'm no longer alive tomorrow, be so good as to inform the authorities, would you?

Henry got up from Martha's bed. No. She wouldn't do that to him; public denunciation wasn't her style. Resentment and retribution were as alien to her as the desire for fame. Henry wouldn't even have dreamed of marrying a woman with such base instincts. Martha's revenge would be the silence that already covered everything like a poisonous dust. And there it was again, that ugly gnawing. You could hear it through the wall. The marten must be directly above him.

Henry searched the house until dawn. There was no paper ash in the fireplace—only little balls from Martha's melted swimsuit. In the meticulously sorted kitchen rubbish there was nothing to be found either. In the end he gave up and, tired and at a loss, went into his bedroom to lie down. On his pillow he found the manuscript, held together with a rubber seal from a preserving jar. *White Darkness*, it said in pencil on the title page. Martha had found a title. Henry tore off the rubber band. The last chapter was missing. *Darling*, Martha had written in pencil on the last page . . . *hang on a little while longer. Can you guess how it ends? Kisses, Martha.*

*   *   *

Betty didn't come. Claus Moreany put the latest MRI scan in his desk drawer and locked it. The metastases had already spread from his hip to his spine, but there was still time. In August, Henry's manuscript would be there. That left enough time for a late summer honeymoon in Venice before the book was published. Betty loved Venice. She loved Renaissance art, the seaweed-green water of the lagoons and the Italian sun. If she were his wife, she'd inherit his entire fortune—why would she say no? In return, Moreany wouldn't expect or demand anything of her except the occasional privilege of having her near him. She didn't even have to touch him. He could still recall the revulsion of the young at the odours of old age. He'd smelt old age again only recently when he had shared his opera box with a classmate from his last year at school. Her bullish, down-covered neck protruded from her evening dress, and the smell of life that's slipped away ruined the whole of *La Traviata* for him. He was particularly troubled by the thought that he too might smell like that without being able to do anything about it.

Moreany was now seventy-one, almost forty years older than Betty. Chemotherapy was out of the question: it would cost him his hair and all that remained of his manliness. He might gain a year that way, but at what cost? Happily the cancer was carrying out its destructive work with slow deliberation, as if it too wanted to see Venice again before the end. Moreany didn't believe that he would live to see next summer—let alone father a child. But Betty was young; she could marry again after his death, have children with another man, start a family. Her children would live in Moreany's house, play in his garden and grow up in the shade of the maple trees that his father had planted in the middle of the last century. Betty would be financially secure for the rest of her life, and she would run the publishing house and watch over it with the same devotion she now brought to her work. Claus Moreany was quite convinced of that.

The door to his wood-panelled office stood open as usual. It was now ten o'clock. Impatiently, Moreany got up from his desk, fished a sheet of paper out of his wooden in-tray and stepped into the outer office where his secretary worked.

Honor Eisendraht stopped her proofreading and looked at the meaningless piece of paper he was holding out to her. She'd been working in Moreany's outer office for over twenty years. After the early years, the good years, she had witnessed the creeping decline of the publishing house, Moreany's battle against old age, and falling sales. When the figures turned red, she began to wear brighter clothes and went to the hairdresser to keep Moreany's hopes up.

She believed in the power of invisible signs that, like hidden markers, guide to their destinations those who seek. One by one, she had replaced the gloomy illustrated calendars in Moreany's office and removed the non-sellers from the bookshelves—and for years now she had been making decaffeinated mocha with a pinch of cardamom. The relaxing powers of this member of the ginger family are said to have prevented world wars. Moreany seemed not to notice any positive effects, which strengthened Honor in her conviction that she'd got the dose just right. He was clearly improved since the shadowy semi-darkness of his office smelt subtly of Maghrebi mint and sandalwood, and the flowers on his desk were no longer left to wilt.

In spite of her gentle interventions, however, insolvency drew nearer. The energy with which Moreany had run the firm for so long began to wane. Honor now dealt with his private correspondence and took control of that holiest of holies, the bookkeeping. An intuitive understanding of numbers and sums is a gift that cannot be learnt. Reading the annual accounts like a musical score, Honor could see the dynamic nature of a business; she found sources of income in foreign rights and film options. It did not escape her attention that Moreany had been incurring losses for years. She also noticed that he was already making arrangements for his will and paying regular visits to a doctor. Potential buyers materialised. They had smelt blood and brought their numbers men along even on their first visit. While these vultures were casting an eye over the inventory, Honor served coffee that she'd made out of old flower water, and passed round biscuits. She sat in the outer office and waited. It wasn't long before the first of them asked for the bathroom. He did not return.

Even so, as things stood, it was only a matter of time before the company died a death. Honor Eisendraht's quiet hope, that her time at Moreany's side was approaching, evaporated when that woman—vain, ignorant and far too young—entered the outer office with the manuscript of *Frank Ellis* under her arm.

Honor put the woman at half her age. Betty was smooth and well rounded and beautiful. In an open declaration of war, she was wearing a short black-and-white-checked skirt. The gun barrels of her thighs were pointed straight at Moreany, who had got up from his desk when she entered his office. After a few words, Moreany shut the door, something he never did. It proved to be a horrifically long day. The woman stayed for four hours. Honor heard her boss on the phone. He didn't have his calls put through from the outer office as he usually did, but dialled direct—another bad sign. In the end he came out, manuscript in hand, in a state of excitement, and asked her to go and get champagne. The smell of cigarettes and lily-of-the-valley perfume emanated from his office. Honor could see the toe seam of Betty's stockinged foot bobbing up and down in Moreany's Eames chair, which was usually reserved for guests of state.

Honor went to the supermarket on the corner, bought the champagne and then got a few glasses from the kitchen. She herself was not invited to have a glass of champagne. After closing hours she aired the outer office and cleared up Moreany's room. She washed up the glasses, emptied the full ashtrays on Moreany's desk and counted the lipstick-stained butts. It was the twenty-third of March. Moreany had forgotten her birthday. Man is his own worst enemy; woman's worst enemy is other women.

The success of *Frank Ellis* changed everything. Moreany blossomed. Betty put in a daily appearance to discuss who knows what. After a deliberately patronising 'Good morning, Honor,' as if addressing a servant, she shut Moreany's door behind her. Only her revolting, cheap-smelling lily-of-the-valley perfume lingered in the outer office.

It is said that dragon trees grant unspoken wishes. Honor bought one and put it in the window of her office. The plant put out sword-shaped leaves like little daggers, and half a year later Betty's visits did indeed grow less frequent. Honor saw the first sweet-scented flowers on the dragon tree. 'Betty's started to take work home with her,' Moreany explained, and didn't look particularly happy about it. Honor had absolutely no desire to know what kind of work. So he'd realised he was too old for her. Or, better still, Betty had found another man, some stupid young lout who'd succumbed to her lure. The door to Moreany's office was left ajar once more—the dragon tree came into full flower.

'Isn't Betty here yet?' Moreany asked, paper in hand. Honor Eisendraht got up, went to the window and looked down at the car park.

'Her car's not there.'

Moreany was annoyed. Why had he betrayed the impatience of his heart instead of looking out the window himself? At that moment, Betty walked through the door. She was wearing a grey-green suit that accentuated her phenomenal waist. She looked a little tired, and paler than usual.

'Sorry, Claus, my car's broken down. I had to get a rental car.'

Honor Eisendraht observed that Betty's apology was not directed at her. It was a long time since the women had deigned to look at one another. Moreany withdrew into his office so as not to get wet, for as soon as Betty's warm front met Honor's cold front, it started to rain in the outer office.

Betty shut the door behind her as usual and put two editor's reports on Moreany's desk. She took the inevitable menthol cigarette out of a packet; Moreany gave her a light.

'I spoke to Henry yesterday,' said Moreany. 'His manuscript will be finished in August. Has he rung you?'

'Me? No.'

'It sounds as if he's having trouble with the end.'

Betty inhaled the smoke. 'Doesn't everyone? I mean, isn't it necessary? Isn't it normal?'

'He can't make up his mind.'

'Is that what he said? What did he mean?'

Honor brought in the coffee; the two of them waited in silence until she'd disappeared again. Moreany noticed grains of sand on Betty's right heel. His gaze lingered on the little veins on her ankle.

'Give him a ring, Betty. Maybe he needs help.'

She shrugged. 'I can try, but who can help Beethoven with the Ninth, eh?'

Moreany laughed. Be my wife this instant! he wanted to shout. Let me kiss your feet, touch your breasts, comb your golden hair! But he didn't speak. Betty stubbed out her unfinished cigarette in the brass ashtray that Moreany had put on his desk specially for her. He didn't smoke himself. So far she hadn't noticed.

110

'What's the matter with your car?'

'It wouldn't start this morning. Maybe I left the lights on.'

'Do you have time to accompany me to Venice?'

She didn't seem overjoyed by the idea.

'When?'

The telephone on his desk began to buzz. The white light flashed. Honor was trying to put a call through. Moreany ignored it.

'What's the matter with your car?'

'You just asked me that. It wouldn't start, that's all. Don't you want to take the call?'

Venice then.

Moreany picked up the receiver. 'Put him through, Honor.' He signalled to Betty that Henry was on the line, but she already knew.

'Henry, old boy, how are you?'

Moreany listened for a while; Betty saw his expression darken. She could hear Henry's deep voice; he was speaking slowly.

'I'll come over at once.'

Moreany hung up distraitly, looking at the floor as if searching for a lost answer.

'What's happened?'

'Henry's wife has drowned.'

'When?'

'Last night.'

'That's not possible.'

'She's drowned. He just told me. Just now.'

'In the night? *Last* night?'

Moreany looked up from the floor. 'I must go to him straight away.'

Betty handed Moreany his coat, wondering whether Henry had already known Martha was dead when she'd returned Martha's car. Would he have run up to her room to look, if he had?

Honor Eisendraht came into the office and sat down ashen-faced in the Eames chair.

'You must have heard everything, Honor. Please cancel my appointments, for tomorrow too. Betty . . .'

'Yes?'

'We'll have to postpone Venice. Would you accompany me, please?'

From the window, Honor saw the two of them in the car park, getting into Moreany's dark green Jaguar. He opened Betty's door and let her get in first. Honor took her pack of tarot cards out of her handbag and shuffled them thoroughly. It was the Tower. A singularly inauspicious card.

During the hour-long drive neither spoke a word. Moreany drove fast, concentrating. Decades ago he had come second in the Mille Miglia and was still an excellent driver. The car was quiet; only the indicator ticked when he turned a corner. Betty felt a wave of nausea and wondered whether it was fear or just a symptom of pregnancy. Martha's unexpected call had not been a goodwill visit. 'You ought to know,' she had said even before she was inside, 'that I don't hate you. The man we both love is in a serious crisis. He can't finish his novel; I see him suffering.' Martha had been so touchingly cheerful as she had sat with her on the sofa. She had spoken of the friendship that comes from love, of good times and of urgently required changes. It is well known that people in despair grow calm once they have decided to take the final step, their spirits soothed at the prospect of the sweet release of death.

Betty lowered the car window. Why hadn't Martha jumped into the sea before last night if she'd known everything for so long? Maybe it was revenge, after all. She wanted to destroy our happiness by committing suicide, Betty thought. Quite possible that Henry would blame her for Martha's death. How would Moreany react when he found out about it all? Venice would be just the ticket now. Far enough away to think things over, but near enough to get back to Henry in three hours. Again the violent twinge in her womb. His child. It was inside her, growing, communicating with her. She'd have it all to herself.

8

The corpse was floating face down, its outspread arms parallel to the coast. A young cormorant landed on its back and spread its wings to dry its feathers. The bird drifted past Obradin's cutter on the back of the corpse and was carried by the current on towards the promontory, whose northern tip extended into the sea for miles.

Obradin had gone out to sea, not in order to fish, but to collect his thoughts. He went slowly so as to spare the gasping engine. When the mainland was out of sight he turned it off and let the cutter drift. He sat down on the foredeck to smoke a Bosnian cigarette. He could have been mistaken, in which case it wasn't Henry's car he'd seen so clearly the night before. Then the man at the wheel wasn't Henry either—or his double had just stolen his Maserati. It had been nothing but a disconcertingly detailed dream, right down to the butts that Helga had cleared off the windowsill and put on his bedside table.

And even if he hadn't been mistaken—and there was reason to believe that this was the case—a man is entitled to drive wherever he likes at night with his lights off, and his wife's entitled to drown wherever and whenever she likes. Coincidence without connection, and nobody's business anyway. But then there was that matter of the bike.

Before sunrise, Obradin had woken up after only an hour's sleep, and got out of bed at once. He dressed quietly and drove to the harbour a few minutes later. *Drina* lay rocking sluggishly at the pier. Obradin checked the ropes and the lashed-down nets, opened and closed all the hatches, made sure that the anchor was in place, jumped back onto the pier and climbed over the concrete breakwaters that had been built by forced labourers in the last months of the war.

The sun rose. Obradin covered the few hundred metres to the beach on foot. He saw Martha's bike propped up against a rock; every day she rode it past his shop down to the bay. But never before lunchtime. Her neatly folded clothes lay next to the bike. He shielded his eyes from the intense rays of the rising sun. After searching the bay in vain for Henry's wife, he returned to his cutter.

*

Obradin gazed after the cormorant as it flew over the radio mast of his cutter towards the coast. Then he started up the diesel again. The current had pulled him a few nautical miles out to sea. He sailed slowly back to the harbour, moored *Drina* and was soon walking through the door of his fishmonger's shop.

'The diesel's had it,' he said. 'And without the cutter we may as well give up.'

Without another word he strode past Helga (who as usual was on the phone instead of working), opened the wooden hatch in the floor and disappeared into the cellar. He re-emerged with a barrel of slivovitz on his shoulder and kicked the hatch shut.

Helga covered the receiver with her hand. 'What are you up to?'

'What does it look like?'

'What about the shop?'

'We're closing.'

'What about the fish soup?'

'There won't be any.'

'When are you coming back?'

Obradin went round the fish counter to his Helga, stroked her cheek with his hairy fingers and kissed her goodbye on the mouth.

'You know when.'

Only minutes later, Helga rang the game warden and the doctor from the neighbouring town. The two of them were to stand by at the ready; in about two hours it would be time to act again. The doctor packed his bag when he heard this; the game warden opened his weapons cupboard and took out a special gun.

* * *

Pale and unshaven, Henry stood outside the house in his rubber boots, his shirt hanging out of his trousers. He was leaning on a shovel when Moreany's Jaguar came over the hill. The car was trailing a cloud of dust. Even from a distance, Henry could see that Moreany was not alone. Poncho ran to meet the car and leapt about, barking. Henry saw Betty in the passenger seat. She made no move to get out. Poncho stood up on his hind legs, curious, and sniffed at the window.

The two men embraced in silence. Moreany's smooth, rosy cheeks with their white sideburns smelt of Old Spice. Henry looked over at Betty. Why didn't she get out? Had she already confessed everything to Moreany?

Moreany extricated himself from Henry's embrace with reddened eyes.

'I don't know what to say.'

'What can one say?'

'I asked Betty to come too. She was in my office when you rang.'

Henry opened the door and held out his hand to Betty. The smell of her perfume flooded out of the car. She felt his firm, warning hold as he embraced her; his stubbly chin scratched her cheek. They kissed each other like brother and sister; she felt another fierce twinge in her womb.

'Please try not to hate me, my darling.'

'I love you. How's our baby?'

'It just moved. I can feel it.'

'Have you told Moreany anything about us?'

'Of course not. Are you sure she's dead?'

Disconcerted, Henry gave her an icy stare. 'Do you want her to come back?' he whispered.

In Henry's studio it smelt of cold tobacco. The manuscript was next to the typewriter on his desk. A broken elastic band was rolled up beside his fountain pen. The slats of the blinds at the enormous picture window were half closed. Notes and crumpled-up paper lay scattered all over the floor.

Henry had spent all morning shuffling things around in his studio and decking it out with creative mess. To indicate the trace elements of complex thought, he'd made little stacks of unread books, inserting a bookmark here and there. He'd even remembered a half-full coffee cup and chewed cigar butt. All the sports supplements and men's magazines had vanished, and he'd rolled the drilling rig into a corner underneath the Botero painting of fat children. It looked like a place where work was done. Apart from the manuscript, it was all his.

Betty caught sight of the manuscript immediately and made a beeline for it, her hand outstretched.

'Don't touch!'

She stopped in her tracks.

'Please don't. It's not finished yet.'

'Sorry. You work on a *typewriter*?'

'Yes. Why not?'

'There is a copy of the text, isn't there?' Moreany put in.

'Not yet. That's the original. It goes in the safe every evening.'

Moreany and Betty exchanged glances. 'That's risky, Henry, to put it mildly.'

Henry opened a bottle of single malt and filled three glasses. Moreany disappeared briefly into the visitors' loo, walking unsteadily. Betty looked about her. The room had been very tidy when she'd examined it in the dark the night before. Now everything was a mess and it reeked of tobacco. She scrutinised the hairy dog blanket next to the desk chair and the waste-paper basket overflowing with rejected ideas, probably worth millions even half full. In the darkness she'd discerned the drilling rig as an unidentifiable structure standing in the room. Now it had vanished.

Moreany came back looking even worse, his hands smelling of soap. Henry handed him a glass.

'Ice?'

'One cube, if you have some.'

'Martha didn't leave a note.' Returning from the kitchen with the ice, Henry began his report. 'Her bike was on the beach.'

Moreany stirred the ice in his glass with his index finger. 'Did *you* find her?'

'No one's found her. The current pulled Martha out to sea. Her rubber sandals, her things, the bike— everything was still there.'

'On the beach?' Betty asked.

Henry saw her astonished look.

'Yes. Down in the little bay next to the harbour where she always goes swimming.'

Henry took a large swig of Scotch, sucked the ice cube briefly and spat it back into the glass. He didn't seem to be suffering much, Betty thought, but then what does suffering look like?

'When she didn't come back for lunch, I went to the beach. Down by the water there was a woman in Martha's green parka, but it was someone else.' Again, Henry saw Betty's astonished look. 'The wind had blown it over the beach and she was cold. She'd put it on.'

'How old was she?'

'A little younger than you.'

'Do you know her?'

'No. Does it matter?'

Moreany cleared his throat. 'Excuse me for blurting this out, but is it out of the question that Martha's still alive? I mean, couldn't something unusual have happened?'

'And what might that be?' Henry asked.

'Well . . . you live here without any kind of security at all. Isn't it conceivable that Martha'—Moreany paused to formulate the thought—'was kidnapped in order to blackmail you?'

'Who'd be that stupid, Claus? Any sensible person would kidnap *me* and then blackmail Martha, wouldn't they?'

Betty lit a cigarette and snapped the lighter shut with a flourish. 'Such people exist, Henry. Stupid, evil people.'

Henry didn't like her tone. 'And who might they be?'

For a while it was quiet in the room. Henry saw smoke streaming out of Betty's narrow nostrils like dragon's breath. She was punishing him, because she knew he was lying.

'Who called the police?' It was Moreany who broke the silence.

'No one so far.'

'I'm going to do it now,' Moreany said, patting his pockets.

Henry put his glass down. 'I think I'd better do that.'

He went into the kitchen to make the call. He should have done it ages ago. How annoying. He had clean forgotten.

Betty was playing with the hovawart in the garden while Moreany and Henry waited in the kitchen for the police. The dog jumped up at her; she threw a stick. Word must have got around among dogs that, if you bring human beings sticks or balls, they will throw them tirelessly. Betty's immaculate skin shone in the sun; there wasn't a cloud in the sky. The two men watched her, each deep in his own thoughts.

Henry noticed that Moreany was clutching the benchtop, swaying slightly. He'd grown old in the last few months and lost weight. Tiny beads of sweat glistened at his hairline. His fingers had felt cold when Henry had handed him the Scotch.

'Would you like a bite to eat, Claus? I've made some lentil soup. It won't take a moment to warm up.'

Without waiting for a reply, he got the bowl of soup out of the fridge, peeled off the foil and sniffed it.

'Today's not the day to talk about this, Henry, but I was going to propose to Betty earlier on.'

'What?'

Henry turned his back on Moreany, put the bowl in the microwave and wondered whether the news was bad or absurdly good. He could see Moreany's distorted outline reflected in the microwave door.

'You heard me. I'd like to marry Betty. I know I'm too old for her, but I love her. What do you think about that?'

Henry peered out of the window. Betty was nowhere to be seen.

'This was *today*?'

'A little while ago in my office. She comes in and I want to ask her if she'd like to be my wife, but I'm completely tongue-tied. Instead, I ask her twice what's the matter with her car. Isn't that ridiculous?'

I don't deserve to be this lucky, Henry thought. 'What is the matter with her car?'

'She has some problem or other with it. And then you rang up, and then it was too late.'

'What kind of problem?'

'You'll have to ask her yourself. I don't know.'

Again Henry looked into the future. Assuming this unlikely stroke of luck really did happen and Betty married Moreany, he would of course be best man. Betty would give birth to his child, who was sure to be a beautiful baby. Henry would be godfather to his own child, and would of course be the best godfather in the world. All these *interpersonal* problems would be solved—at least in part. But how to convince Betty about a marriage of convenience in this day and age? With the secret joy of a prospector who's found a nugget as big as your fist, Henry laid both his hands on the shoulders of his friend and publisher.

'I'm so pleased for you, Claus. It's never too late. Just follow your heart and pop the question.'

Moreany embraced Henry. Even in such desperate circumstances, Henry was magnanimous enough to be pleased at the happiness of others. Moreany couldn't say anything, he was so touched.

The microwave chirped. Henry took out the soup bowl and set it down on the table in front of Moreany. Henry was visibly moved too.

'Would you like a slice of bread with it?'

* * *

Obradin's incisors lay in the damp sand of the cellar floor. The steep steps which you had to go down backwards at the best of times were now extra slippery with bloody saliva. Earlier on, Obradin had smashed the glass door of his shop, presumably because he couldn't find his key, and had plunged headlong down the steps trying to fetch a second barrel of slivovitz from the cellar.

A big pile of shit next to the slivovitz barrels furnished evidence that Obradin must have been in the cellar since eleven in the morning. At lunchtime the little harbour pub opened, where Obradin lost a further tooth, because his idea of payment in kind did not correspond with that of the landlord. As it later turned out, the tooth was rotten and would have had to come out sooner or later in any case. Not one of the men who came rushing up to help managed to pacify the raging Serb.

He was finally hit by a tranquilliser dart from the game warden's gun. The anaesthetic, known as Hellabrunn mixture, was dosed for a rhinoceros; even so, Obradin had enough time to sing the Serbian national anthem before falling into a death-like sleep.

Helga, who had accurately predicted the course and duration of his rampage, was waiting outside the fishmonger's together with the doctor when her husband was returned to her more dead than alive. It was heartbreaking to watch her suffer. In twenty years of married life she'd experienced half-a-dozen of these attacks, without ever finding out what caused them. The eruptions remained as unpredictable as earthquakes. Obradin claimed not to be able to remember what triggered them, which from a toxico-logical point of view was hardly surprising. The doctor diagnosed various haematoma and tooth loss in Obradin, but otherwise normal vital functions; the men carried him to the double bed he shared with Helga and there he remained for the time being.

Outside, Poncho was barking. A vehicle drew up. Henry saw that it wasn't the police. Lashed tight with blue cord, Martha's bicycle stood like a monument on the pick-up tray. Henry had seen the bike countless times without feeling anything. What is there to feel at the sight of an old rusty bike? But now it was different. Standing at right angles to the frame, the handlebars and the old lamp were pointing straight at him. The rust at the neck of the saddle was gleaming like dried blood—and there in the wheel was the broken spoke he'd never replaced.

At the steering wheel sat Elenor Reens, the mayor, and next to her the young woman from the beach. She was wearing a baseball cap and had pushed her sunglasses up onto the peak. Elenor got out and took a packet containing Martha's things from the back seat; the rubber sandals and Martha's parka were in a plastic bag. She put everything on the bonnet.

'Just let us know if there's anything we can do. No matter what. We'll always be here for you. I'm speaking on behalf of everyone—you and your wife are in the thoughts of the whole town.'

'Thank you.'

Elenor followed Henry's gaze.

'This is my daughter, Sonja.'

Sonja opened the door hesitantly, got out, walked round the car to Henry and clasped his outstretched hand. She was wearing white trainers and faded blue jeans; her khaki jacket was buttoned up to the neck as if she was cold. Her hand was cool and slender, her eyes were of topaz-blue earnestness, the line of her lips looked as if it had been drawn with a fine brush.

Aphrodite stops at nothing to torment me, Henry thought. 'How could I have forgotten? We've already met,' he said. Sonja nodded. Henry had the feeling she wanted to tell him something she couldn't say in her mother's presence.

Elenor went back to her car. 'Oh, by the way, Obradin went berserk again. The game warden brought him down with a tranquilliser gun.'

* * *

Every murderer ought to know that, as the science of criminal investigation, modern forensics are very thorough. If a person disappears, no stone is left unturned. The murderer has to prepare himself for an investigation that may go on for a long time and will brook no logical contradiction.

A murderer must be alert. His enemy is detail. The thoughtless word, the mere nothing he forgot, the trifling mistake that wrecks everything. He has to keep the memory of his crime alive and kindle it within himself every day, but still keep silent. But keeping silent is against human nature. It's not easy to keep a secret. A lifetime spent keeping silent is agony. Looked at that way, a murderer's punishment begins on the day of his crime.

The wife killers and husband murderers among us should take particular note that any personal advantage derived from the disappearance of one's spouse, whether it be life insurance or the understandable desire for freedom, will bring an even more thorough investigation in its wake.

No one knew this better than Henry. In his long days of leisure he had extended his knowledge of forensics, learning among other things that the police notify the insurance companies in cases of unexplained death. As everyone knows, insurance companies are not fond of paying back money they've already collected, no matter how small the sum. If they do settle, it should always be interpreted as an act of tempering justice with mercy. When it comes to paying out life insurance, they get particularly suspicious and let loose their detectives. You have to beware of these specialists, who work on commission and are paid by results. They know that all the world's a stage and act accordingly, searching not for truth, but always for untruth. Murder, fraud and self-inflicted injury are insurance scams as far as these gentlemen are concerned—there's no other way to describe them. In this way they deny the psychological aspect of the struggle for existence—and for them a policy payment is tantamount to the triumph of evil. So, as a basic rule, murder should look like an accident. That is harder than it may seem to begin with, because even an accident has a plausible story behind it; accidents don't just happen. But more on this later.

Strictly speaking, Martha's death wasn't murder; it was an accident. Nevertheless, Henry had already made two crucial mistakes. He had failed to ring the police straight away, and the whereabouts of Betty's Subaru shouldn't have been associated with him. Whatever the police found out, it should in the end be clear beyond doubt that Henry would not derive any advantage from Martha's disappearance.

That corresponded entirely with the truth. There was no life insurance in his favour, only in hers. Henry wouldn't inherit a thing from Martha, because it wasn't Martha who was rich but him. Nor had she been in the public eye—that was just him. So far, so good. Thanks to his experience of lying, or merely making excuses, Henry was confident that people would continue to believe him as long as he lied. It was only the truth he had to be sparing and prudent with.

He put the packet containing Martha's clothes on the kitchen island. Then he said goodbye to Betty and Moreany, who were going back to the office together. Henry saw them to the Jaguar, embraced them both affectionately and with equal intensity, and whispered in Betty's ear as he said goodbye, 'Report the car stolen; I'll explain everything to you later.' She waved to him. She's got me in the palm of her hand, Henry thought, and waved back.

* * *

Jenssen was a young detective with butter-yellow hair and watery blue eyes. He was descended from Vikings; Henry could see that at a glance. He was athletic and clearly worked out. His manicured hand felt strangely fat. He had read Henry's novels, was a big fan of *Aggravating Circumstances* and would have liked to be a court reporter, but, as he told Henry, he couldn't write. Well, who can? Henry thought.

'Your heroes are men of action, Herr Hayden,' Jenssen enthused by way of greeting. 'Always something going on. And you never know what's going to happen next. Strange happenings, dark secrets, dangers lurking everywhere and really brilliant villains.'

Henry took to him at once. He wasn't so keen on his female colleague, who always stood half a pace behind him. She was skinny and obviously unqualified, because she didn't know any of Henry's novels.

'Do you have a photo of your wife?' she asked, without a trace of sympathy or understanding.

Henry went into his study and returned with a holiday photo of Martha and him together in Portugal. The policewoman examined it for a long time as if she wanted to creep inside it. Her pinched face with its narrow eyes under a bushy monobrow made Henry think of an opossum. Maybe he could pair her off with the marten in his roof at some point;

it might result in some interesting offspring. The silver streaks in her dark hair seemed to suggest that she was severely over-acidified as a result of professional mistrust.

She passed the photo on to Jenssen and curiously sniffed at the air, which Henry found irritating. Was she somehow checking for molecules of guilt and fear? All dogs can smell fear; some can even smell epilepsy and cancer. Why not guilt? Guilt emissions must linger around everyone who is afraid of discovery or punishment. Fortunately, there are not yet any devices finely tuned enough to detect such molecules. But they may yet come.

Henry's suspicion intensified in the kitchen when the woman bent over the packet containing Martha's clothes and sniffed it.

'What colour is her swimsuit?'

'Blue. What do you smell?' he asked.

'Can we take this with us?' came her reply.

'Will I get them back again? They're very private things.'

'How often did your wife go swimming in the sea?'

Her habit of not answering Henry's questions was getting on his nerves. 'My wife goes swimming every day. Even in the winter when it snows. She's a fantastic swimmer. Do you swim too?'

'Do you know the sea here?'

'Only to look at. I don't go in.'

Jenssen now showed off his nautical knowledge—
no doubt a legacy from his ancestors—and described
the strong north-westerly currents. There were often
shoes washed ashore after swimming accidents,
especially plastic shoes; they drifted as far as
Greenland, sometimes with a foot still inside. Henry
remembered Obradin telling him he occasionally
saw ownerless shoes floating on the sea. He suddenly
thought of Obradin. Why hadn't he come to offer his
condolences?

'But your wife wasn't wearing swimming shoes
when she went in the water.'

The opossum was pointing at Martha's swimming
shoes with her spindly finger. The blood rose in
Henry's throat when he realised his annoying mistake.
He hadn't been thinking. It was logical that Martha
would have gone in the water *wearing* her swimming
shoes—why would she leave them on the beach?

'To be honest, I'm surprised at that too,' Henry
replied. 'My wife *always* wears her rubber sandals
when she goes in the water, because of the sharp
stones. She has sensitive feet.'

'It's possible,' put in Jenssen, who had noticed
Henry's stoical use of the present tense, 'that her
shoes were washed up and then blown over the beach
by the wind. That's why you found them.'

A good explanation. Henry was coming to like the
fellow more and more. He decided to take a risk.

'You know all about this kind of thing, Herr Jenssen. Is it possible that my wife was kidnapped?'

The policeman knit his brows. 'Has anyone been in touch?'

Henry shook his head.

'Would you pay a ransom for your wife?' the evil colleague asked.

This question showed that her sense of smell was considerably better developed than her cerebral cortex. Of course he'd pay! No sum would be too large if it would bring back his wife.

'Money's no object,' Henry replied with emphasis.

'Did your wife leave a farewell letter?'

Oh, these uneducated people! They didn't know Martha. She wouldn't have announced her suicide in writing or—worse still—given reasons for it. Everything she did, she did without giving reasons; everything was *l'art pour l'art* for her. Besides, it went against Martha's fine sense of drama to announce something which then happened in any case.

'No. She didn't want to say goodbye, definitely not. Not to me, and not to life.'

'Did she suffer from depression? Was she on medication?'

'She laughs a lot and likes eating fish, if that's what you mean.'

The policeman ran his hand thoughtfully through his butter-yellow hair. He had no sense of humour. 'If

I may ask a rather straight question—you didn't have any marital problems, weren't planning to get divorced, were you? Just a question.'

Henry touched the skin under his right eye. The numb feeling was coming back.

'No way. Never.'

Afterwards, Henry showed the two of them through every room in the house. He spoke quietly, answered all their questions, gave a detailed and truthful description of the search for his wife, and of how he'd made dinner for her the evening before—and then burst into tears standing in front of her empty bed.

Henry continued to speak of Martha in the present tense, as if she were still alive. He finished by showing them round the cellar, stables, barn, garden and chapel. He gave them an old cardboard box for Martha's clothes and then helped them to lift her bicycle into the police car.

Janssen gave Henry his card.

'Please let me know immediately if you find any trace of my wife,' Henry said as they parted. 'No matter what it is.'

After they'd left, he fetched a heavy mallet from the barn and started to smash up the wall behind Martha's bed.

9

There was something not quite right about Henry's story. Martha hadn't drowned on the beach. Betty didn't believe she had returned home from the cliffs. What was clear was that her Subaru was still missing—who knows, maybe it was rusting away at the bottom of the sea with Martha in the driver's seat. This all meant that Betty herself was mixed up in the affair. Strictly speaking she was even partly to blame for Martha's death, because she had stolen her husband from her—or had that been fate? If the car were to be found, there'd be a great many awkward questions. Betty decided to look on the bright side for the time being. Martha's death had cleared the way for a life with Henry and the baby.

She remembered how Henry had once said that if you make your dreams come true you have to live with them. He'd made happiness sound like a traumatic experience you could never entirely come to terms with. He himself no longer had any dreams, Henry had added; he'd already achieved everything. Apart from that, Henry revealed hardly anything about himself. He never spoke of his past, as if it was some unsavoury thing that had to be hidden away before the guests arrived for dinner. If at all, he spoke about the time after Betty had met him. She had the feeling that, for each person, Henry chose a past to suit the occasion. He twisted it like a kaleidoscope, always revealing a different aspect of the same thing.

Moreany had proposed to her in his Jaguar in the car park outside the office. He spoke frankly of his feelings for her and of the fortune she would inherit when he was no longer around. Betty was surprised and genuinely touched. At the same time she felt another wave of nausea and asked him for some time to think it over, which she later regretted, because there wasn't anything to think over. They parted with a kiss on the cheek. Moreany walked across the car park with a spring in his step; Betty unlocked her rental car to drive to the police. From long-established habit, she glanced up at the third floor. Honor Eisendraht was standing at the window.

Honor tore a leaf off the dragon tree and crushed it between her fingers. She had observed the kiss by the Jaguar and now, watching Moreany cross the car park on winged feet, she felt a strong desire to flay the skin off her own face. When Honor had started to work for Moreany all those years ago, she had been young and desirable. Why, oh why, had she kept quiet all those years in her office chair, serving and waiting until someone younger came along and took everything away from her? It is well known that our worst mistakes are the ones we don't notice.

Moreany came into the outer office, breathing heavily; he must have taken the stairs instead of the lift. Honor wondered whether he really believed that death would make an exception for him and grant him an extra day for this ludicrous exercise.

'Have they found the poor woman?' she asked.

Moreany understood at once whom she meant. 'No. She must have been caught by a current. They'll never find her.'

Moreany went into his office. He left the door ajar as usual. Honor could hear paper rustling. She got up from her chair, smoothed her skirt and stepped into his office. Moreany was rummaging around on his desk; he was still out of breath.

'How's Herr Hayden?'

'Amazingly well,' Moreany replied. '*Amazing.*'

'Can I do anything? Shall I prepare a statement for the press?'

Moreany interrupted his search, propping himself up on the desk with both hands. 'Honor, that would be wonderful. Please don't write "deceased", no details, and put it on my desk.'

'I'll make some valerian tea.'

'No need to do that. I have to leave again in a second.'

'A Herr Fasch rang up three times.'

'Who is he?'

'He says he's an old school friend of Herr Hayden.'

Honor Eisendraht waited at the window until Moreany had got in his car and driven off. She went into his office. After she'd poured herself a double Scotch from the glass decanter that stood on the little black ebony table, she sat down at his desk. 'We'll have to postpone Venice,' Moreany had said to Betty when they'd heard about Martha Hayden's death. Yes, Honor thought, go to Venice, just you go. There's a *laguna morta* there. I'll wait there for you, Betty, you bloody whore, and I'll drown you.

She drained the glass and began to rifle through the drawers. She removed a blonde hair and a big fat fly from the pen groove. Honor was looking for travel documents, plane tickets or a hotel reservation in Venice. The middle drawer was locked. Honor felt for the key under the leather desk mat and unlocked it. Along with notes and press cuttings, she found an empty pill box and some cash. Right at the bottom was a yellow A5 envelope, unmarked. It wasn't sealed. She opened it gingerly. Inside were two MRI images of Moreany's lumbar vertebrae and histological findings of the tumours that had permeated his vertebral body.

Reports in hand, Honor hurried back into the outer office, shuffled the tarot deck and turned over the top card. It was the Tower again. Now there was no longer the shadow of a doubt.

At the police station, Betty reported her Subaru stolen. As she was filling out the insurance form beneath the searching gaze of the duty officer, she could feel her breasts ache and the nausea return. She couldn't remember when she'd last had anything to eat. Moments later, she was throwing up sour water in a urinal, because the women's toilet was occupied. The reason for her nausea was not Moreany's proposal, nor was it Henry's absurd story about his wife's death on the beach. It was clearly the baby in her belly. It wouldn't be possible to conceal it for much longer. She urgently needed to decide on a plan of action with Henry.

She left the police station through the steel security door and leaned against the sunlit brick wall surrounding its grounds. Mechanically, she took a cigarette from the packet, lit it and inhaled. The menthol smoke tasted revolting. Betty threw the cigarette onto the street along with the packet and bought herself a newspaper at a kiosk.

Author Henry Hayden's wife drowned, it said on the bottom of the front page in smallish print. It was just a brief report without a photograph. Betty dug her telephone out of her bag and rang Henry. Because she knew he didn't have a message machine, she let it ring for a long time. Henry didn't answer. Betty waited about a minute and then tried again.

The brute had bitten him. Henry rinsed the wound in clean water and examined it. The sharp teeth had cut right through to the bone, leaving blue-red holes below his wrist. Downstairs in the kitchen the phone was ringing. Henry ignored it and looked in Martha's bathroom mirror.

His face was black with dust and wood shavings; cobwebs and mummified larvae hung in his hair. He looked like Indiana Jones without the hat. His left ear was encrusted with blood; his shirt was ripped to shreds; arms, belly and legs were studded with splinters of wood.

After opening up the wall behind Martha's bed in a fit of frustrated pique, he'd gone on a marten hunt armed with a small spear gun. It was a completely absurd undertaking—an example of what Freud rightly calls 'symptomatic actions', because they 'give expression to something which the agent himself does not suspect in them and which he does not as a rule intend to let others know about, but to keep to himself'. Well, who could be blamed?

Between the roof tiles and the thermal insulation there was a narrow crawling space. Henry had climbed through the hole in Martha's wall into the roof cavity and crawled on his stomach like a soldier over the rough-hewn planks. He kept pausing, listening and then working his way forward again. He could smell the animal's secretions. After a while he heard the patter of curved claws on the wood, cocked the trigger on the spear gun, switched off his head torch, and held his breath.

But martens are hunters too. It could see, hear and smell better than Henry—and this was its territory. The animal could sense danger and didn't leave its hiding place; its instincts protected it. Animals don't understand much, but they know everything. Humans make mistakes, because they believe; humans rush headlong towards ruin, because they hope. Animals don't hope, they don't look into the future and they don't doubt themselves. That's why the marten didn't leave its hiding place.

Henry found eggshells, feathers, bones and pungent-smelling droppings that were still soft and oily. As he squeezed his way on through the labyrinth of old oak beams, long splinters of wood pushed their way into his skin. He ignored the pain. So much the better, he thought. If the filthy brute smells my blood it might make the mistake of coming closer. But the filthy brute did not appear.

143

At some point, Henry realised he'd lost his bearings. Martha's room was on the west side of the house; the roof here was a good thirty metres long. He had crawled maybe twenty metres. Wind whistled through a crack from somewhere and blew dried insects up his nose. He had to sneeze and tried to turn over in the tight space.

As he was performing this manoeuvre, he knocked his head torch off, the light went out and the battery rolled out of its plastic compartment. When Henry tried to roll onto his back in the dark he accidentally pulled the trigger. With a dull thud the steel spear landed in the beam right next to his ear. It had been driven half a finger deep into the oak. If the spear had hit him in the face, it would have pierced his brain stem. Henry had to laugh. It was ridiculous. A man who manages to shoot himself with a spear gun in his own attic has earned his place in the Darwin Awards. Henry remained lying there, doubled up, for a while.

The marten came up from behind him and climbed over his legs. Henry felt its claws in his calves. Its fur was warm and silky-soft as it slid along Henry's waist to his upper arm. The animal sniffed at him, a whisker tickling his shoulder. The marten had come to inspect its prey.

Henry took stock of the situation. If he kept lying there, the marten would eat his corpse and start a family. He made a grab for it and caught its tail; the brute squeaked and bit him. Its sharp teeth pierced the nerve above his wrist. Henry recoiled, let go, went to kick out at the marten and managed to ram the spear gun into his own ear. After the pain had subsided, Henry decided to let things rest for the time being. He closed his eyes and, after a few breaths, fell asleep.

Threads of light were shining through the cracks in the roof. As he awoke, Henry could smell the putrid secretion that the marten had sprayed onto his shirt. The marten had left its mark on him! *You've no business being here* was the meaning of its stinking autograph, you've invaded my territory, you can't get the better of me here.

Henry began his retreat, crawling between the beams. More splinters pushed their way into his skin. It was an eternity before he reached the hole in Martha's bedroom wall and squeezed through the opening into his own territory. Poncho was lying on Martha's bed, wagging his tail in delight. The faithful soul had waited there for him. The dog sniffed his hand; he could smell the marten. Henry felt a warm rush of gratitude. He hugged the dog. 'My friend, my good friend,' he whispered to him. 'You know I'm a completely worthless idiot and you still stand by me.' Henry began to pull the splinters out of his skin.

Downstairs the phone was ringing. Henry looked

up and listened. The ringing stopped and then started again. It must be Betty. It was time he told her what had really happened on the cliffs.

When he came into the kitchen, after showering and bandaging his wrist, the telephone had stopped ringing. Henry saw on the display that Betty had rung four times. Uncertain whether to call her back or not, he opened a tin of Premium dog food for Poncho and spread truffle paste on a slice of bread. The phone rang again. Henry saw that it wasn't Betty and picked it up. The friendly Jenssen gave his name in a matter-of-fact tone.

'We've found your wife, Herr Hayden.'

Martha's corpse had been found on the coast nearby. Height, weight and hair colour tallied. Jenssen asked with sensitivity whether Henry thought he would be able to come to forensics to identify the dead woman.

The cold embrace of fear choked Henry. After making a note of the address of the Institute of Forensic Medicine, he put the phone down carefully as if it was made of unfired porcelain, and felt the floor give way beneath him. He clutched the corner of the kitchen island. The room, all the house around him, shot deep down into the earth as if through an invisible shaft. As he gathered speed he became weightless and, bewildered by the effect of the levitation, he stretched out his arms and came crashing down with his chin on the benchtop.

10

Gisbert Fasch had also seen the news of Henry's wife's fatal swimming accident. There was no mention of her name; there wasn't even a photograph of her. In death, as in life, she wasn't granted a title of her own—even post-mortem she remained *the wife of*.

For four hours now he'd been sitting in his hot and stuffy car, squashing creepy-crawlies as they made their way over the roof. Shadowing your opponent is always so exciting in books and films; in real life it turns time into mouldy old cheese. You sit there producing carbon dioxide; the minutes drag on for ever; you want to sleep, but can't, because you can never be sure that something noteworthy isn't about to happen, and in your misery you turn to squashing insects.

Fasch fanned himself with the newspaper he'd already read to death and looked up at Henry's property on the hill. His eyes were watering from so much surveillance. In an English lifestyle magazine, he'd come across a large-format photograph of Henry's living room, showing the master of the house on his Chesterfield sofa together with his wife and dog. Fasch had studied the photo for a long time, looking for hidden clues to location. The woman at Henry's side looked educated and pleasant, with a remote, saintly air about her. In the picture she was wearing lined boots and a reversible tweed poncho. Henry, quite the old trophy gatherer, lay sprawled on the sofa with an arm around her shoulder. In the background, somewhat blurred, a picture window, dark wooden shelves full of books, a fireplace—how absolutely essential—and to the side a black dog sitting upright like a Spanish grandee. It was such a cliché, this living room, so utterly tasteful, exactly what he would have expected of someone like Hayden, who disguised his malign personality with refined junk and the mammals to match. Made you puke.

Fasch had by now completed the crossword, including all subsidiary rivers and Nordic divinities; the roof of the car was a sea of bloody stains. Every now and then a slight breeze blew through the open side window, bringing with it the smell of cut grass, and making the little photo of his mother Amalie swing on the rear-view mirror.

On the back seat lay his old briefcase. It had now acquired the weight of a twenty-week-old infant and contained everything ever written by and about Henry Hayden. Fasch no longer left the bag for a second. Several times during the last weeks he had woken up screaming, because he'd dreamt he'd lost it.

The information Fasch had managed to gather about Henry so far allowed for a reliable reconstruction of the first eleven and the last nine years of his life. In between, there was still a gaping hole of almost twenty-five years. There are blind spots and dark matter in everyone's biographies—amongst them things people prefer to leave out because they are embarrassing or simply unimportant. But suppressing a time span of twenty-five years is too much to go unnoticed. His entire youth was missing.

Henry had led a secret life—somewhere and somehow. That in itself was an achievement, for vanishing is an art. It means renunciation and abstention. Renouncing home, family and friends, language and familiar habits. And who do you tell? Who do you share it with? Even Dr Mengele, who had to change his hiding place several times over, left clues and a diary. *Keeping silent goes against human nature*, it said at the beginning of *Frank Ellis*. Clearly a hidden reference to Henry's secret biography.

Suddenly, then, he re-emerges and starts publishing novels. Just like that. Without a first shot, without practice, without a mistake. All novels tell you something about their authors, no matter how cleverly they try to conceal themselves. Whether Hayden had actually written his novels himself or simply stolen them, Gisbert Fasch believed they were just teeming with clues; it was only a question of finding the key to decipher them.

Henry's car came along the avenue of poplars at high speed, a cloud of dust in its wake. Fasch threw his half-drunk paper cup of tea out of the window, switched on the engine and put his foot to the floor. He had trouble tailing the car because he was an unpractised driver. The worn tyres on his sixteen-year-old Peugeot skidded on the bends, and the car lurched from side to side, making hysterical noises.

By the time he'd gone about five kilometres and come to a fork in the road where you take a right for the freeway and a left for the coastal road, he'd already lost Henry. Judging by the speed at which Henry had set off, he was in quite a hurry. People in a hurry take the freeway, you'd think. Fasch hesitated briefly and turned left.

Henry had indeed chosen the narrow, winding coastal road, because he wanted to make the most of his last opportunity to drive the Maserati flat out. He was expecting the police to detain him on the spot, so he'd taken with him a small travel toothbrush, his reading glasses and a paperback edition of Paul Auster's *Sunset Park*, in case there was nothing to read in the cell—word has it that being held in custody is much more unpleasant than the prison term after sentencing.

It was about forty kilometres from his property to the Institute of Forensic Medicine; he would get there over an hour early. Henry thought of his dog. He hadn't been able to bring himself to kill it with the spade. Who was to look after Poncho if he didn't return? He'd wanted to uncover the old well in the summer and have the leadlight windows in the chapel restored. But now everything would go to rack and ruin, or be auctioned off or razed to the ground by bulldozers.

Presumably, the police divers had recovered Martha's corpse from the Subaru. In that case the homicide squad already knew that the car belonged to Betty and were doubtless tapping his phone. That would explain why Betty had been so persistent in trying to get hold of him. She was cooperating with the police, so as not to be punished for Martha's murder—and who could blame her? Henry would have done the same if he'd been in her shoes. After all, Betty's pragmatism was the thing Henry really valued about her. It would be difficult now to pronounce Martha's death a swimming accident, but what were lawyers for? They get paid to come up with explanations. Henry was able to afford the best lawyers and, since O. J. Simpson's acquittal, nothing has seemed impossible.

Henry could see his pursuer in the rear-view mirror. The red car came nearer, then remained at a distance of about two hundred metres. He couldn't make out how many people were sitting in the car, especially with the sunlight reflecting off its windscreen. The police would hardly send such amateurs after him. Henry slowed down; the car behind him slowed down too. As soon as he put on speed again, the red car closed up. Maybe it was tourists or those bird lovers who came to the coast at this time of year to watch the mating flights of the sea birds. Alternatively, Henry thought, his pursuer might be a mere figment of his conscience; after all, the world is full of perils for anyone with a sense of foreboding.

Henry accelerated and the little car fell a long way behind. After rounding a bend concealed by high bushes, he slammed on the brakes, put on his sunglasses, got out of the car and waited for his pursuer. Sea spray settled on his sunglasses like a veil. The coast dropped away here, falling some thirty metres and hefty concrete blocks were set in front of the precipice to prevent accidents. The wind howled up between the cliffs; clouds drove shadows over the coastal road. Henry saw seagulls circling overhead. Half a minute passed, then he heard the car coming. It rounded the bend at high speed, its tyres screeching.

Fasch saw Henry standing in front of his car. It was him all right. He stood there nonchalantly, his hands in his trouser pockets. His hair was still thick, his shoulders broad; he was wearing a checked English cashmere jacket with leather patches on the elbows just like in the showy portrait photo that ruined the covers of all his books.

With the impact on the concrete block, the windscreen shattered into a million fractals. His face crashed through the glass and then back again. Everything slowed down and began to rotate. In the centre of this revolving world, Fasch saw the photo of his mother Amalie hanging motionless while, all around it, everything moved. He wondered when he'd last rung her and what he should give her for her seventieth birthday. Then there was an implosion in his chest and something pushed in on him from the sides and grew hot.

The Peugeot ended up lying on its roof. A shower of glass pelted down onto the road. Henry sprinted the thirty metres to the remains of the car. He nearly tripped over the fat brown briefcase that was lying on the road. Paper came fluttering out of it. The wrecked car hissed like a wounded dragon. A mixture of fluids flowed out of its gaping metal jaws and down the road. The roof was in shreds; one door and all the windows were gone, the rear right wheel was still turning.

Henry took off his jacket—first things first—and knelt down in the iridescent pool to look inside the smashed-up car. First he saw the arm, the fingers on the hand twitching, and then the man, lying twisted and whimpering on the back seat. He was still alive, but he didn't know a lot about driving.

Henry took hold of the arm and pulled. The man groaned. Henry let go, crawled into the wrecked car as far as he could, clasped the man round his bloody chest and pulled him out. With no resistance to speak of, the body slid onto the road. The eyes were open, but the man didn't seem to understand; his face was already beginning to swell. A trickle of blood ran out of his ear. Sticking out of the right-hand side of his chest was the broken-off shaft of a headrest. Henry put his ear to the open mouth of the injured man and heard his gurgling breathing.

Henry grasped the shaft in his chest and pulled it out; the ribs cracked. He listened again. After a few breaths the gurgling grew fainter; the man's chest rose and fell quickly. There was now a lot of blood gushing out of the wound. Henry ripped a strip of cloth from his favourite shirt and pushed it into the hole in the man's chest with his finger, the way you might fill a pipe.

At the eight-kilometre marker, only a short distance from the junction where the forest track led off to the left towards the cliffs, Henry took a right in the direction of town. Fasch was lying on the back seat, his head on the briefcase which Henry had been considerate enough to rescue. A bloodstain was spreading around the bag on the soft Nappa leather. Fasch's legs were raised up and sticking out of the back window. He was whimpering softly, but was not conscious. The traffic was growing heavier. Henry was in complete control of the car at every overtaking manoeuvre—it has to be said that he was driving the race of his life—and he reached the hospital in under twenty minutes.

An ambulance was parked outside the emergency department with its rear doors open. A paramedic in fluorescent orange was sitting on a gurney reading a newspaper as Henry rolled up the ramp tooting his horn. 'I've got an injured man!' Henry called out of the car window.

Stoically and without a single superfluous movement, the paramedic folded his newspaper. He saw a dozen injured people every day—dead people and dying people, delirious drunks, weeping mothers—and not for one damn minute was he left in peace to read his newspaper. Without a word he helped to heave the unconscious man onto the gurney and push him into emergency.

Tired, and uncertain whether or not he could still be of any use, Henry got back in his car and wondered whether he should ring Jenssen to cancel his appointment at forensics. He was now dreading the thought of seeing Martha's body again. It would have begun to decompose. All the same, he did want to see her face, to touch it. He quite simply owed it to her. No doubt her expression would reflect the horror of the final moment when she had realised her mistake. For all her synaesthetic sixth sense and her great knowledge of human nature, she'd been wrong about him. Wrong out of love for him, until the cowardly moment he'd come up from behind and pushed her into the black water. It had been murder, even if it had been a mistake. Who else but he would see the disappointment on her face?

There was a knock on the window. A young doctor was standing at the car. Henry got out again.

'Are you injured?'

Henry looked down. It was only now that he noticed his stained trousers, and remembered ripping a strip off his favourite shirt. Its sleeves were stained with congealed blood.

'The blood's from the other man. Is he still alive?'

The doctor nodded. 'There's a fair amount broken,

including his skull, and he's lost a lot of blood, but he'll pull through. Did you bring him here?'

* * *

He was given a glass of water. In the doctor's room in the emergency department, Henry washed the blood off his hands and described where the accident had happened and what he'd seen and done. He didn't mention the fact that he'd lain in wait for his pursuer round the corner—why should he? On a table, Henry saw half-full cups and partly eaten salami sandwiches, abandoned in the rush to help others.

'Did you pull anything out of his chest?'

'Yes, there was a piece of metal in it—it was bubbling terribly. I thought it might get in the way of his breathing.'

'He has a collapsed lung; he would have suffocated.'

'Then it was the right thing to do?'

'You saved his life.'

Henry produced his ID. A statement was drawn up, which Henry signed. A pretty nurse brought his jacket from the car. Her white overall suited her fantastically well. Why is it, Henry wondered, that men love women in uniform?

'The police will be in touch with you, Herr Hayden.'

'I dare say they will.'

He looked at the clock. Time was running short; too much was happening. He could still make his appointment at forensics, because he'd set off early. But should he drive to his own arrest in this state?

'You don't happen to have a pair of trousers and a clean shirt for me, do you?'

The doctor disappeared briefly into the room next door and returned with trousers and a shirt. 'These are the consultant's; the shirt's mine.' They both fitted, although the trousers were a little tight. 'Just send everything back to the hospital afterwards.'

As Henry was walking along the grey corridor of the emergency department, the nurse came running after him. She was bringing him his jacket for the second time.

'You're a writer, aren't you?'

'And you?'

'If I could write like you, I certainly wouldn't be a nurse. My condolences, Herr Hayden.'

'What for?'

'Your wife. I saw it in the newspaper. Can I take a photo of us?'

'Another time. When I'm wearing something appropriate.'

Henry put his jacket on after he got back in the car. He unwound the blood-encrusted bandage on his wrist and dropped it into the footwell. He examined the wound where the marten had bitten him. The skin around it was reddened and slightly swollen. For a moment he considered going back to emergency to have the scratch looked at, but then he rejected the idea. It was too ridiculous. Just now he'd pulled a stake out of a stranger's chest, there was his dead wife lying in forensics, and he had life imprisonment to look forward to. When Henry set off, his memory of the accident was already fading, like a dream that is blotted out when you awake.

He had no concrete notion of what awaited him. He would make no confession when he was arrested, but wait and see what charges were brought against him. A defendant should say little in court. Or, better still, keep silent. You can lie, too. An accused person enjoys the rare privilege of being allowed to lie. Besides, you're the centre of attention. It's no rare thing for criminals in the dock to feel a sense of endorsement and a genuine interest in them and their mucked-up lives for the first time. Some of them are so taken with this that they confess more than is necessary, for the sole purpose of having people listen to them. It is possible that people of this type would never have become criminals if they'd been given a taste of the precious elixir of recognition a little earlier. The victims of a crime, the bereaved, wait to be acknowledged in vain, for it is well known that the reward for suffering consists in evading punishment. Recognition is rarely just.

Henry had all the time in the world now. He would spend the rest of his life waiting and remembering. Maybe he'd even write a book and become a better person. He would also, of course, have his regrets.

The Institute of Forensic Medicine was a grey rough-cast building, plain and functional, without any kind of ornamentation at all. Jenssen was sitting on the front steps with a plastic coffee cup in his hand, leafing through a thin folder. When he caught sight of Henry, he put the cup down on the steps and walked towards him with an outstretched hand. His eyes took in the Maserati, then Henry's shoes.

'What happened?'

Henry examined his blood-smeared shoes. There you are, he thought, you forgot about them. That's how quickly it happens.

'A road accident in front of me. It's not my blood. Shall we go in?'

Jenssen refrained from asking any more questions. A thoroughly agreeable trait of character. 'You don't have to do this,' he said to Henry on the stairs. 'We could just wait for the results from the DNA analysis instead.'

'Of course we could. But I'd like to see my wife. I'm grateful to you for ringing me up straight away. Does she look terrible?'

'I haven't seen her yet either. To be honest, I've never seen a drowned body.' Jenssen scratched himself. 'But there's a first time for everything, eh?'

That's what you want in a police officer, Henry thought. There's nothing he doesn't know about human nature, and yet he remains a decent bloke, sympathetic, open to basic emotions and not indifferent to other people's suffering.

'Where's your charming colleague who looks a bit like . . .'

'An opossum?' Jenssen laughed loudly. Henry nodded. 'She really is the spitting image of an opossum. She never comes to forensics. She says it stinks too much for her.'

Jenssen realised this was less than professional, and became serious again. 'Would you like a cup of coffee?'

'Maybe later,' Henry replied. 'Let's get it over and done with.'

Jenssen let Henry go on ahead. Henry suspected that Jenssen's exceptionally polite treatment of him had little to do with respect and a lot to do with his investigative techniques. A locked door opened with a buzz; they crossed a corridor where a vending machine was humming and stopped in front of a sheet of glass. Behind the glass sat a woman who was scowling. No wonder—it would put you in a bad mood, sitting in that glass box all day long, being stared at like a monkey. The corridor smelt of cleaning agent and instant coffee, and there was something else unidentifiable in the air, rising up from the basement.

Henry signed another form, cast a glance back towards the daylight coming in at the window and passed through blue double doors. A flight of stairs led down to the basement to a change room where Jenssen handed Henry green plastic overshoes and overalls. As Henry was putting on the overalls, he noticed the other man observing him. But he wasn't going to make it that easy for him.

'What happened to your wrist?'

A delayed question, Henry thought. So Jenssen had noticed the wound earlier on. The question came later, as a surprise. Part of his tactics, Henry thought. I must make a note of that.

'Something bit me.'

Henry followed Jenssen into the Hades of the dissecting room. The smell of putrefying flesh was intense. *This is the place where death delights to help the living*, read an inscription on the wall. Jenssen laid a hand on Henry's shoulder.

'May I give you some advice?'

'By all means.'

'You might as well start breathing through your nose now.'

*

No previous knowledge is required to know how death smells. There's no smell like it. When you enter a dissecting room you can't shake a sense of grim foreboding.

No corpse is beautiful. First, Henry saw the feet. The toes were black and swollen. The corpse lay, oddly bulky, on the farthest of four big, clean, stainless-steel tables under a vertical light. The chest was already open. The head lay on a plastic block, something dark covered the face. At the table stood a woman of about fifty with short hair and stained overalls, who was putting something soft—we don't want to know what—in a steel dish. The forensic pathologist had adopted the sombre air of the dissecting room to delight in helping death in this place. A few paces from the dissecting table, Jenssen paused again and held Henry back.

'Just a moment, please.'

He hurried on ahead and spoke to the pathologist in a low voice. Henry saw her quick glance, then she nodded, took a green cloth and laid it over the open chest of the corpse. Now, Henry noticed the swollen hand sticking out at the side beneath the cloth. The crisp, black skin on the fingers had cracked open. Flaps of skin had peeled off and hung down at the side. Parts of the bone could be seen. The ring finger was missing.

Jenssen came back and stood between Henry and the corpse. He had grown noticeably paler.

'You must excuse us, we weren't quite sure when you were coming. You can see for yourself, they've already started the post-mortem, and the face is . . .' Jenssen couldn't find the words to complete his sentence. 'It's better if you don't see it.'

'Please, I want to see my wife.'

Jenssen stepped aside and Henry walked past him to the table. The pathologist pushed something that looked like a spatula under the torso. The skull had been sawn open, the brain lay in a dish beside it. The face had been pulled down from the forehead like on a furry animal that's been skinned. The severed ring finger lay in a little dish next to the brain, a gold ring gleaming on it. The pathologist reached into the corpse's copper-green hair with her latex gloves and, with an unsentimental tug, she pulled the face back over the skull.

'Your wife drowned,' the pathologist explained.

My wife? Henry thought. The face of the drowned body looked like a *quattro stagioni* pizza topped with seasonal ingredients such as you might tuck into at the Italian on the corner. A doughy black tongue bulged out of the mouth; the eyes had sunk to shrivelled olives; the nose had opened out like an artichoke, exposing two black holes. None of it resembled Martha. Her features weren't even remotely recognisable. This face, dehumanised by rot, belonged to a stranger, as did the rest of the bulky body.

Although he was already quite sure, Henry also had a look at the cracked-up finger in the dish. The ring it wore was broad and less beautiful than the one which Henry had slipped onto Martha's finger in the registry office. A DNA test was hardly necessary. It wasn't her.

Henry turned away, shaking his head. 'That's not my wife.'

Jenssen nodded in agreement, as if Henry had just said it really was Martha. 'You're right. It doesn't look like your wife any more, but it is.'

Jesus Christ, Henry thought, if I say the truth, no one believes me. 'What did she have on?' he asked, knowing quite well that this might be a major blunder.

'She was fully clothed.'

'Then how can it be my wife? I found her clothes on the beach. And besides, my wife's petite, and this lady here'—Henry pointed at the corpse—'is massive. And the ring on the finger there isn't Martha's wedding ring.'

Jenssen glanced in his folder. 'There's nothing here about a ring.'

He leafed through the pages, as if the missing clue might be there. Then he looked across at the pathologist.

'The ring was concealed under the epidermis on the palm,' she remarked matter-of-factly.

Henry held up his hand to show his wedding ring. 'I chose our rings; they're identical and narrower than that one. We had our names engraved on them. Her ring ought to have my name on it.'

For the first time in years, he pulled off his ring—it hurt a little—and handed it to Jenssen, who looked at the inscription of Martha's name on the inside, and then went over to the table and bent over the finger in the dish.

The pathologist took some pincers and pulled the ring off the bone tissue. Not a nice noise. She rinsed the ring in clean water and passed it to Jenssen. To look at the inside, Jenssen had to hold the ring right up to his eye. It can't have smelt good. There was no inscription. Shame and irritation at having notified Henry in such a premature and unprofessional way made Jenssen blush. 'Damn!' he stammered. 'I'm so sorry.'

'Don't mention it.' Henry took the opportunity to reward the detective's kindheartedness. Anyone can make a mistake after all. 'Do you know what, Jenssen?' he said, putting his hand on his shoulder. 'You've convinced me that my wife's still alive and I'm grateful to you for that. Would you like a coffee?'

Everything was up in the air again. No one suspected him; no one was going to arrest him. He didn't need the toothbrush or the book, and he would drive home a free man. Like sunshine piercing the clouds after a storm, artificial light fell from the ceiling of the dissecting room onto the lady lying open on the table. Henry felt sympathy for the dead woman. What was it that had driven the poor thing into the water? Had she been tired of life, or fatally ill? Did she have children? Who was waiting for her now, in vain?

It later turned out that the dead woman was a retired police officer who'd fallen off a bridge trying to take a photo of a seagull.

Henry treated Jenssen to a coffee from the vending machine in the corridor. They stood next to each other for a while without speaking, sipping from their plastic cups.

'Sometimes people disappear,' Jenssen said after quite some time. He took a gulp of coffee and scrunched up the cup in his fist. 'And some return.'

Henry flinched. 'What do you mean by that?'

'Well, just recently, we had a bloke turn up—he'd been gone fourteen years, no mean feat, completely vanished, because, he says, his children got on his nerves.'

Jenssen giggled. Henry remained serious. A man who knows how hard it is to disappear doesn't find that kind of thing funny.

'It's ten years now since he was pronounced dead, his wife has married the man next door, and now the mongrel comes back and wants his wife to pay him his life insurance. He's even brought charges against her—can you believe it?'

Henry could understand the man perfectly, but he didn't reply. Jenssen took a piece of paper out of his folder and handed it to him. It had clearly been torn from a book. Four words from a line of printed text were visible.

'We found this in your wife's jacket.'

Henry put on his reading glasses, which he'd brought with him specially for his stay in custody. A message had been scribbled over the scrap of print in a biro that had pierced the paper in several places; the writing surface had evidently been soft. The hand was rounded, feminine.

'It says: *If I can do anything* and there's a phone number.' He gave the scrap of paper back to Jenssen. 'That's not Martha's writing.'

'We rang up. The number belongs to a certain Sonja Reens.'

Henry saw the young woman before him, standing in Martha's parka by the sea, huddled up with cold.

'She's the daughter of Elenor Reens, our mayor. I met her on the beach when I was looking for my wife.'

'That's right. She sends her regards and asked how you were.'

'And?' Henry asked. 'How am I?'

'I don't want to begin to imagine,' Jenssen replied and pointed at the scrap of paper in Henry's hand. 'Do the words seem familiar to you?'

Henry read the printed words out loud: '*Always alone than never.*' He didn't have the shimmer of an idea what this crap was supposed to mean.

'Doesn't ring any bells?'

Triumph flared in Jenssen's eyes as if he'd just landed on the Planet of the Apes. An inner voice told Henry it would be better if he did know the phrase, so he decided—as so often—to play the odds and make a wild guess. We don't, incidentally, make use of our hidden talent for guesswork half often enough. Beyond comprehension and consciousness, an army of anonymous neurones are working things out for us. Electric charges are transformed into memories; deep down inside us, knowledge emerges and generates the visions of the unconscious. You just have to trust them.

'It's mine. The phrase is mine.'

Jenssen was as surprised as he was disappointed. 'Bingo,' he said appreciatively. 'I recognised it straight away too and looked it up. Bottom of page one hundred and two. Only "better" is missing. "*Better always alone than never.*" It's from your novel, Herr Hayden. *Aggravating Circumstances.* I think it's your best book.'

'Very impressive,' Henry murmured with admiration. 'Just goes to show how valuable an attentive reader is.'

11

He decided to go and have a look. At the eight-kilometre marker, he turned off towards the cliffs—instead of driving home, which would have been a lot more sensible. As every amateur knows, murderers often return to the scene of their crime, only to be arrested when they get there. They go because they are sentimental, or because they are curious, just like everyone else. Some go out of vanity and others, listening to the voice of conscience, go out of regret; they return because they can't believe they were really capable of such an act. Henry, for his part, after his visit to forensics, had arrived at the conclusion that the police believed it was an accident. That meant there was no reason *not* to visit the place where his wife was and see how things had been going for her in the interim. Martha would have expected it, in Henry's opinion.

*

Even from a long way off he could see flashing danger signs. As he rounded the fatal bend where that poor twit had simply kept straight on and driven into the concrete bollards, the tow truck came the other way with the car on its tray. It was a write-off—a miracle that anyone had survived in it. Now, Henry remembered that their eyes had met just before the car had crashed. Instead of watching the road, the driver had looked at him, as if in surprise, as if he'd recognised him. Well, a lot of people on the road recognise me, Henry thought, and who cares—the lucky devil survived the crash thanks to me.

On the forest track, Henry parked the car in the usual place and walked over the perforated concrete slabs towards the cliffs, whistling. Here and there little white clouds scudded across the sky; the scent of fresh pine needles filled the warm air. Ought to go for more walks, he thought. It does one good.

On the cliffs, just where the Subaru had been parked, there was now a campervan. If number plates are to be trusted, an English family with children was holidaying there amid an impressive amount of camping equipment, which lay spread about the ground in a kind of organised chaos. A treasure trove for the forensic team. The whole area was sprinkled with saliva and sweat, not to mention excrement, hair, dandruff and goodness knows what else. God bless this family, Henry exulted. Even the best forensic scientists in the world would be kept busy here for a thousand years.

He hid in a clump of bushes and watched in delight as a naked woman in wooden sandals threw washing over a line strung up between two trees. This Late Neolithic Venus must be the mother. Her palely gleaming breasts with their neat areolae hung down, heavy but shapely; her waist had been noticeably thickened by the birth of her three children who were throwing pine cones at one another not far from the campervan. Henry's expert eye did not miss the caesarean scar that ran horizontally above her pudenda—very nicely healed and not at all ugly.

In an aluminium chair, the naked family patriarch was sitting reading the newspaper, a straw hat on his head, his crossed legs marbled with varicose veins, and—what was he doing?—he was smoking cigarettes! Not hurriedly like Betty, but relishing every life-shortening drag. This cultivated Brit carefully stubbed out the butt on the aluminium chair leg, flicked it onto the ground, and proceeded to light up the next one. Henry would have liked to give him a whole truckload of cigarettes. His thriving, naked kiddies were tirelessly gathering and throwing pine cones, laughing and shouting—it was a joy to watch them. Henry had an overwhelming desire to join in their playing and throwing. What a long time it was since he had played as boisterously as that and how very rarely it had happened! Yes, it was a good idea to go on summer holiday with children once in a while—they have such a lot of fun.

If there were still any tyre tracks from the Subaru, they were now rolled flat and obliterated by the broad tyres of the van. How fantastic! Henry decided to come back sometime. He would have loved to saunter past these nudists to the cliffs, just to have a quick look at Martha—but you shouldn't tempt the devil, even when he's in a good mood.

* * *

Fat, black flies were crawling in various directions over the windows of the Maserati. The sun had heated up the inside of the car, and when Henry opened the door a swarm of flies escaped in a stream of stinking air. The smell was coming from the brief-case on the back seat, which was caked in brown bloodstains. Flies had already deposited symmetrical clusters of white eggs here.

Nauseated, he grasped the briefcase by the handle and pulled it away. It was stuck to the seat. The handle was stained with sweat. He studied the bloody curd cheese on the reddish brown Nappa leather in dismay—the best leather from hand-massaged cattle. An issue for the insurance. Yellowing sheets of paper were pouring out of the briefcase. Henry was just about to throw the bag into the bushes, when he noticed a page with words circled in coloured pencil. It was his third-form school report. *His* name was circled in blue.

Right at the bottom of the page were illegible signatures. The two years he spent in Year Three had been particularly bad—he preferred not to think about them. The marks all ranged from Unsatisfactory to Poor—with the exception of PE. In the comments it said, among other things: *Henry will not be moved up. He is disruptive in class and copies from fellow pupils. His participation in lessons and his behaviour leave much to be desired*. Exclamation mark. 'Copies from fellow pupils' had a red ring round it and was flanked by another exclamation mark in the margin.

Henry saw, carefully filed and sorted in chronological order, a copy of his birth certificate, school reports, legal documents concerning his parents, records of his admission to various children's homes, psychological assessments, newspaper articles about Henry Hayden and his novels, even a copy of his marriage certificate—all marked with coloured circles. Henry suppressed the urge to burn the briefcase then and there. He threw it back onto the seat, let down all the windows, and a few minutes later was rounding the bend again at a modest speed. Some firemen were sweeping the last splinters of glass from the road. So the fellow *had* been following him. He should have trusted his instincts and let him perish.

The belief in human goodness is a prejudice hard to refute. Wouldn't it be more sensible, Henry wondered, as he drove angrily along the avenue of poplars to his property, to believe in the self-evident badness of human beings? In his case, for instance, sporadic acts of goodness, such as rescuing the man from the wrecked car or strangling the deer in the field, were nothing but brief interruptions to his innate wickedness. He was a murderer, a liar and a fraud. Not to be asked who you really are—that is the *ne plus ultra* of imposture. Millions of readers devoured his books, he was desirable to a lot of women, and Martha, who knew better than all the others that he was no good, had never stopped loving him. Is it possible, Henry sometimes wondered, to love a monster? Is it permissible? It is in fact obligatory, if you believe in human goodness. That belief, Henry concluded, bringing his train of thought to a close, leads inescapably to punishment. For the very belief in human goodness makes punishment necessary.

That morning he had driven to forensics in the certainty that he would spend the rest of his life in prison for the murder of his wife. On the way there, quite by the by, he had saved someone he didn't know from Adam, helping him without a thought for the potential disadvantages. He was nearly late for his own arrest. But did that make up for the murder of his wife? No, it most certainly did not. No good deed can offset a bad one—but that's not why you do good deeds. Is it?

He'd been gone a few hours, and yet it seemed to Henry as if he was returning from a long journey. Something was different. Poncho didn't come barking and running to meet him as he usually did. Then he saw Sonja Reens, the mayor's daughter, standing on the old millstone in the garden, the dog at her feet looking up at her, riveted as if hypnotised. Even when Henry called him, he didn't turn his head, but kept his eyes fixed on the woman. She was wearing blue jeans, flip-flops and a white, tight-fitting T-shirt. The brown skin of her upper arms shone; her T-shirt left a narrow strip of skin exposed at her waist. She raised a hand and the dog lay on its belly. She lowered it, turning her palms outwards, and the dog sat up again as if pulled by strings.

Henry snapped the central locking open and shut. Usually, Poncho came running to the car at this sound, because it activated his driving reflex, but he didn't so much as prick up an ear. For years, Henry hadn't managed to teach his dog anything except to do exactly as it pleased.

She clapped her hands. Poncho awoke from his catalepsy and, wagging his tail, chewed the biscuit she'd given him in reward.

Henry raised his index finger in reproach. 'Poncho, we'd agreed that you only do that for me.' He looked at her admiringly. 'How did you get him to do that?'

Her expression betrayed an expert's pride. 'It's so easy. Dogs love to learn. They're grateful for the challenge. Poncho's a nice name. It suits him. He's a clever dog.'

'I'm glad. Up until now, I could have sworn he was stupid.'

Henry noticed a wicker basket next to the millstone. There was a checked cloth covering it. She saw his glance.

'I thought maybe you could do with some company, Herr Hayden. My mother has baked rhubarb cake for you.'

'For me?'

Henry would have preferred waterboarding. For him, rhubarb belonged to those bitter varieties of vegetable which are made into a revolting-tasting jelly to torment defenceless children in institutional dining halls. During his odyssey through various homes and disciplinary establishments, his experience had always been the same: there's a punishment to fit every crime and as a reward there's stewed rhubarb. But now was not the time for resentment.

Sonja jumped down from the millstone—she almost seemed to glide—bent over the basket, picked it up and swung it to and fro. Henry watched, captivated, as his shadow walked towards hers.

'Or do you seriously mean *better always alone than never?*' she asked, smiling. Henry immediately recalled the scrap of paper Jenssen had shown him outside the Institute of Forensic Medicine. There are days when everything comes back to haunt me, he thought.

'No, I didn't write that. My wife did.'

Her laughter rang out, irreverently. She didn't believe him. How could she? He was telling the truth. Henry noticed that their shadows were already embracing.

'You must excuse me, Herr Hayden . . .'

'Henry.'

She blushed slightly. 'Henry. I'm sorry about the page from your book, but I wanted to write you a message and didn't have anything with me except your novel. The book belongs to my mother, by the way. She's a big fan of yours.'

Blessed be anyone with a mother, he thought.

'Do you have any crème fraîche, Herr Hayden?' She had forgotten to call him Henry.

'Yes, why?'

'*Everything* tastes better with crème fraîche.'

'I can quite imagine,' Henry replied, and heaven be his witness that he meant it.

*

The last thing he needed now was any kind of complication. The novel wasn't finished, and the question of who was to finish writing it was nowhere near being answered. The baby in Betty's belly was already growing little fingers, there was a demon of conscience living in the roof in the form of a marten, and an unknown snooper secretly gathering clues to his past in the hope of uncovering his biggest secret. It wouldn't be easy to find solutions to all these problems and to restore order; now was not the time for amorous experiments. There are phases in life when it's best to act on principle, not on impulse.

But Sonja was magnetic. Everything about the young woman attracted him. While he was making tea their eyes met in the reflection in the open kitchen window. Afterwards, they sat in his studio. She talked about her veterinary studies and how much she'd like to open a practice in the country, while he sucked on his cold pipe in silence, wishing it was her clitoris. Nothing would have been easier than to set her up in a practice; his lustful thoughts rose to heights too elevated for words. Every time she leaned forward to spread crème fraîche on the rhubarb cake with her teaspoon, previously inactive glands released hormones into his bloodstream. No doubt about it, *everything* tastes better with crème fraîche, and danger is more erotic than reason.

A quarter of an hour later, he would have eaten rhubarb cake with rusty nails if it had amused her. They discussed the pleasant isolation of country life; he talked about inspiration; she told him of her weakness for rural machinery. Just as he was about to confide in her that he'd bought a John Deere tractor to dig out the old well behind the chapel, the telephone rang. The bloody telephone. The most insidious invention since the hand grenade.

It was Betty. Sonja understood his silent glance and left the room at once. Her flip-flops were left next to the sofa in the shape of a V—if that isn't a sign, Henry thought. Her spontaneous response suggested that their brief acquaintanceship was already becoming conspiratorial. An emotionally detached person would simply have remained sitting there. All that was needed now was to overcome small-town conventions, get through the process of grieving, remove any inconvenient people and, last but not least, wait for Martha's official death statement. Henry counted to five in his head and picked up the receiver.

Betty's voice on the phone was tense and deeper than usual. 'I'm here for you,' she said. As if scorched by a hot iron, Henry spun round on his axis and looked out of the picture window.

'*Where* are you?'

'I'm right here for you, Henry. I'd just like you to

know that I love you, I want to be with you, our baby . . .'

Yes, our baby, our baby, tra la la, et cetera. Henry was no longer listening. Any residual feeling for Betty had already been atomised by the charisma of the unknown—he could feel himself no longer feeling anything. For Betty, that is. This would have been the time for speaking frankly, coming to a financial understanding, for instance, promising to safeguard the future of their child and to part in truly sympathetic friendship. But men are never more cowardly and their lies never more pathetic than when they're caught with their pants down. Isn't that so, gentlemen?

'I have to see you,' he said.

'I thought you never wanted to see me again.'

How right she was. He never wanted to see her again. It was high time to tell her what had really happened on the cliffs.

12

The longest days of the year came. They met in the Four Seasons Hotel at about eight in the evening. Not under a false name as in the past, their sunglasses on and their mobiles off, but quite openly in the foyer. People recognised Henry, greeted him, offered their condolences; it was like being at a funeral. Henry remained as unassuming and nonchalant as ever and led Betty to the Oyster Bar where a waiter showed him to the best table and swiftly cleared away the lilies.

Betty felt uneasy. His correctness, his choice of a public rendezvous, and above all the positively gooey gentleness with which he touched her, reinforced her suspicions that he was going to confess to his wife's murder. What do you say when you hear a thing like that? Do you treat it as a proof of love and then call the police? Would she have to testify against the father of her child? Or should she maintain a sympathetic silence and spend the rest of her life with a murderer? A dilemma. She ordered a glass of water.

The maître d' recommended the Belon oysters from the mudflats of Brittany. Betty had no appetite. Henry went for steak and chips as always. He never looked at the menu. If there was no steak, well, then schnitzel. Betty was poring over the menu, but Henry could see that she wasn't going to order anything—good God, how it got on his nerves when women made a big thing about a plate of pasta. Betty clapped the menu shut at last and shook her head. The waiter slunk off, offended.

'Now tell me.'

Henry cleared his throat as if about to read out a school essay. He'd never been good at this kind of thing. 'I don't think Martha would have ever wanted you to go to prison for her death—for fifteen years, if not more. No, she definitely would not have wanted that.'

This was not a confession. This sounded somehow worse. Betty wasn't ready to rule out the possibility that it was a bad joke, and she kept her cool. 'Me—in prison? Ah ha. For what?'

'Now just imagine,' Henry continued in a worried tone, 'that the police find my wife dead in your car. You did report it stolen?'

She nodded.

'What are they going to think? There's no farewell note, nothing that points to suicide. The only thing they *can* think is that you did it.'

'Me?' Her voice rose an octave. '*You* were the one who was last with her on the cliffs.'

Henry sadly shook his head. 'No, darling. It wasn't like that.'

She leaned forward. Henry spotted an alluring vein on her forehead that he'd never seen before.

'You *didn't* go?'

'Nope, I didn't.'

'Then where were you?'

'I went to the cinema. Korean film. Completely fascinating.'

The steak arrived. Betty waited, controlling herself with difficulty. Her nails quietly scraped the damask tablecloth. The smell of the deep-fried potatoes on his plate made her want to throw up. She fiddled with the cloth, the vein on her forehead throbbing. If it burst, then my problem would be taken care of, Henry mused as he spun the steak around on his plate. She leaned back and looked out of the window onto the street, still drawing fine lines on the tablecloth with her fingernails. Henry could tell that she was replaying the events of that evening. He let her take her time, spearing chips with his fork, rubbing them over the steak and putting them in his mouth.

Betty finally got to the point.

'You ran upstairs to her room to look for her. Did you think your wife was at home? Or was that all play-acting?'

'I thought she was at home, my love. I was absolutely certain she was in her room. She's always in bed at that time.'

Betty's eyes narrowed. 'If you thought that, then why did you stage her death on the beach?'

'I didn't. Her bike really was there. Martha had left it there. God knows why. Do you remember how I took you home that evening?'

Of course she remembered. 'After that I went straight to the cliffs. Your car wasn't there any more. The tyre tracks led straight into the sea. And there were butts on the ground. She smoked *your* cigarettes and then . . .'

Betty covered her mouth with her hands. 'Oh, my God, how awful!'

She had understood. Henry put down his knife and fork on the edge of his plate. 'Don't worry. It rained all night. You can't see anything any more.'

'Don't worry? Why didn't you ring the police straight away?'

'I wanted to. Then I thought about it. I don't know whether it was right, but I decided that you . . . that the two of you are all I have. You and the baby.'

He stretched his open hand across the table. Betty took it in hers. Her fingers were clammy.

'You did it for me?'

'And the baby. Our baby.'

Baby. He saw her tears. Why is it women always cry over that word? How can one word do that?

'We must go to the police, Henry. Straight away!'

'No need. They've already been to me. After you left with Moreany. How is he, by the way?'

Betty didn't want to talk about Moreany and his silly proposal just now. She clutched Henry's hand like a prayer book.

'Henry, we're going to the police now and we're going to tell them what happened.'

Henry played a quick round of pick-up-sticks with his chips. 'What did happen, darling?' he asked softly, but insistently. 'What really happened?'

Unsurprisingly, she let go of his hand.

'What do you mean by *really*?'

'Are you going to drink that?'

Without waiting for a reply, he downed her glass of water. Now he lowered his voice even further. 'Did Martha drive to the cliffs alone or did you take her there?'

Betty half rose from her chair in indignation. 'You don't really think *I* killed your wife?'

'Did you?'

Betty looked around desperately for justice, but there was none. She was visibly fighting back the urge to get up and walk away. She didn't. She sat there—she didn't have the strength. Henry felt sympathy for her, but unfortunately, he was going to have to strangle her now like the dying deer in the field.

'To be frank,' he continued, 'I did think that for a while, yes. I'm ashamed to admit it, but I thought you'd killed her.'

'Why?'

'Out of love for me. What was I supposed to think, for God's sake? Martha drives to your flat in her car. Then she drives to the cliffs in your car and disappears. And where were you?'

Betty closed her eyes briefly. 'I was at home. You know that.'

'*I* know, but do you have an alibi?'

She began to blink. 'That's a stupid word, Henry. I was at home, that's all. I was waiting for you to ring.'

'I did have my doubts,' Henry admitted.

'But you don't any more?'

'No. None.'

'What do you think now?'

'I think Martha drowned. And the police think so too. You're not implicated at all. That's what I think.'

'But she was sitting in my car.'

'Yes, that was a mistake. It must be the last one we make.'

Betty pressed herself up against the chair back, her arms folded in front of her chest. 'What mistakes can we make now?' she asked in a quiet voice.

Henry pushed his plate aside and made an unsuccessful attempt to take her hand.

'*Everyone* will think I'm your lover if you have a baby with me.'

'So what? Aren't you my lover?'

'Of course I am. But the timing. It would be fatal if it came out shortly after the death of my wife that *you're* pregnant by me.'

'What are we to do?' Betty asked, hardly audible. Henry lip-read the words.

'No one needs to know that the baby is mine.'

Betty got up from the table and raised her hand. 'You scare me, Henry. You've always scared me. But you can depend on one thing: your baby is going to be born. It's going to be born and you're its father whether you like it or not. Make up your mind where you stand in all this—I'm not going to make any difficulties for you. I'll even keep it a secret if that's what you want.'

'Now you're being unfair, Betty. I want it. I *already* love our baby.'

She opened her handbag. Henry ducked to avoid being shrouded in pepper spray. But she only looked into the bag, rifled through it and then closed it again.

'What are you up to?' he asked suspiciously.

'I'm going to go and puke.'

'The police don't know anything. There's absolutely no problem as long as we don't do anything. Not a thing, do you understand?'

'Henry . . .'

'Yes?'

'Your wife knew everything. Not from you—you didn't tell her about us. Of course you didn't. You never tell anyone anything.'

Betty pushed a strand of hair off her forehead. She looked ravishing in her anger and disappointment. Why is it that I always want her the most when she's about to leave? Henry wondered.

'Do you know what, Henry? As she was leaving, your wife said to me: We have to love Henry without knowing him. *I* don't know how that's possible and I don't believe I can do it.'

Betty turned and left. He watched her go without regret, but not without respect, because she did have class. He wasn't interested in where she was going or whether she'd come back. Was it really possible that Martha could have known about his affair with Betty all along without letting on or making any changes in her life? Who could endure such a thing? Right up to the last moment, their love had remained warm, their daily routine unchanged. And then suddenly she visits her rival for afternoon tea? *Can you guess how it ends?* was Martha's last message to him, written in pencil under the chapter she had just completed. Was it a warning, a threat, a prophecy? Henry didn't know the answer. It exhausted him, endlessly thinking about this kind of thing. The bullet was out of the barrel and pondering got you nowhere. Aggrieved, he flicked a half-eaten chip onto the carpet and looked around for the waiter.

Sitting in her armchair next to a stout column, Honor Eisendraht saw Betty hurry through the foyer and head for the marble stairs that led to the women's toilet. She had an impossibly garish handbag under her arm. Her face was decidedly pale. Gone was the usual provocative swing of her hips; she almost staggered down the stairs. Something must have happened, no doubt something unpleasant.

Honor had just left the stuffy, overfilled seminar room on the first floor of the hotel to have a cup of liqueur coffee. The so-called Numerology Seminar had been a complete farce, a rip-off. For that kind of money you deserve more than a porky woman with a pointer blathering on about trivial mathematical patterns, cosmically connected phone numbers and hidden traits of character. Who believes in such nonsense?

Honor had hoped to meet someone who knew a thing or two at the seminar, some spiritual person with whom she could discuss the full significance of the Tower, the sixteenth card of the Major Arcana in the Tarot. The card had come up for her twice already: it had to mean something. But there were only know-alls and half-wits in the seminar.

As all initiates are well aware, the Tower is a drastic card. Lightning strikes from a black sky, and a young man and his sweetheart plunge, burning, to their deaths. The card heralds annihilation and rebirth or, equally, solitude and the end of things. It is culpably reckless to ignore it. But sometimes the signs of an imminent event remain hidden and it is impossible to foresee the full extent of their significance. That is why you have to be prepared for anything, and sharpen your senses to find the vital clue in the shapeless mass of everyday life.

Honor left her coffee and a big tip on the table. She took her handbag and crossed the azure blue carpet in the direction from which Betty had come. If it's Moreany, she vowed to herself, then the thing with the Tower card is settled and I shall hand in my resignation.

At the window table in the wood-panelled bar, Henry Hayden was fiddling with his shirtsleeve. The poor thing looked pale and pain-stricken. How unbearable his wife's death must have been for him. There's no one who'll grieve for me when I'm no longer around, and I have only myself to blame, Honor thought. She wanted to go up to him and hug him, but the waiter approached his table. Henry paid the bill. Honor saw something in his look that stopped her from offering him her condolences.

Of course there's no connection between the sum of the digits in a phone number and hidden traits of character. On the other hand, there's no such thing as a chance encounter in a hotel; there are only inattentive observers. In the corner of the Oyster Bar, Honor realised that the fateful turn of events heralded by the Tower card was already under way. Before Hayden could spot her, she returned to the armchair next to the column, from which vantage point she could survey the entire foyer, her face concealed behind a newspaper.

Henry came out of the bar. He shook hands, signed one of his novels at reception and exchanged a few words with a hotel guest, glancing discreetly towards the toilets as he did so. Betty didn't emerge. Shortly afterwards, he left the hotel alone. He didn't turn round again.

How energetic he was, Honor thought. His predator's gait and his athletic, broad-shouldered physique had impressed her from the start. 'Heart, yield or break,' she had read in *Aggravating Circumstances*. Until she saw Henry, she had always believed that men of letters walked with a stoop, weighed down by the burden of their thoughts, propelled by an inner force or dragged through the world by a dark hostility. The true artist is sick—so thought the Portuguese poet Fernando Pessoa, and spent all his life waiting for the carriage from the abyss. A blind Borges wrestled with God's irony in the infinite library of symbols. But Henry Hayden was sporty, disciplined, always in control. And ever the artist. Quite fabulous.

Her tip was still lying next to her coffee cup. She did a quick sum to work out how many hours it had taken to earn that much, and exchanged it for a smaller amount.

Gagging noises were coming from the third cubicle on the left. There was flushing, then more gagging. Honor could smell lily-of-the-valley perfume and saw the hideous bag through the gap at the bottom of the door. She went into the next-door cubicle, lifted the lid and pulled up her skirt so as to produce an authentic sound. Between individual gagging attacks she heard a soft sobbing sound—strictly speaking, a whimper.

It was a gift, a sweet reward, this chance to be privy to such an intimate moment with her rival. She nearly forgot to flush. The death of Hayden's wife could hardly have grieved the hussy to this extent; she wasn't capable of genuine feelings. Something must have happened between the two of them that was dramatic enough to make her cry and him leave. Honor listened in delight as her rival coughed—blood perhaps—and then left the cubicle to rinse out her mouth at the washbasin.

The obligatory spell elapsed that women devote to making adjustments in front of the mirror. Honor tore off loo paper and flushed again. Her cover was perfect. At last she heard the clack of heels, and the door close. She let a minute pass, then left the cubicle, prepared for the possibility that Betty was still there, lying in wait for her at the door. She wouldn't have put it past her. Honor would have simulated surprise, maybe even exchanged a few words, but not too many. She was, however, alone.

An empty packet of gastric pills was in the plastic bin next to the basin. *Sample—Not For Resale* was diagonally printed across it, and beneath that the stamp of a gynaecological practice. The information leaflet was missing from the packet. Honor rifled through the bin, but found nothing except fake eyelashes, stained tissues and empty lipstick tubes.

In the chemist's not far from the hotel, Honor had it explained to her that women in the first trimester of pregnancy are advised *not* to take antiemetic tablets. But in their desperation, said the pharmacist, with an expression of concern, lots of women took them all the same. She herself had found the nausea of the first months of pregnancy her greatest ordeal in becoming a mother.

Honor Eisendraht took the bus home. She got out one stop earlier than usual so as to walk the last few metres to her flat. In the hall she put on her felt slippers, gave the budgie some water, lay down on her stomach on her reading couch, buried her face in a cushion and screamed as loud as she could.

13

Unshaven and without his incisors, Obradin looked like a jack-o'-lantern with a full beard. He spent most of the day smoking at the open bedroom window above his fish shop, baring the yawning gap in his teeth at every passer-by and looking out at the sea hidden behind the houses opposite. By now the entire town was preoccupied with the mysterious cause of his rampage. Helga remained silent, determined not to add grist to the rumour mill. Some reckoned it was schizophrenia; others suspected that something size-able had burst in his brain. It was all conjecture.

In the days that followed, Obradin still made no move to leave his bedroom and resume work. Helga took over the shop. She never got off the phone, but she did take the opportunity to have a lock put on the cellar door and to peel the silly fish pictures off the window.

On Assumption Day, a glorious day in August, Henry came driving up in the best of spirits, wearing a white Panama hat. Two weeks earlier his wife had drowned. You would never have guessed that he was in mourning, but everyone mourns in his own way—who's to say what mourning looks like? He parked on the pavement in front of the fishmonger's. He'd brought flowers and Spanish soap for Helga, and a badger-hair shaving brush for Obradin.

Helga related the whole story about Obradin to Henry, who already knew most of it. He slipped Helga an envelope containing money for the secret purchase of a new engine for *Drina*.

'Wait till the lottery numbers are announced,' he whispered in her ear. 'Then fill in a slip with five winning numbers maximum, do you understand?'

Helga understood and kissed both his hands. Henry fetched a cardboard box from the Maserati and climbed up to Obradin's flat via the stairs at the back of the shop. Because he had his hands full, he didn't knock, but pushed down the door handle with his elbow.

'Hey, what's the matter with you, old pal?' he asked, putting the box and the present on the bed. It didn't escape Henry's notice that one half of the double bed was untouched. Helga must be sleeping somewhere else just now.

'I've brought you something to shave with.'

198

The Serb was standing beside a pile of cigarette butts about the size of an ant hill.

'Wok goo you wonk?'

Henry eyed the gap in Obradin's teeth with respect. 'Wow. You could string a clothes line in there. Now have a look at this.' He took a solar-powered marten deterrent from the cardboard box. 'Ultrasound. This is the solution. Listen.'

Henry switched on the device. *YEEEEEEK*—an ultra-unbearable sound shrilled out. Each man put his fingers in his ears. Henry turned it off.

'And that's the problem. I don't know what frequency you need to drive away the marten and not the dog.'

'Wok?' Obradin asked, without interest.

'Hey, you know Poncho—he's sensitive, just like you. He goes crazy when I switch on this infernal machine. Help me to adjust it. We'll set the thing up, scare away the marten and have a smoke. It'll never come back. Wok goo you fink?'

Henry chuckled. He'd always been of the opinion that feeling sorry for people only delays their recovery. A little joke helps a sick man back on his feet faster than a sympathy suppository.

Obradin did indeed smile. Henry put out his hand and held his mouth shut. 'Don't say anything, you Serbian bean stew, or you'll make me laugh again. Come on. Let's go to the dentist.'

It was the best private practice for miles. Obradin got new teeth. First, temporary ones, which didn't look bad at all—just a little rabbit-like. Later, an oral surgeon put in implants, two veritable works of art, each one more expensive than a middle-of-the-range car. The molar was replaced too, and a piece of bone taken from his palate to reconstruct his jaw. It goes without saying that Henry footed the bill and never mentioned it. As we have seen, Henry could be great.

* * *

Sixty kilometres further south, Gisbert Fasch was transferred from the intensive care unit to a four-bed ward. Badly mangled but in full possession of his faculties. With his broken legs and one arm dangling in an aluminium noose, he looked like poor Gregor Samsa who awoke one morning to find himself transformed into a giant insect.

Brown pus flowed out of Fasch's chest through a tube into a little contraption beside his bed. This pumped out septic fluid, which then gathered in a transparent plastic pouch. The shaft of the backrest which had pierced his chest had been full of bacteria. Once every twelve hours the pouch was emptied by a nurse who seemed only to be qualified for this one task and was correspondingly bad-tempered. She also changed his nappies, and washed and moisturised his behind. Her firm fingers on his scrotum were indisputably the highlight of the day.

Every breath hurt. He had a taste in his mouth that was difficult to describe, and a whispering sound in his lung. Something in there had become infected in a big way—he could smell it. A high whistling sound pierced the walls of the ward day and night. No one seemed to hear it but him.

The three other men on the ward all wore nappies. Anyone without a room of his own learns a lot. Such as, for instance, what dirty nappies smell like. Human beings, as Leonardo da Vinci realised long ago, are merely passageways for food and drink; all they leave behind them is a pile of shit.

In the artificial twilight of the ward a fly was buzzing around. Fasch saw it double; he saw everything double since coming round after the anaesthetic. Lured by the smell of pus, the fly orbited the patients, alighting here and there. It nibbled at the gangrenous foot of the man in the bed on his left—a nameless diabetic, who only groaned—and then vanished into the gaping maw of the motionless man on his right to lay eggs on his tongue.

Gisbert's head was fixed in a head clamp on account of his fractured skull. Only with a little pocket mirror was he able to see a back-to-front image of his surroundings. So as not to see everything double, he had to shut one eye. He would have liked a bed at the window and to be able to stretch out his legs. He missed Miss Wong, his long-standing partner, and on top of that his anus itched and he couldn't scratch himself because he had a venous catheter full of nutrient solution stuck in the back of his right hand. In the mornings the resident doctor dropped in on his rounds, a cluster of medicos surrounding him like bodyguards, and asked Gisbert how *we* were. Well, how does he think *we* are, with an itchy arse and no way of scratching *ourselves*? It was wretched.

The most painful thing for Gisbert was the lost briefcase. When he came to after the operation, it was his first thought. Like a mother searching for her lost child, he called out for his briefcase. They thought he was hallucinating. He was given sedatives and in his fitful dreams he continued to search for the briefcase—with no success. Fasch wasn't told who had rescued him and brought him to the hospital. Only that he'd been driven to the emergency department after a bad car crash.

His hunt for Henry Hayden was over. He'd invested two years of his life in the search and they'd been the best two. Now all the precious evidence, every tiny detail, all the questions without answers, all the irreplaceable documents were lost. Henry had got the better of him with a silly trick. He'd simply lain in wait for him around the corner and then *bang*, *crash*, it was over—what a defeat.

If Fasch had lost all memory of the accident, as is usually the case with cranio-cerebral trauma, he could have recovered in peace and been grateful for his second life. But he couldn't forget. His memory ceaselessly projected the same sequence of images onto his retina. No sooner had he closed his eyes than he was approaching the bend again, racing straight towards Henry. Over and over again— Henry. Hallucinations arise out of nothing, figments of the imagination, but this was no figment, this was a documentary film on endless loop. It was torture. Over and over again—Henry. If this doesn't stop, Fasch decided, I'll kill myself.

And then one day the door opened and in walked Henry Hayden. Not a ghost, waiting around a bend in the road, but the man himself. With the same professional nonchalance as a doctor, he drew up a metal stool and sat down at the bedside. He looked just the same as in the lifestyle magazine. Only now there was no woman or dog at his side. What you might call a pared-down version of perfection.

The diabetic in the next bed let out a soft hissing sound. Otherwise it was absolutely silent on the ward. 'How are you?' Hayden asked in a pleasantly matter-of-fact baritone. The question may not have been original, but it was appropriate; they were in hospital after all, the house of the sick. During the conversation that followed, Fasch kept one eye screwed up, so as not to have to see two of his enemy.

'Who are you?' Fasch asked, after some hesitation.

'I happened to be present when you crashed your car. My name is Henry Hayden.'

The bloke's got a nerve, Fasch thought. *Happened* to be lying in wait around the bend, happened to disappear from the scene for thirty years and now just happens to drop in. As if.

'Haydn . . . like the composer?'

'Something like that. Hayden with an *e*, like the writer.'

'Ah? I know your books. But I'm afraid I have trouble reading just now. As you can see.' Fasch swung the arm in the noose to and fro. 'No can do.'

Hayden moved his stool a millimetre closer to the bed. 'I'd be happy to get you a few audiobooks, if you'd like.'

Fasch wondered why Hayden had visited him. Not to deliver audiobooks, that was for sure. Perhaps Hayden had been expecting to find a human vegetable and was now disappointed. Did he have any idea who he was? *Could* he have any idea? Fasch tried to sit up a bit, but the iron clamp prevented it. The whistling grew louder.

'Can you hear that?' asked Fasch, to change the subject.

'What?'

'The whistling. There's a whistling noise here. Something's whistling. It's coming through the wall.'

Henry looked about him, listened, shrugged his shoulders.

'Can't hear a thing.'

Fasch sighed. 'So you can't hear anything either. No one can except me.'

'In *that* case, it's a conspiracy.' Henry leaned towards him over the bed. 'If I see or hear something and everyone else pretends there's nothing there, then I know it's a conspiracy.'

Fasch had to laugh. That hurt, and not just his chest. Most of all it hurt his soul. He didn't want to laugh. Laughter means reconciliation. It connects people, and undoes grudges. But he had already invested a lot in this grudge of his. He had tended it and watched it grow. Why should he discard it now?

'You saw what happened?' he asked, trying to change the subject again.

Henry nodded. 'You took the bend too quickly and rammed into the barrier. Then the car overturned.'

'I don't remember anything.'

'That's for the best. It wasn't pretty. Hardly possible to believe anyone could survive a thing like that.'

'Where was I? How did I look?'

Henry adopted a thoughtful expression. Fasch looked at his manicured hands resting on his thighs.

He was wearing an IWC with a brown strap. Must have cost a packet.

'Your car was lying on its roof. There was broken glass all over the place . . . You were trapped on the back seat, unconscious. I pulled you free. You were completely out to it.'

'You? *You* pulled me free?'

Henry gave a cheerful laugh. 'Of course. There was no one else about. You looked at me—your eyes were open—but you didn't notice anything, did you?'

'I can't remember a thing. Did I say anything?'

'You just gurgled.'

'And then?'

'A few people have asked me that. Well, there was this piece of metal stuck in your chest. Pretty big, about so big.' Henry held up two fingers to show just how big it had been.

With his right hand, Fasch felt the painful spot where the tube disappeared into his chest. 'You pulled it out?'

'Yes.'

'Then you saved me.'

'Oh, I don't know about that! The doctors saved you. I just happened to be there.'

Silent implosion of emotion. Fasch could feel his hatred turning into something else. He was overcome by sadness, but he could do nothing to prevent the transformation from taking place, and felt sympathy and gratitude towards Henry Hayden. There was no more reason to hate him.

Henry put his head on one side. 'I wonder why you didn't brake?'

'Didn't I?'

'No, you didn't brake. You just drove straight on.'

Fasch closed his eyes. Once more he was speeding into the bend with the blazing sea before him . . . he was shooting towards Henry, light reflecting on his sunglasses, a fleeting glimpse of his mother's photo, and then . . . Hayden was right, he really hadn't braked.

When Fasch opened his eyes, Henry was standing over him with compressed lips, looking at him with cold fascination. There he was again: Grendel, the monster from the swamp.

'Don't you feel well?' asked Henry. 'Should I fetch a doctor?'

'Please don't!' Fasch replied. 'I have enough problems as it is.'

Henry pressed the bell next to his bed.

'What are you doing?'

'I'm leaving you on your own now. You need to sleep.'

The door opened and two male nurses came into the ward. Henry gave them a nod. They fiddled around with the contraptions at the side of the bed. Fasch felt a sense of panic.

'What's going on? What are you doing?'

One of the nurses bent over him. 'Keep calm, we're just taking you to another room, all right?'

'Why? It's nice here. I don't want to leave.'

One storey higher, Fasch was wheeled into a room for private patients. It was peaceful and clean. It had a floor-to-ceiling window with white curtains. There were flowers on a round glass table, a plasma screen on the wall, a Kandinsky print over the washbasin, a brand new tablet computer on a mobile table. Only the minibar's missing, Fasch thought, and coughed up a lump of catarrh. His bed was wheeled to the window so that he could see the park. The pus-hoovering contraption was plugged in again, and then at last he was left alone. Gisbert Fasch looked out of the window and thought of his partner, the silent Miss Wong. She never came to visit.

14

The bloke's not a cop, Henry decided, as the lift door closed behind him. He's not a private detective either. He's a perfectly normal man with a bee in his bonnet. An amateur. He must have been after Henry for quite some time. Why had he put on an act, pretended not to know him? If he were just a fan who had made a clumsy attempt to get close to his idol, he would have owned up to it in the hospital, if not sooner. Maybe he just wanted to make his mark and write a biography of him. Perhaps during his research he'd come across the gap in Henry's past and smelt blood.

Whoever uncovers me will undoubtedly become famous, Henry thought, and pressed the button for the ground floor. On his way down it occurred to him that Fasch hadn't asked about the briefcase. Of course, he would have given himself away then, but how could he not miss it? Gathering all that stuff would have cost time, effort and money. He would surely set great store on getting it back.

So much was clear to Henry: this fellow had come perilously close to uncovering his secret and wanted to do him harm, but didn't know how. Now he has a problem because he owes me. Maybe he'll never walk again, thought Henry with a flicker of compassion. Nevertheless, Henry had to keep ahead of him, find out his plan, which wouldn't be so difficult—anyone looking for clues invariably leaves his own clues along the way. Deep down inside, Henry had the feeling he'd met Fasch before. Some time and somewhere.

He strolled through the little park in front of the hospital to the car park. It was hot. Flakes of blossom floated between the lime trees, a gardener was mowing the lawn, a sprinkler was soaking a stray newspaper. People in dressing-gowns sat on benches. A bald woman on crutches was with her family. She'd obviously survived chemo and was glad to be alive. Congratulations are in order, thought Henry, feeling moved.

He stopped and turned round. His gaze wandered up the façade to the open window on the third floor. Fasch waved to him from his bed. Henry waved back. You can buy silence, but you can't buy good will. No one knew that better than Henry.

*

He took the Maserati to Car Wash Royale to have the congealed blood removed from the seat leather. A troop of cleaners in silly paper caps hurled themselves at the job. Henry explained to the suspicious boss's son that a wounded deer was responsible.

While the troop set to work, Henry sauntered out of pure curiosity into the nearest multistorey car park, where he rummaged through the bin next to the ticket machine for the red telephone. He ignored the camera diagonally above him; after all, he wasn't doing anything illegal. The phone was of course long gone—crushed to pulp when the bin was emptied, or in Africa.

An hour later, the car was sparkling clean and the interior once more smelt of leather. The boss's son came running out from his little glass cabin where his father had sat before him for forty years. He didn't like the way Henry was distributing generous tips to the cleaning slaves, but he couldn't do anything about it. Henry saw his braces straining over his belly.

'Herr Hayden,' he murmured in respectfully low tones, 'I didn't recognise you straight away, but I saw your book in the boot. My wife is a big fan of yours and I wanted to ask you . . .'

'Would you like an autograph?'

'My wife would be delighted, and so would I, of course.'

Henry took the book out of the boot and thumbed the pages. 'It's a little the worse for wear, but of course I'll sign it for you. Was it you who came up with the name Car Wash Royale?'

The boss's son already had a pen to hand. 'Oh, no, that was my father.' He watched, curious what Henry would write.

'What's your wife's name?'

'Sarah. She's . . . um, yes. Sarah with an h.'

He wrote: *Best wishes to Sarah from Henry Hayden.*

'May I ask you another thing?' the boss's son blurted out as Henry gave him the book. 'My wife writes, you see.'

'How funny,' Henry replied. 'So does mine.'

'Just to amuse herself—for the drawer, you know, but she's gifted. I'm not just saying that because she's my . . . um, yes. Well now, I'm to ask you what's the most important thing a writer should remember.'

'That's a complicated question to spring on someone in the afternoon. The most important thing'—Henry scratched himself under his right eyebrow with a little finger—'the most important thing is to write only about things you know.'

'Things you know. Ah ha.'

'And to allow plenty of time for leaving things out. Leaving things out makes for more work than anything else.'

'Leaving things out?'

'Everything you *don't* write, everything you leave out on purpose or delete—that's what gives you the most trouble and takes the longest. Don't tell anyone you got that from me.'

Then Henry drove to his favourite fast-food stand behind the station and ate a meatball. It was time for a good plan. And it was here he had the best ideas.

Where to begin? That amiable idiot, Detective Superintendent Jenssen, wasn't a threat just yet, because he believed in Martha's swimming accident. The homicide squad wouldn't stir themselves while the corpse hadn't surfaced. But *that* was just the point. The corpse could surface—in every sense—at any moment. It's well known that it takes ages for human bones to disintegrate in sea water. Algae hinder the process, unfavourable temperatures slow down decomposition, and the low concentration of oxygen also plays a part. Only depth is any help. The deep sea is a gratifyingly uncharted place.

Then there was Betty. She was so angry and disappointed that she would leave him in peace for a little while. But sooner or later the baby would be born. Henry wasn't sure whether the explanatory lecture in the Oyster Bar on the topic of *What Really Happened on the Cliffs* would prevent her from running to the police and blurting it all out. She was afraid. Fear is a truth drug: it speaks even with its mouth shut. You

213

should never frighten anyone who could grass on you—Henry knew that. One word from Betty about their meeting-place on the cliffs, and even the most useless policeman would put two and two together.

And then there was Sonja. He didn't want to disappoint *her*. Henry had searched his heart and decided that his desire for her was as physical as it was spiritual, a stroke of pure luck at his age. During their dramatic encounter on the beach and later on the millstone in his garden, they hadn't touched once, but the invisible current of libido between them and the union of their shadows had been sheer magic. And she liked his dog. It was all going swimmingly. Which took Henry back to point number two: Betty. He had to compensate her in some way, placate her, reassure her—in other words, she must be got rid of.

He opened the glove compartment and took out the receipt for a certain *Surveillance Manual*, which he had found in Fasch's brown briefcase. 'Office' had been noted on the receipt in red pen, presumably for tax purposes. Next to his address was the date of purchase. Fasch had bought this undoubtedly useful book on 3 May of the previous year. Just look at that, Henry thought—my birthday.

His sat nav took him straight to the right street. Cobbled and with a slight downhill slope, it ran parallel to a busy main road. The noise of the traffic splashed over the roofs and broke between the house walls. Henry turned off and parked the gleaming Maserati in a side street. It stood out in this neighbourhood amongst all the small cars, but he only needed a quarter of an hour.

The crumbling façade and front door were smeared with graffiti. The door was open. *Fasch* was scrawled in biro on the little nameplate next to the bell. Henry put on disposable gloves and rang the bell—you never know. Then he stepped into the dark hallway. Fasch's letterbox was overflowing with mail. Henry went up to the second floor.

The door wasn't deadlocked and it was child's play to push back the latch with a penknife. Opening it didn't take five seconds. He noted with satisfaction that he had not yet forgotten the time-honoured motions—but you don't forget how to ski, either. The door only opened a crack, then it met with an obstacle. The gap was just big enough to squeeze through. Henry was met by a strong smell of drains. Entering the flat, he had the absurd feeling he was conducting an endoscopic tour through the body of a stranger, beginning in the musty rectum of the hall.

Henry had never stolen more cash or jewellery than he needed to live off. Because he respected people's privacy, he always left personal effects untouched, which made the theft more tolerable. He never went near art on principle—that kind of thing is hard to turn into money. Ideally the theft would go unnoticed, but that rarely happened. Once, many years earlier, he'd broken into a dental practice and stolen dental gold. When days later he read about the doomed special units who had forced open the mouths of the dead and quarried gold out of them behind the gas chambers of Auschwitz-Birkenau, he returned the gold immediately and left two opera tickets by way of apology. Thrilled, the dentist and his wife watched *La Traviata* from the best seats. When they got home, their diamond jewellery had vanished. But that was a long time ago.

Printed paper was piled up to the ceiling on both sides of the hall. Newspapers, magazines, books, photocopies by the tonne. The dust had strung threads, and clouds of disintegrating cellulose snowed down on him. The paper was elaborately held together with string, and shored up with broom handles and all manner of laths and slats, so that the hall resembled a mineshaft. Between the mountains of paper ran a path less than fifteen centimetres wide. It was only thanks to his early participation in boy-scout field trips that Henry was able to negotiate it.

Silverfish scuttled under the shower tray, shunning the light, when Henry looked into the bathroom. The vile smell was coming from here. Henry closed the door. The bedroom floor was covered with semi-disembowelled appliances, rotten fruit and dirty washing. In the bed lay an almond-eyed creature with her thighs spread and her mouth open wide. Her perfectly proportioned body and expressionless face were turned a little to one side. Curling tongs were lodged in her hairless vagina. Out of sheer curiosity Henry lifted the doll up and discovered that she weighed the same as a living woman; he put her at over fifty kilos. Her name was stamped on the sole of her dainty foot: *Miss Wong*. The doll can't have been cheap. The flesh colour was convincing, but the silicon skin felt cold to the touch, which would explain the tongs to heat her vinyl vagina. This still life with curling tongs seemed to Henry like a joke in poor taste.

A telephone was ringing somewhere. Henry felt his way back along the paper bowels of the hall and followed the sound until he came to Gisbert Fasch's surprisingly tidy, spartan study. On a big double-sided pinboard Henry saw himself. His life in the form of a flow chart, with pictures, dates and hundreds of different-coloured circles. Henry was touched. It was as if he'd just entered a lost-and-found office for vanished memories. There were polaroids of buildings and places, press photos, pictures of him at readings and, in the top third of the chart, an old postcard showing a photo of an arched gateway. On the arch, in cast-iron letters, it said: *Saint Renata*. In this instant, Henry knew where he'd met Fasch.

The almost antique answering machine started up. A cassette began to whirr. *This is Gisbert Fasch speaking. I can't take your call right now. I'll get back to you.* Beep!

Herr Fasch, this is Honor Eisendraht from Moreany Publishing House. As we have already communicated to you, we do not release personal information about the life of Herr Hayden. Furthermore, I must point out to you that an unauthorised biography of Herr Hayden could have legal consequences for you. I would ask you not to address any further written enquiries concerning the matter to the publishing house. I wish you a pleasant day.

Henry barely heard the end of the message. He had already stepped back into the bedroom and switched on the curling tongs in the doll's plastic vulva. He left the flat in silence. No one saw him drive away.

The black smoke alerted the neighbours. It rose through the cracked bedroom window and up the front of the building. A little later, the windows in the living room shattered. The fire brigade came with three large engines and put out the fire with foam. Anxious tenants rescued their children, animals and most valuable possessions, and assisted the fire-fighting operations with their silent prayers. Outside the cordoned-off area, a number of onlookers videoed the event on their phones. Some of the videos appeared the same day on YouTube. The one to get the most hits was by a thirteen-year-old grammar-school girl who filmed the rescue of two burnt cats from the second floor and set it to music she'd composed herself. After the smoke had dispersed and the static equilibrium of the building had been tested, the majority of the tenants returned to their flats. The arson squad set to work in the charred flat. They came across what was left of a melted silicon doll; the foot had survived and belonged to the 'Miss Wong' model. Her remains were salvaged. The forensic investigation into the cause of the fire dragged on in the usual way.

* * *

The friendly gentleman from the insurance company waited patiently while Betty hunted for the car key. She had gone to the door in wooden sandals and a dressing-gown, assuming it was the courier service bringing her typeset pages to proofread. The man waited in the hallway outside the door. He had put down his bag and folded his arms over his belly. He enjoyed contemplative moments such as this.

Betty knew perfectly well that she wouldn't find the key, because it was rusting away in the Subaru at the bottom of the sea. For a long time, she'd driven the Subaru with the spare key, because the original key had got lost at some point. Nevertheless she rummaged around in the drawer of her desk, theatrically pushing it open and shut.

'I can't find the key just now,' she explained in embarrassment as she handed the car's papers to the friendly gentleman at the door. 'Does it matter?'

'What about the spare?'

'The spare? Lost that ages ago.'

'That's bad,' the insurance expert said with regret. 'Because without the key to the vehicle we can't accept liability for the loss.'

'Never mind,' Betty let slip far too quickly, 'I didn't report it because I wanted money from you.'

'Then why?' he asked, clearly surprised.

'Well, because I thought it's what you *have* to do when your car's stolen. Isn't that right?'

'No. You just have to cancel the car's registration, because you no longer drive it or because you've sold it.'

'I haven't sold it!' she protested, and immediately lowered her voice. 'It was stolen.'

'That'—he bent down lithely to open his bag—'is why your vehicle is being searched for. The police are looking for it all over Europe.'

He took out his documents and a questionnaire, put

the papers from the Subaru into a transparent folder and slipped it into his bag. Then he licked his index finger, opened up the questionnaire, suddenly and inexplicably had a biro to hand and clicked the doodah.

'Now then. Where was your vehicle stolen?'

'Right outside my front door.' Betty tried to remain polite. 'Listen, I don't have any time; I have to drive to work in a second.'

'In which car?'

The chap was getting more impertinent by the minute. 'I'm driving a rental car at the moment.'

'We undertake to pay part of the cost of that if your vehicle has been stolen.'

'No need. The company pays for the car.'

'That is'—he looked in his documents—'Moreany Publishing House?'

She wanted to poke the biro in his eye, but left it at a dry 'Correct'.

'You're renting the car from Avis.' He smiled when he saw her surprise. 'The rental car is insured with us as well. Your company'—he looked in his documents again—'Moreany Publishing House, has not received a rental agreement.'

Betty felt the blood shoot up her throat. He noticed that too, but stuck to the facts.

'I've spoken to Accounts. Frau . . .' He looked at his cursed documents for the third time.

'Eisendraht?'

'That's right. She knows of no rental agreement in your name. But Frau Eisendraht knows a Herr Henry Hayden.'

Henry's name fell like a sword. She felt suddenly dizzy. How on earth had this bloke got onto Henry? The friendly gentleman from the insurance company studied her face, registered the increased frequency of her pulse, her twitching eyelid, the way she turned down the corner of her mouth and shifted the position of her feet. With increasing experience, he got more and more pleasure out of his job.

'You showed a Visa partner card as security. The amount will be debited from Herr Hayden's account.'

Betty tore the questionnaire out of the man's hand. 'OK. I'll fill this in and send it to you. You don't have to pay a thing. Oh, and by the way, I'm going to terminate my insurance agreement.' Then she shut the door and leaned up against it. Her heart was pounding. She felt her hot cheeks with the back of her hand.

She hadn't thought of that. Henry had given her the card for emergencies, so she could make transactions and purchases for him when they went on business journeys abroad together. Because she had of course presumed that Henry would pay for the rental car, she had used his card. Just the once. Now her connection with Henry was documented. She dressed hastily. In her hurry, she tore a ladder in her tights. It was only in the mirrored wall of the lift on the way up to Moreany's office that she noticed that the rip had risen from calf to thigh like blood poisoning.

15

Frau Eisendraht was at the window, watering the dragon tree, and didn't turn round when Betty walked through the outer office into Moreany's room without a word of greeting. Moreany was sitting pale and very quiet behind his desk and didn't get up to give her his hand. Betty shut the office door.

'I'd like to clarify something, Claus,' she began, but before she could continue, Moreany motioned towards the Eames chair.

'Sit down, please.'

She sat down, crossing her legs to conceal the ladder. It might be something nice or something really awful, but there was no way it was the trifling matter of the car rental. She hadn't put in an appearance at the office for two days, and a foreboding rose up in her that a number of events must have overlapped in the interim. Moreany took off his reading glasses and set them on his immaculate desk. It was never tidy—that wasn't a good sign either.

'I've put you in a very awkward situation.' Moreany breathed deeply. He screwed up his eyes. The whole thing was obviously difficult for him. 'Please accept my apologies and forgive me my—how should I put it?—passionate stupidity.'

Then he said no more. Betty waited until the silence was unbearable.

'What's happened?'

Moreany slid open the drawer of his desk, took out an opened envelope and held it out to Betty. She got up and accepted it after some hesitation.

'I only opened it because it was addressed to me.'

Betty felt the envelope and saw the stamp of her gynaecological practice on the back. With two fingers she pulled out the CD with the ultrasound images of her baby stored on it.

'It's a girl,' Moreany said gently. 'The bill's enclosed. Allow me to settle it for you.'

Back to the beginnings of humankind. A Cro-Magnon man returns exhausted but happy after a day's hunting. In his comfortable cave in, let us say, present-day Apulia, he throws freshly killed game down next to the fire and looks around for his wife. He is tired, he is hungry, he wants to tell her about his hunting success. In the dark of the cave he hears her groaning.

He takes up a burning piece of wood and goes to look for her. He finds her lying in a side passage, her newborn baby beside her. The bitten-off umbilical cord is still hanging out of her womb. The woman is clutching the baby, covering the fine small face with her hands. He tears it out of her arms. The baby begins to scream, and he sniffs it and scrutinises it. It's a little Neanderthal. He knows at once that he is not the father of this bastard. He kills the child with one swipe against the rock wall and returns to the fire. The woman cowers in her corner of the cave, not knowing whether she'll survive the night.

Since the Pleistocene, things have moved on, it is true, but the question of paternity remains a delicate one, even for women now. No matter who had sent the ultrasound images to Moreany, there was no way it was a misunderstanding and even less chance it was a wrong address. It was simply the work of a very bad person. Henry can be ruled out, thought Betty, as she stood at Moreany's desk, taking stock, because it wouldn't be in his interest. Henry's never done anything that wasn't in his interest. But no one except him could have known about her pregnancy. She hadn't even told her mother. An obscure enemy had done it, invisible and yet very close. After this brief analysis, Betty sat back down in Moreany's Eames chair and, by way of explanation, said the only sensible thing she could think of—nothing.

As Moreany, likewise speechless, sat at his desk looking at Betty, his heart was weeping. The last plan of his life had failed. His late-summer romance in Venice was to remain a foolish old man's dream. The end would be lonely. There's no more to be done, he thought. I've reached the end of my journey. He got up, walked a little unsteadily to the black ebony side table, poured cognac into two balloon glasses and handed one to Betty.

'I'd like you to do something for me. Drive to Henry's and discuss the novel with him. I can imagine that he needs you at present. Time's running short; it's almost too late for the book fair. He told me he's only got twenty pages to go, but I can't believe he's able to write just now. It would be a real shame if he couldn't finish the novel before I go on holiday, eh?'

Her mouth was so dry that her lips stuck together when she sipped the cognac. The alcohol burnt in her throat. *He doesn't know*, she realised all of a sudden. *He doesn't know it's Henry's.* She got up, put the glass down on the table and hugged Moreany. She pressed him tightly to her. Never had she been so close to him, or felt so grateful. What a noble man, what a wonderful man, she thought.

'I'll call him now, Claus, I promise.'

Moreany nodded, a little tired. 'Thanks. Don't tell him anything about me, if you can help it.'

If Moreany had asked for her hand just then, she would have said yes without hesitation.

'Of course I won't, Claus.'

Honor took from her ear the glass she'd been using to eavesdrop at the dividing wall and quickly sat down at the computer. In a single gesture she slipped on her headphones and placed her fingers on the keyboard. Betty didn't walk through the outer office in silence as she usually did, but stopped in front of Honor and rested her palms on the desk.

'Honor,' she said softly, 'can I ask you a favour?'

Honor took off the headphones. It really was the first time that this person had addressed her respectfully and, above all, directly. She wanted to hear it again.

'Pardon?'

'May I ask you a favour?'

'Any time. What can I do for you?'

'Next time one of those insurance chappies rings you, please don't pass on confidential information about Herr Hayden.'

Eisendraht's head jerked, like a chicken that has just spotted a grain of corn. 'He asked me about Herr Hayden!'

'Yes. A lot of people do. And we protect the privacy of our authors, do we not?'

This 'do we not' left Honor no alternative. 'I've been working here for many years, *Betty*,' she said, 'and if there's anything that's sacred to me it's the privacy of our authors. You ought to know that.'

'All I know is that it was *you*.'

Betty was already out of the door, leaving Honor Eisendraht in a state of turbulence.

'She did *what*?'

Henry leapt up and began to pace in front of the picture window in his studio. The hovawart immediately got up from its place under the coffee table and slunk out of the room with its tail between its legs. It wouldn't come back until its finely tuned ability to pick up on bad vibes had given it the all-clear.

On the table in front of Betty was the envelope with the ultrasound images of the foetus. She followed Henry from the sofa with her eyes. Against the light she could see his silhouette flitting back and forth, a restless shadow.

'The envelope went straight to Moreany,' she went on. 'She rang up the practice and asked them to send the pictures to him at the company.'

'Eisendraht?'

'It must be her. It was a woman. She pretended to be me. She knows how old I am, where I live and that I'm pregnant.'

Henry turned his back on Betty for a moment and looked out at the fields. It wasn't yet ten in the morning and the sun was already blazing down. Not a cloud was in the sky. There was just a stork circling high, high up. It was going to be a hot day.

'How can she know that?' he asked, without turning round.

'Not from me.' Betty took off a shoe and pulled her leg up onto the sofa. 'And no,' she added, 'I haven't told Moreany anything. No one except the doctor knew about it. By the way, the insurance man dropped in yesterday and wanted the car key for the Subaru. I didn't have a key to give him.'

Although she couldn't see Henry's eyes against the light, she thought she could feel his penetrating gaze.

'No key? You don't have a key at all?'

'No.' Betty leaned forward and took the envelope from the coffee table. 'It was your idea to report it stolen. Why are we behaving like criminals, Henry? Why are we doing this to ourselves instead of simply grieving for your wife and being pleased about our baby?' She shaded her eyes, so she could see Henry.

'Can you come out of the light, please? I can't see you.'

Henry let down the electric blinds; it was at once cooler and pleasantly dim in the large room. He was visible once again.

'I'm going to the police, Henry. It doesn't make sense any longer.'

'Ah,' he said quietly—and then, after a long pause—'you know what will happen then?'

Betty took the CD out of the envelope. The light was refracted into the colours of the spectrum. She spun it in her hand. She's already gone into defensive mother mode, thought Henry all of a sudden. She's not scared of me any more. She just wants to keep the baby safe.

'What happens then I quite frankly don't care,' Betty replied. 'I think truth is the best policy for us. I don't want our baby to be born in prison. Wouldn't you like to have a look?'

Henry stared at the silver disc in her hand. It had all begun with that image. A little photo of a living piece of tissue, no bigger than a matchbox. At the sight of the foetus, the demon in him had been aroused, his old mate and protector from difficult times. *Follow me*, it had whispered, and Henry had once again followed. It had driven with him to the cliffs to kill his wife and crept in after him amongst the rafters of his house where the marten lurked. The demon had told him the right bend to lie in wait for his enemy, and was even now whispering its dark plan in his ear.

'The novel's finished.'

Betty looked at him in surprise. 'Really?'

'Yes. I suddenly saw the end. Then I sat down and wrote. I've been working through the night.'

She put the CD back on the table. 'I can't believe it. Can I read it?'

'By all means. Read it, tell me what you think and then we'll celebrate.' Henry went over to his desk and took the manuscript. He weighed it in his hand and passed it to her. 'I haven't had time to type it up on the computer yet. That's the only version. There's still no copy.' He saw that Betty was about to object, and raised his hand.

'I'd like you to read it before Moreany. And afterwards, we'll go to the police together and clear up this whole business. And now'—Henry joined her on the sofa and reached for the CD—'show me our baby.'

16

The *Drina* pitched and rolled in the light swell that was blown into the harbour by the west wind. Obradin pushed a can with the top sliced off under the oil drain outlet of the diesel engine and opened the valve. A change of oil might do the engine good—or it might be the extreme unction. He pursed his lips to whistle his usual little tune, but no sound came out—only air. He could chew much better with his nice new incisors, and cold things didn't hurt any more, but he could no longer whistle.

Black with powdered metal, the oil flowed into the can, shimmering in the sunlight that fell through the hatch into the engine room. Obradin dipped in an index finger and rubbed the black grease experimentally between finger and thumb. A shadow fell into the engine room. Obradin turned his massive skull. Glancing up, he saw Henry standing over him, his arms folded. He'd pulled his hat low down over his forehead. If the expression on his face was anything to go by, it must be something serious.

Henry inhaled tobacco smoke and let his gaze wander along the quayside wall.

'I have to get away from here, my friend.'

Obradin saw the smoke stream out of Henry's nostrils like cold winter breath. It curled and dispersed over the seaweed-green nets. There just couldn't be a better place for a man-to-man talk than his pitching, rolling, wonderfully hideous *Drina*.

'I'm in deep shit and don't know any other way out, so I'm going to make myself scarce. But first'— Henry laid his hand holding the cigarette on Obradin's oil-stained trousers—'I wanted to see you again. You don't know what my life's been like; you've never asked. You've never wanted to know where I come from, or what I've done, or what I get up to during the day.' He pushed the brim of his hat a little higher up his forehead and smiled sadly at Obradin. 'You don't know how much good that does me.'

'Where are you going to go?'

'Away from here. I'll lie low until everyone's given up searching for me.' Henry looked dreamily at the leather tips of his shoes. 'I've gone underground a few times in my life. Once, I did it for years. I lived by myself in a house with bricked-up windows and no one

236

noticed. The house belonged to my parents; they had been dead for many years. I only went to school until Year Six, just imagine. I can't even do mental arithmetic. Can you believe it?'

Obradin spat a flake of tobacco into the water. 'Just goes to show how little is actually enough.'

Henry took off his hat and wiped the sweat from his forehead. He spun the hat between his fingers.

'My wife didn't drown on the beach.'

Obradin jumped up and raised both arms imploringly. The *Drina* started to rock.

'Don't tell me, Henry. I don't want to know. You're my friend—I don't care. It's better you keep it to yourself.'

Henry stood up too and stretched out his hands to him.

'Calm down, Obradin, you have to know. The night Martha disappeared, I drove to the bay.'

Obradin put his hands over his ears. 'Don't tell me any more. Please.'

'I'm not leaving until you know what happened that night. I saw Martha's bike and her swimming things on the beach, but she wasn't there.'

Troubled, Obradin sat down again, kneading his hairy hands together. Henry saw tears in his dark eyes.

'I know. I saw you, Henry. You drove to the bay at night with your lights off and I saw you drive back again.'

'And what did you think?' asked Henry, taken aback. 'Come on, tell me, what did you think?'

'I didn't think anything. You can do whatever you like.' Obradin shook his bull's neck. A tremor racked his huge body. His shirt straining over his belly, he squirmed like a recalcitrant child. 'I don't know what I thought. It's your business, nobody's business but yours.'

'There's a woman,' Henry said softly, and sat down next to his friend again. 'Another woman. A wicked woman. She's called Betty and works at the publisher's. She's been pursuing me for years—claims she's going to have a baby by me. She's using it to blackmail me. She wants my money, but most of all she wants me.'

And then Henry told his friend, the fishmonger Obradin, what had really gone on at the cliffs that night. The *Drina* pitched and rolled, wavelets sloshed against the seaweed-covered side of the boat, miniature fish passed by in little schools. Obradin listened with closed eyes; he didn't interrupt Henry once. Only his hirsute index finger played over the seam of his trousers, as if he was taking notes.

'She told me Martha went to visit her in order to confront her,' Henry concluded, 'but Martha's car's still in the barn. Martha didn't come back from the meeting. I looked for her everywhere. Betty's car has disappeared. She's reported it stolen. This woman's even started using my credit cards. She's putting it about that she's pregnant by me. In court she'll say I did it. I'll be locked up for murder and she'll get the lot—the house, the rights to the novels, the whole lot.'

Obradin opened his eyes and blinked into the sun. 'Why don't you just send her away?'

Henry peered into Obradin's face. 'Send her where?'

'Send her to a place from which no one returns.'

'And where might that be?'

'It's quite simple,' Obradin replied quietly. 'Believe me.'

Henry shook his head violently. 'I couldn't bring myself to do that. I've often thought about it, I admit, but I'm too soft.'

'Not in your novels.'

'That's different. That's imagination, pure invention. In real life I can't even kill a marten. You were in the war, Obradin. You lost your daughter. You know how to hate. I don't know how to hate.'

'You don't have to hate a fish to kill it. It's quite simple.'

'A person's not a fish, Obradin.' Henry slapped his thighs and got up. 'Martha was the love of my life. I miss her. The house is too empty without her. I can't write any more. My friend, in a year or two you might get a postcard. From a stranger. That'll be me. Until then . . .'

Henry reached into his pocket and took out a key.

'This opens my safe. If you ever fall on hard times, if you're ever at your wits' end, then use it. You'll find the bank on page 363 of *Frank Ellis*. Farewell, my friend.'

17

The Old Harbour was the only restaurant in the region with a Michelin star. The sweeping terrace of revamped ship decking rose up above the sea on tarred struts. From here—afloat, as it were—you could enjoy the sunset. Initiates could enjoy one of the house's signature cocktails at the same time.

Henry parked his Maserati next to an open-topped Bentley in Tudor Grey and walked across the meticulously raked white gravel of the car park, past other landmarks in automobile history. He had his sleeves rolled up and his jacket flung casually over his shoulder. He'd just had a shower, he was hungry and he could smell his own aftershave. With a spring in his heel he took the steps two at a time and entered the sandalwood-lined lobby of the Old Harbour. Anyone who, like Henry, can reach this lobby after passing the gleaming chrome of those status symbols, without any feelings of envy or inferiority, can be said to have made it, to be one of the club.

Although Henry was wearing dark glasses, he was recognised by the head waiter and led to the *table pour deux* at the side of the terrace. It was the corner table right up against the balustrade, which offered the best view of the sun disappearing into the sea and of new guests appearing in the restaurant. There was enough room to stretch out your legs or to make an easy getaway. Henry had a quick look around him. The concept of informal dining requires only a casual dress code. Most of the male guests were wearing canvas shoes like him, sunglasses like him and expensive watches like him. Here one could mingle with a like-minded crowd—the young-at-heart fifty-plus, as they say nowadays. The balustrade tables were in high demand and booked months in advance. On his table was a white cloth, two long-stemmed water glasses, two sets of cutlery, two little hors d'oeuvres dishes and two discreetly patterned, laundered napkins. He glanced at his watch: 6.46 pm. He'd come a quarter of an hour early.

Betty had been reading all day. The blinds of her office were drawn. She had only made one brief sortie into the staff kitchen to make herself some peppermint tea. When she turned the last page, she paused, baffled. 'That's not possible,' she said out loud to herself. 'That's just not possible.' The end of the novel was missing. It didn't say 'The End' underneath either; it simply wasn't there.

White Darkness was an unbearably gripping novel. Betty had turned the pages with clammy fingers— now it had to happen!—and then the book just stopped. Betty stared at the large blank space on the last page as if there was a microdot hidden there that contained the secret of the ending. But there was only a speck of brown fly dirt.

Chekhov was famous for reducing his stories to the bare minimum. He would lop the beginning and the end off each one because he thought they weren't necessary to the plot. There is an unconfirmed rumour that his friends wanted to break into his study to rescue these endings. Countless readers of 'The Lady with the Dog' have realised with horror . . . just as the tormented love of two lonely people is about to overcome convention, undo their endless Russian hesitancy, send them into raptures and finally set them free . . . that suddenly it's over, and they've turned the last page. The fiercely longed-for ending is no longer part of the story. It's ghastly, but you have to accept it.

Betty suppressed the urge to ring Henry immediately. It was, after all, conceivable that he had simply forgotten to append the missing pages. 'The novel's finished,' he had said to her, smiling mysteriously.

Had he by any chance withheld the end in order to torment her? How irrational would that be? This novel was different from its predecessors. It was more passionate and more emphatic in every detail, but without the missing pages it was nothing but a torso. Incredible, the intuitive power with which Henry could develop his characters from within his armour of indifference, thought Betty, as she drank the remains of the cold peppermint tea. She put the manuscript down beside her.

Henry had painted her portrait. Betty had recognised herself from the very first pages. The same man who took her for his wife's murderer and didn't seem capable of developing the slightest feeling for his unborn baby had painted a precise and sympathetic portrait of her. As an editor you learn to separate author and work. It's not the person but the personality that is reflected in the artist's work. *We have to love Henry without knowing him*, Martha had said in parting at the door of her flat. She had apparently loved Henry as the man he was—as the man she didn't know.

* * *

At about five in the afternoon, Betty went into the photocopy room in the office and closed the door. She put Henry's 380-page manuscript into the paper feeder, plugged in her USB stick and pressed *Scan*. The machine began to suck in the pages one by one and save them on the stick as a PDF file. Then it spat each page out again. Betty stowed the manuscript in a plastic folder and put it in her handbag. She put the stick in a small Murano glass dish on her desk.

She took the lift up to Moreany's office. On the way she felt the movements of the baby, now growing noticeably stronger, and placed her hand on her belly. The movements immediately subsided. The horrific attacks of nausea had vanished. Betty no longer took medication, and for weeks now she had entirely avoided alcohol and cigarettes. She drank tea instead of coffee. Contrary to what she had expected, going without her daily dose of poison was easy, and the abstinence made her even more beautiful. Men openly turned and stared at her. Even the female employees at Moreany's threw furtive glances at her.

Most of her colleagues had already gone home to drive to the coast for the weekend. Betty cleared the dirty cups away as she passed the central coffee counter. She said hello to the attractive young fellow from the publicity department who was always throwing paper darts at her. Then she went into Moreany's outer office, where Honor Eisendraht stood sorting accounts at her top-secret Bisley filing cabinet—the heart-lung machine of the company, as Moreany called it. Her monitor already had its cover on. Betty saw a pack of Tarot cards next to the keyboard on her desk. The door to Moreany's office was closed.

'Has Moreany already left?'

Eisendraht spirited away the Tarot deck and took her handbag from the back of the chair. Betty noticed her subtle perfume, her smart hairdo and her outfit that offset the colour tones of the office.

'He left for an appointment at three.'

Betty tried to gauge from Eisendraht's eyes whether she was withholding information from her, but the secretary's face was an unreadable mask, something like what you see on totem poles in anthropological museums. Only the way her glance strayed to Betty's belly betrayed what was going on inside her.

'Is there anything else?' asked Eisendraht, smoothing her jumper over her navel in a presumably unconscious gesture.

'Yes, I've never shown you my appreciation. That was stupid of me and I'm honestly sorry. I respect you and I admire your work. Have a nice day.'

Alone in the outer office, Honor stood motionless for a while. The dragon tree shed a leaf, otherwise nothing changed. And yet. There is a certain irony in hearing the most touching compliments emerge from the mouth of your very enemy, on whose cold disdain you have come to rely. Honor Eisendraht knew too much about women not to see with perfect lucidity that Betty meant her apology seriously, sincerely and without expecting anything in return. She took her bag and went out of the office, shrugging her shoulders. Such things happen. Nothing you can do about it.

Henry decided on steak and chips. No ordinary fries these, but *pommes allumettes*. The Thai-style red snapper at the next table looked tempting too, as did the lady with the silicon breasts who had ordered it and who would have simply loved to join Henry if circumstances permitted, which they didn't. But a steak was enough for Henry. He savoured the last of his sundowner. The sun was still high over the sea. His watch now showed 7.07 pm. He looked in the direction of the restaurant lobby; the head waiter saw his glance and came to his table at once. Of course he saw the empty place, and naturally he understood that Henry wanted to wait to order. There couldn't be the shadow of a doubt that Henry's dining companion was female, so he suggested vermouth, the proper drink for a gentleman who is waiting for a lady and does not wish to appear to have an indecent thirst. A moment later, Henry's phone vibrated. It was Betty.

'Henry, I'm driving along this ghastly dust track. Can that be right?'

'Yes, that's right.'

The air in the car shimmered. Betty looked out of the side window that was clouded with dust and let it down a little further. A fine mist of particles rolled into the car, formed clouds, deposited tiny crystals on her skin, got into her hair and lungs, mingled with the moisture of her mucous membranes.

'What can you see?'

'Well, on the right I can see fields and pylons, and on the left there are these kinds of bushes and, apart from that, absolutely nothing. It's ridiculously dusty here. I'm going to look like Ben-Hur after the chariot race when I get there.'

Henry knew she'd taken the right road. 'The pylons lead you straight here.'

Betty looked at the GPS device. 'The sat nav only shows a dotted road. Four point nine kilometres to go. Is that possible?'

'You're doing fine. Keep straight on till you get to the water. It's an old harbour. That's the name of the restaurant: Old Harbour. You're really close. Have you got my manuscript with you?'

'Of course.'

'Great. Shall I order you a sundowner?'

'No alcohol for me, thanks. OK, see you soon.'

Betty put the phone on top of her notebook computer and Henry's manuscript in the open hand-bag beside her. She'd had a good feeling when she'd left work to meet Henry for dinner. The first step towards reconciliation with Honor Eisendraht had been taken. Malicious it may have been, but Eisendraht's betrayal had had a purgative effect. She'd done Betty a real favour, even if it can't have been her intention. The ultrasound images had brought the silly secretiveness to an end. No affair is worth denying a child for.

The potholes in the track were getting deeper and deeper. Betty reined in the speed. Rust-ravaged metal containers lay dotted about the side of the road. Here and there she saw shreds of truck tyres. Fountains of dust flew up in the air like powder. She tried to drive in the ruts of the broad tyre tracks which had been washed out by the rain and baked into rock-hard furrows by the sun.

The more slowly she drove, the more interminable and absurd the trip seemed to her. But Henry had always had a good nose for remote and stunningly beautiful places. Betty remembered Es Verger on the Puig de Alaró on Majorca. Henry had driven doggedly upwards; the engine had shrieked; the car had creaked and clattered. 'We'll get there at some point,' he said, and she had trusted him. After an endless ascent on a narrow winding track, they had finally reached the mother of all mountain restaurants and eaten the most delicious lamb of their lives. It was that night the baby had been conceived, Betty was quite sure of it.

A sign appeared in the distance. It stood half sunken on rusty steel posts, almost illegible from so much dust and sun. Betty could make out what looked like a fishing boat and in faded letters *Harbour*. That must be it. Her sat nav showed she was less than a kilometre away. In rough outline the display showed an oblong site on the seafront. 'In seven hundred metres you will reach your destination. You are approaching your destination.' A metal fence surrounded the place. The ugly concrete frontage of an industrial building came into view and seagulls sat on skeletal cranes.

Betty passed through the open gate at a crawl and followed the concrete slabs that were overgrown with weeds. Heaps of fly-blown rubbish were piled up. Yellow and blue plastic drums rolled around in the wind. A putrid smell hung over everything. Betty let the car roll up to a waist-high wall, where a sign in faded paint read: *No Access*. She stopped the car, got out and looked about her.

'Follow the arrows,' chirped the sat nav.

The terrace was bathed in red evening light. More guests had sat down. A woman was just being led past Henry's table. He followed her tanned ankles in their backless heels. Henry's phone buzzed.

'Betty, where are you?'

'I've ended up in a rubbish dump and there's a *No Access* sign in front of me. Is this supposed to be a joke? There's no restaurant here.'

'Then you're standing in front of a wall, right?'

'Yes, and I'm not driving any further. It's really spooky here.'

Henry laughed. 'Just ignore the sign. Keep driving a bit. I'll come to meet you.'

His laughter reassured her. After a brief hesitation, Betty got back in the car and drove slowly along the ugly wall. She kept the phone at her ear. She could hear his steady breathing. After fifty metres the countryside opened out on her left and the sea came into view.

'OK, I'm right by the water now. There's a hangar here. There are dustbins and old rail tracks all over the place. No one in sight, no car. Where are you?'

'On my way to you. Stop next to the hangar. I'll be there in a second.'

Betty stopped the car next to the hangar. Its enormous door stood open like the jaws of a crocodile. The dust on the windows reflected the light so brightly that she couldn't make out what might be hidden in the darkness within.

'The restaurant's not in *there*, is it?'

'I can see you, Betty. Get out, turn round, can you see me?

Betty opened the car door and got out. A cold wind blew out of the darkness of the hangar. She clutched the phone in her fist and peered about.

'Henry, where are you,?'

18

Jenssen liked statistics. Like most of his colleagues he was of course acquainted with the annual crime stats. Numbers tell stories. Especially if you compare them with one another—for instance, the fact that in Germany, in 2009, precisely 38,117 women underwent facial laser treatment compared with 42,623 German men over the same period of time. 'What does that tell us?' Jenssen liked to ask, whenever he cited such figures in the police headquarters canteen.

Homicide offences, counting both murder and manslaughter, had gone down by 2.2 per cent compared with the previous year. The rate of solving crimes had now reached 95.9 per cent, which throws a good light on the investigative work of the authorities and a bad light on the acumen of your average perpetrator of violence. It would seem that the almost one hundred per cent likelihood of being convicted of murder and severely punished is regarded by most offenders as acceptable. Maybe for the simple reason that it's only *almost one hundred per cent*, and because the statistics don't affect them personally— just the others. And not least because crime statistics provide information about detected murders, while the undetected ones, not to say the *successful* ones, remain in the paradise of darkness. Thus it can be assumed with a kind of foreboding that the coming years will see a similar percentage of murders committed and punished.

Martha Hayden's death by drowning had for Jenssen been a classic case of death by misadventure, because there was no motive or evidence pointing to anything else. The bike on the beach convinced him. It had convinced *everyone*. And yet 'fatal swimming accident' was only a hypothesis, based solely on the discovery of the bicycle—a discovery made by her husband of all people. Purely hypothetically, the bike on the beach allowed the conclusion that the owner had been kidnapped by aliens and was now having a whale of a time with underage exomorphs on board their spaceship. Why not?

The disappearance of Bettina Hansen, a thirty-four-year-old editor at Moreany Publishing House, however, was no accident. It certainly wasn't suicide, either. A coastguard helicopter had sighted the burning car wreck at about 10 pm on a routine nightly flight. By the time the fire brigade arrived forty-five minutes later, they could only smother the glowing plastic car parts with foam. This foam destroyed valuable evidence in the immediate vicinity of the wrecked car. The arson squad did not find the remains of a human body.

An hour after the beginning of the early shift, Jenssen arrived on the site of the derelict fish factory. It had been out of use for a decade and made him think of an apocalyptic seaside resort on the Costa Brava. Every muscle in his body was aching because he'd tried to catch up on three weeks of missed training in the gym the evening before. In spite of 1500 milligrams of Ibuprofen, he couldn't walk properly. He could only waddle sideways, his arms dangling like an orang-utan's.

The powder-fine white dust had turned into grey mush in the extinguishing foam around the car. Jenssen's colleagues from the forensic unit were crawling around in it, looking for a trace of blood or hair, for vestiges of body fat or bone ash. Jenssen blessed his far-sightedness in deciding at the beginning of his career not to work in forensics. Not because he found the work dull or pointless—no, the tedious thing was that the clues tended to be microscopic. You found a hair and it assumed the dimensions of a tree trunk. For Jenssen, poking around in the nanosphere like that took away the sensuous pleasures of detection.

Jenssen paced out the distance to the sea, counting forty-two steps. Abandoned rail tracks led down a slightly sloping concrete road into the water where the skeletons of old freight wagons had been left to rust—wagons that had once been used to haul cargo from the cutters up onto land, in the good old days when there were still fish.

After a fruitless search the tracker dogs were loaded back into the van. A few police officers were still snorkelling in the reinforced shore area. Naval divers had been sent for and were expected in the course of the afternoon. They wouldn't find anything either, Jenssen was convinced of that. He sat down on the tyre of a heavy goods vehicle that had already received forensic treatment, and did some surreptitious stretching exercises to regain control of his upper arms. He was sure they would find neither a corpse, nor evidence of the perpetrators, nor indeed anything that might help solve the crime. Once again, he took out the crumpled-up fax paper from his pocket and read the transcript of the emergency call.

At 9.16 pm, Henry Hayden had dialled the emergency number of the police on his mobile phone. First, he had asked whether a road accident had been reported. Then Hayden had related that Betty Hansen, an editor from his publishing house, had not turned up at their arranged meeting-place with the original manuscript of his latest novel. He said that she had rung him twice on her way there. Once to ask the way, a second time to tell him she'd be late. He'd been trying to ring her for hours, but it hadn't been possible to get hold of her. The police officer on the emergency services line told Henry that no one had reported an accident and that it was still too early for a missing person search. Entirely correct procedure. Jenssen was sure that an examination of the phone company's records would confirm Hayden's statements as to length of call and location.

* * *

It was the proliferation of similarities that he found so remarkable. Two women had gone missing in less than a month—both of them closely connected with Hayden. One of them he was married to, the other he worked with. But wouldn't everyone have called the police in this situation? Jenssen wondered. Also striking was the fact that both women had disappeared altogether—not a single trace, not a hair, not a particle to be found. Martha Hayden was a practised swimmer. Her death was plausible. No one can get the better of a strong current. But how could a healthy, sensible woman like this editor manage to get quite so lost? It was five kilometres of cratered dust track from the coastal road to here. No sign, no signpost and no sat nav entry indicated a restaurant in this wilderness. And what had happened to her corpse?

Jenssen got up and waddled past his colleagues to the hangar. He took five steps into the darkness, then turned round and yelled, 'HELP!'

They all stopped in sync and looked about—but no one could see him. Only five paces away and yet invisible, Jenssen noted. This was probably the exact spot where the murderer had come from.

* * *

After the fifth futile call, Honor Eisendraht phoned a taxi and had it take her straight from the office to Moreany's villa. She entered the old park through the garden gate and pressed the bell at the front door until she got a cramp in her index finger. Then she walked round the house and entered the library through the open veranda door. Filled with anxiety, she searched all over the big house. Countless rooms were empty or crammed with books and boxes. She called his name; she listened out.

In the end she found Moreany in his bedroom on the first floor. He was lying on his side in his enormous box-spring bed, his face covered in sweat. Long seconds passed between one breath and the next. She saw an open packet of prescription morphine beside him. There were three ten milligram tablets missing. She turned Moreany onto his back. He opened his eyes, gasping for breath, recognised her and smiled. She fetched water, carefully poured it into his mouth, helped him onto his feet and supported him as he staggered to the bathroom. Moreany was clearly in pain. He was so weak that she had to hold onto him as he sat on the lavatory.

Four cups of coffee later he was a little better. He looked into her anxious face.

'I already know. Henry rang me last night. The novel's lost too.'

'*Lost?*' Honor held her hands to her mouth in horror.

'Betty had the manuscript with her in the car.'

'No! Isn't there a copy? He must have made a copy.'

Moreany shook his head. 'He always writes on a typewriter. I've seen the manuscript. This is the end, Honor. And if you want to cry now, be a dear and fetch me my English shortbread first.'

Honor found the biscuit tin he had described in a larder full of delicacies that had gone off. Everything was covered in cloths spun from the finest insect secretions—Spanish ham coated in a blue lawn of mould, mummified sausages, shrivelled fruit, dangerously bulging tins, the shelves interconnected by a myriad of bored tunnels. No doubt about it, the house was lacking a woman's touch. Honor hardly dared open the biscuit tin, but to her relief the biscuits inside were perfectly edible.

'Did you see the vultures on the roof, Honor, my dear? I hope they're vegetarian. I don't know how much longer I can hang on.'

Moreany had spoken tenderly to her for the first time. Honor took his hand and pressed it. He munched a biscuit with relish. 'Now, my little honorific,' he said, and closed his eyes, 'give me the good news. Is there any?'

* * *

The small three-roomed flat was neat and tidy. There was a faint smell of lily-of-the-valley and of the freshly washed laundry that was hanging on a clothes horse in the living room. Jenssen made his way through the rooms, looking at the furniture, the small collection of Venetian glass, the clothes and shoes. A large black-and-white portrait of Betty hung on the wall. It showed her in semi-profile with the light shining on her blonde hair, and reminded Jenssen of the 1940s Hollywood star Lana Turner. He took a photo of it with his phone. In the kitchen the breakfast dishes were still on the table. An apple with a bite out of it lay next to an open newspaper and a magnetic calendar was stuck on the fridge. There was a date circled. 'Gynaecologist' was written beside it in felt-tip pen. Jenssen glanced at his watch. The appointment was today.

On the small desk in Betty's bedroom, Jenssen found some photographs. In a few pictures he could recognise Henry Hayden. The pictures had obviously been taken at readings or literary festivals. Jenssen couldn't find a computer, but there was a modem, evidence that she had internet access. On a pile of manuscripts lay the blank car-insurance claim. The insurance company had already ticked the box for theft and identified the car model. Jenssen was aware that Betty Hansen had reported her car stolen without being able to produce the keys. He also knew that she had rented a car with Henry Hayden's credit card. The question was: why?

Jenssen liked walking through the rooms in dead people's flats. There was a macabre reverence about it, like an atheist in church solemnly contemplating God's absence. A pair of shoes next to a sofa, slipped off with the intention of tidying them away at the next opportunity, could be so tragic. A book left open on a bed was a stopped clock, every calendar entry a message from the hereafter.

In the melancholy grip of these relics, Jenssen reflected on the unknown woman who had lived here. Even before discovering her portrait on the wall, Jenssen had suspected that she had been Henry Hayden's lover. She was well suited to him. She was young and beautiful, obviously educated and successful, and she worked closely with him—most marriages and clandestine affairs begin in the world of work. It was only another vague hypothesis, a hunch, but Jenssen believed that the deaths of the two women were in some mysterious way connected and could be explained by a single motive.

Henry Hayden had not killed Betty Hansen. So much was now certain. He had without question the best alibi in the world. He had waited for her in a public restaurant in full view of everyone. He had even spoken to her on the phone. The old-fashioned telephone on Betty's desk began to ring. Jenssen jumped. After some hesitation he picked it up. It was the receptionist from Dr Hallonquist's gynaecological practice, kindly ringing with a reminder of Betty's next appointment.

'When?'

'This afternoon at three.'

* * *

Henry saw the police car in the car park. The radio antenna was discreetly attached to the rear of the vehicle, but not quite discreetly enough. He said hello to the old porter and asked after his long-suffering rheumatic wife. She was as ever in a wretched way. Then he took the stairs to the third floor to lend some credibility to his quickened pulse.

Honor Eisendraht came to meet him in the corridor as if she'd been waiting for him. Her eyes were reddened, her hairdo was a little dishevelled. She was wearing a coal-grey suit in keeping with the atmosphere. 'The police are here,' she whispered to Henry. 'There are three of them and they're questioning *everyone*. They've sealed off Betty's office. Moreany's in a very bad way. How could all this happen?'

'Have you had your turn yet, Honor?'

'I'm next. After they've finished with Moreany. Henry, is the novel really lost?'

He nodded gravely. 'I can reconstruct it from my notes, but it will take a long time. If Betty's dead, then it's lost.'

'Do you think she might still be alive then?'

Henry saw her lips trembling. Moved, he took Frau Eisendraht in his arms and stroked her back. 'As long as Betty's corpse hasn't been found, I won't believe she's dead.' They extricated themselves from the embrace. Honor wiped away her tears.

'Herr Hayden, you don't think it was *me*, do you?'

'That *what* was you?'

'I didn't send those ultrasound pictures.'

'You? For heaven's sake, no, never in my wildest dreams would I believe that! Do you know what I think? I think it was the child's father.'

When Henry entered the room, Moreany's police interview was already over. The three detectives stood in the room like the last pieces in a game of chess. Grey in the face and unshaven, Moreany was sitting in the Eames chair. He was too weak to get up, and just waved.

'Henry, these are the people from the homicide squad. Excuse me, I've forgotten your names.'

Henry recognised the opossum standing next to Jenssen. She had plucked her eyebrows since he'd last seen her; the monobrow had been erased. He didn't know the dark-haired man with the fine-hewn face. The officer introduced himself. 'Awner Blum,' he said drily. 'I'm leading the investigations.' Henry couldn't gauge whether that was good or bad news. He shook hands with everyone and again felt the power of Jenssen's grip.

'Are there any—how should I put it—breakthroughs yet?' Henry asked, looking round the assembled company.

'We're still in the process of evaluating,' replied Jenssen matter-of-factly. 'The perpetrator or perpetrators set fire to the car to destroy any evidence. We're most interested in whether this was an accident or a premeditated crime.'

'Who could possibly have planned it?' Henry adopted a puzzled expression. 'Betty got lost. Not even she knew where she'd ended up. No one knew.'

'That's just the question, Herr Hayden,' said Blum, butting in. Jenssen was silent.

'You mean whether anyone was in the car with her?'

'For instance. It's possible, isn't it?'

'Whoever could it have been?'

The door opened quietly. Honor Eisendraht entered the room behind Henry. He noticed that the opossum was sniffing around again.

'If you've no objections, Herr Hayden, we'd like to continue the questioning with you.' Jenssen looked at Moreany. 'Do you have another free room for us?'

Before Moreany could reply, Henry raised his hand. 'I'd like to say something that concerns all of us here. A little time ago, I lost my wife.' Henry paused to collect himself. 'As you may already know, the manuscript of the novel I've been working on for a long time disappeared along with Betty.'

Henry glanced at Moreany, who nodded. 'I just told the police that.'

'A few days ago,' Henry continued, 'I met Betty in the Four Seasons. She was distraught and scared, not herself. She was afraid.'

Jenssen whipped out a device. 'Would you mind if I recorded this?'

'Not at all. Well then, we sat in the Oyster Bar and discussed the novel. I talked about the difficulties I was having getting anything written after Martha's death. She hardly listened. I asked her what was wrong with her and then it burst out of her. She told me she was pregnant.'

Honor leaned against the office wall. She felt a little dizzy.

'Did she name anyone?' asked Jenssen, who clearly felt awkward conducting this conversation in front of the other witnesses.

'No. She spoke of the disastrous mistake she'd made. It was already too late for an abortion.'

'Do you think she was raped?' asked the opossum.

'I wouldn't want to rule it out. At any rate she spoke of a man she was afraid of. She said he was dangerous and unpredictable. She'd ended the relationship with him and now she was afraid he might try to get his own back. It seems he was always ringing her up and threatening to send the ultrasound images of the baby to Moreany's office. She said he'd stolen the car.'

'Along with the keys?' asked Jenssen in disbelief.

'I don't know anything about that.'

Shaking his head, Jenssen started to take notes.

'I advised Betty to go to the police and offered to have her to stay for a few days, but she refused. Then she felt sick and had to go to the lavatory, but she didn't come back and I drove home to work on the novel. That was the last I saw of her. Now I blame myself for not going straight to the police. She was in trouble, in danger. I shouldn't have left her alone.'

'I can confirm that,' Honor said in a quiet voice. She was slumped into a heap against the wall. 'I also happened to be in the Four Seasons lobby that day. It was the Tuesday before last. I saw Betty go to the lavatory. She vomited and she was crying. Crying a lot. Herr Hayden came out of the Oyster Bar and left the hotel. He didn't see me.'

Moreany got up out of his chair with difficulty and let Honor have it. He seated himself behind his desk, his face screwed up in pain.

'We interrupted you, Henry.'

'I only want to say one more thing,' Henry declared. 'If Betty is dead and it was, as Herr Jenssen puts it, not an accident, but murder, then you must look for the father of her child.'

Moreany's office was as silent as a concert hall. Only a solitary cougher could be heard.

19

Chief investigator Awner Blum was in charge of three separate homicide squads. He was reputed to be a genius of case analysis, which in film and on television is generally known as 'profiling'. His officers had indeed a number of times drawn up such accurate criminal profiles that convicted murderers had congratulated him from prison.

Blum didn't know the first thing about psychology, but he had a superhuman instinct for managing people. He might have been born to run a murder squad. He had headhunted the most skilled detectives to join his squads and had attained a solved crimes quota of one hundred per cent. He'd done that for three years in a row. Blum was a womaniser and liked the sound of his own voice. His lectures on criminal profiles, larded with quotations, could drag on for ever. Jenssen was of the opinion that just listening to him ought to count as overtime. In the most successful investigations the movement patterns of victim and perpetrator were compared. The method worked well. You drew up the most comprehensive biographies possible of the victim and then looked for areas of overlap with the profiles of potential offenders.

The data crunchers established that Betty Hansen had indeed made regular phone calls to an unknown person over the course of the last six months. His identity however remained a mystery. The SIM card from the prepaid phone had been registered under a made-up name and a false address. Betty's phone also remained missing, as did her notebook computer where her emails were stored. Neither her leather-bound diary nor her private or business correspondence yielded a name.

Jenssen went to see the gynaecologist who had carried out the scan. Betty Hansen hadn't mentioned the father's name to this woman either. Without a sample of tissue from the amniotic sac, it wasn't possible to determine the father's DNA. Members of Betty's family were questioned, along with her friends, her neighbours and her work colleagues, but no one knew anything. Just three sets of prints were found in her flat: Betty's, Jenssen's and those of a neighbour. The only evidence of any use was the scattered movement profile of the caller. A great deal of effort went into following up this evidence.

It is widely believed that telephone companies store data as to *who* telephones *whom, where* and *for how long* for no more than six months. Far too short a period for thorough police work, in Awner Blum's opinion. Universal data mining for the purposes of criminal prosecution would be far more effective if there were no time limit, in as much as *every* caller is a potential offender who ought to be subject to preventative scrutiny. Only the National Security Agency knows everything forever, and the Americans are famous for being extremely tight-fisted when it comes to handing over their valuable knowledge.

Jenssen didn't find the telephone data particularly helpful. He stuck a large transparency of the mystery caller's movement profile on the map on his office wall and ordered a jumbo tuna pizza with extra capers. Place, time and length of call were marked on the transparency in the form of clouds of scattered dots. Joining the dots up yielded an abstract pattern which was aesthetically demanding, but an investigative nightmare. Each call came from a different place. Some were made in town, not far in fact from Betty Hansen's flat. Most of them, however, were made in sparsely populated areas—from remote forests and nature reserves for instance, within a radius of three hundred kilometres. That meant that it was extremely difficult to locate the telephone with any accuracy. What is more, the caller only ever switched the phone on immediately before making the call and then switched it off again immediately after hanging up. There was no movement along roads, no *lines*—only dots.

A special taskforce was already hard at work looking for a nature lover, a forester or a hunter. Hundred-strong police contingents combed the areas where the caller had switched on his phone. Thermal imaging cameras and satellite optics were also deployed in case there was a secret hide-out to be found. Specialised dog teams hunted for underground burrows. They found only poachers' hideaways and an abandoned boy-scout camp. A lot of innocent hikers were detained by the police and had their phones examined—but the search yielded nothing.

As the search for the unknown person wasn't getting them anywhere, Blum's teams reopened murder cases where the trail had gone cold, and applied the same techniques. More experts with new hypotheses arrived on the scene. The homicide squads were expanded further, and the search area widened again. Jenssen, who had started throwing darts at the map in his office, didn't believe in the nature-lover theories. He saw a much more flexible strategy in the guerrilla-like appearance and disappearance of the unknown caller. For Jenssen, it was clear that the mystery man could be none other than Henry Hayden.

At the daily briefings in the meeting room, Awner Blum circulated a photocopy of a new profile. 'We're looking for a man,' he began, 'who's been living a double life for a long time. He's sporty, about thirty to forty-five years old, might well be married, have children and lead an unremarkable middle-class existence. He lives in a radius of three hundred kilometres from here. Perhaps he's a hunter or a forester—he might even be a policeman or a regular soldier by profession, because he's a master of disguise and knows a lot about location technology. He's looking for the kick that his day-to-day life can't provide. Maybe he robs banks in his spare time, or kills people. It's possible that he's on the run from something.'

'From what?' asked Jenssen in the back row.

'Something in his past,' Blum replied. 'A traumatic experience that's still haunting him, or else a crime. He leaves nothing to chance. At some point he gets to know his victim. He must have told her some fanciful story about himself, a story so plausible that she didn't talk about him to anyone, not even to her closest friends and relations. We have to assume that she was unaware of his true identity. Then one day or night she gets pregnant by him. He didn't want that; the thing starts to get too risky for him. He was in the car with her when she was on her way to meet Herr Hayden. That's when the murderer killed her and disposed of her body.'

'How?' asked Jenssen from the back.

'By boat or by ship. The murder took place right by the water.'

Jenssen rose from his seat.

'Excuse me for saying this, but no woman is that stupid. The victim was an editor. Editors read books for a living. They analyse them. They look for logical errors and inconsistencies in them. They're experts in fanciful stories. Nothing escapes them. I think you can fool anyone, but not indefinitely. If our man wanted to disguise himself—and there's no doubt that's what he wanted—then why did he phone her at all?'

Jenssen's reflections aroused a feeling of unease in the room, but he carried on regardless.

'I think this bloke just likes going for walks. Why should he of all people send ultrasound images of the baby to the publisher when no one's supposed to find out?'

Awner Blum looked around at the assembled company. 'Is it possible that the murder victim sent the pictures herself in order to get rid of him?'

'Certainly not if she was afraid of him.'

'OK, Jenssen.' Blum was getting angry. As a certified investigative genius he had no use for time-wasting sceptics. 'So why don't you tell us who you think the unknown person is?'

Jenssen mumbled something.

'Sorry? Speak up, please. We can't hear you.'

'I said, maybe we already know him.'

'Maybe?'

Awner Blum looked at the clock on the wall. Jenssen was getting on his nerves with his 'maybe'. He was still young and relatively inexperienced to be on a homicide squad, and on top of that he was slow on his feet and not a good team player. Blum had been considering a transfer for Jenssen for quite some time. A friendly 'recruitment' by another department would be an excellent method.

'We all know your theory, Jenssen, and we wonder why you persist in defending it. At the time in question, Herr Hayden was sitting on a crowded restaurant terrace. He has no motive other than being famous. He has tried to the best of his ability to assist in solving the crime—what's more, he was talking to the victim on *his* phone when she died. *What* in your opinion would be a possible motive?'

'Sex,' replied Jenssen after clearing his throat noisily. 'The murder victim Betty Hansen was his lover. He's the child's father. Either he or she or both of them together killed his wife, Martha. And something went wrong.'

* * *

In the air-conditioned silence of his private room, Gisbert Fasch realised that he was a man who had problems. Not just since the accident, but also long before. His mother Amalie, who paid him sporadic visits, confirmed this. He'd always been something of an only child, she explained to her son, even though he'd had two older sisters. That was why he'd spent half his childhood in children's homes. After this clarifying conversation, Fasch broke off relations with his mother.

The tiresome whistling sound, Fasch was told by a neurologist by the name of Rosenheimer, was not coming through the wall. It was tinnitus, a disorder of auditory perception caused by his cerebral bleeding. This bleeding incidentally also damaged his visual cortex which, wonder of wonders, is situated right at the back of the brain—according to Rosenheimer that was why he was seeing double. Both afflictions were permanent, along with stiffness in his legs, a fifty per cent lung capacity and an eighty per cent chance of having one or more epileptic seizures in the next sixteen months. Rosenheimer was not a sympathetic person. Gisbert would have liked to talk to a psychiatrist, but psychiatrists are famous for not visiting hospital patients. Three weeks after the accident, he still wasn't capable of getting up by himself. His legs were no longer hanging in nooses, but encased in plastic sleeves. Only a trickle of clear fluid flowed from the drain in his chest.

Gisbert Fasch had never been happier. The knowledge that he was able to enjoy his new-given life with all the possibilities of starting over filled him with joy and gratitude, and made his pains and the ringing in his ears more bearable. He often thought about the man he had to thank for it. Next to his head on the bedside table was a box set of *The Sopranos*, which Henry had brought him and a letter from the public prosecutor's office.

From the letter he gathered there were proceedings against him on a charge of arson by culpable negligence. The entire contents of his flat had been incinerated. Electric curling tongs that had caught fire inside a Miss Wong-brand silicon doll were said to be the cause. It looked very much as if Fasch was going to be homeless on his release from hospital and then thrown into jail soon afterwards. If Fasch had read the underlined paragraph 'Cause of Fire' once, he'd read it a hundred times—he could have sworn he'd switched off the curling tongs in her groin before leaving the house.

There was a knock. The evening duty-sister looked in. Her slim face, her black hair with its pageboy cut, and the thick eyeliner over her expressive eyes all reminded Fasch of his ex, Miss Wong, and, night after night, stimulated his curling-tong fantasies.

'There's a visitor for you,' the sister said.

*

Jenssen came into the room with an unusually large briefcase. Gisbert's heart missed a beat, but then he realised that this case was black, not brown like his. The policeman in the corduroy jacket introduced himself in a friendly way, showed Fasch his badge, and placed the briefcase on the table behind him against the wall. This poor fellow has not got any health insurance, and yet he can afford a private room, Jenssen thought. With his powerful hand he pushed aside the white curtain to cast a glance out over the magnificent park. Then he looked around appreciatively.

'Nice room you've got here.'

This empty phrase might have been a polite prelude to particularly bad news or was it the start of an entirely new topic? At any rate, it was unusually personal for a policeman he didn't know from Adam.

'May I see your ID again?' Fasch asked.

Jenssen obliged.

'Herr Fasch, you don't have to say anything if you don't want to. This isn't a formal interview, and I'm not here because of the fire in your flat either. I'd like to ask you some questions about your road accident.'

Fasch squinted past the man's broad shoulders at the black case on the table. 'You don't have my notes in there, by any chance?'

Jenssen smiled slyly. 'My colleagues from accident investigations found these documents in the wreck of your car.' Jenssen opened the briefcase and handed Fasch an envelope half a centimetre thick. Fasch tore it open. To his disappointment it contained only a Moreany Publishing House catalogue, the photocopy of a 1979 register of names from Saint Renata and a few photo clippings of Henry. One of them was the magazine picture of Henry and his wife on the sofa. Fasch had circled Henry's likeness with a felt-tip pen, which in retrospect seemed ridiculous.

'How do you know Herr Hayden?'

There was no point in denying it. 'He pulled me out of the car and brought me to hospital. But you probably already know that.'

Jenssen nodded. 'How can you remember? You were unconscious, weren't you?'

'It's an inference. The man who brought me to hospital is the same man who pulled me out of the car.'

'Absolutely correct. How did he come to be present at the accident?'

'I can assure you,' replied Fasch, who was prepared for this question, 'that Herr Hayden is in no way to blame for the accident.'

'I believe you there. So he was there purely by chance?'

'Yes. You said this wasn't an interview.'

The athletic policeman cast a melancholic glance out of the window. He'd never get such a lovely private room if he were ever ill. 'I'm going to be quite frank with you. Only an hour after he'd dropped you off at the emergency department, we met at the Institute of Forensic Medicine, where Herr Hayden was to identify his wife.'

'She drowned. I read about it.'

'The dead woman at forensics wasn't his wife.'

'Why are you telling me this?'

'A few days ago, another woman fell victim to a crime of violence. A young woman at Moreany Publishing House who edited among other things the novels of Herr Hayden. Good writer, this Hayden. I like his style. Do you know him well?'

Fasch decided on a reply of moderate precision. 'Who knows anyone well?'

'But you're collecting material about him?'

'Not just . . . I mean, not any longer. It's all burnt, but you know that already.'

'I've been wondering'—Jenssen drew up a chair—'what interests you about Herr Hayden's past.'

'We were at the Saint Renata home together.'

'That was an orphanage?'

'Yes, it's quite a long time ago.'

'You're not writing any kind of biography of him, are you?'

Gisbert Fasch was only one answer away. They could have become friends, he and the policeman. He might have got out of the wretched arson trial and, together with the police, he could have hunted Henry down.

'At the moment I'm working on my autobiography by trying to get better.'

There was a brief silence. Jenssen didn't for an instant believe in a chance encounter between the two men. But he understood that this wasn't going to get him any further. The poor chap wasn't going to say a thing—after all, he owed his life to Hayden. That much was made perfectly clear in the admissions protocol. What was odd was that later at the forensic institute, Hayden hadn't said a word about his selfless act.

'Then I can only offer my heartfelt wishes for a speedy recovery.'

'Thank you.'

Jenssen took the briefcase from the table. It was still heavy. He held out his hand in goodbye.

'Is that all?'

'Yes.'

'My brown briefcase hasn't turned up by any chance?' asked Fasch as he shook Jenssen's hand.

'I'm afraid not. Did you say—brown?'

'Brown with a strap round it. About the size of yours.'

'Perhaps it was flung into the sea by the impact.'

'I'm sure that's it,' Fasch replied. 'It wasn't strapped in.'

20

Henry saw the figure from the kitchen window as he was carving the pheasant. It darted through the half shadow of the blackberry bushes to the barn. One of the double doors was shut but the other stood wide open. Poncho was lying next to him on the cool kitchen floor, perfectly still. He didn't seem to have noticed. Henry put aside the carving knife and climbed backwards over the prostrate dog.

It was the third time in a week that he'd seen the intruder. A few days ago, he'd spotted him in the distance, walking across the fields that belonged to his thirty-hectare estate. Henry had taken him for someone out for a walk who hadn't realised that he was trespassing on private land, as there was no fence or sign to bar the way. When he noticed that the walker was pacing up and down parallel to the house, he fetched his binoculars from the studio. But by then the walker had disappeared.

Two days later, he was on the drive, standing between the poplars only a hundred metres from the house. He was leaning against a tree and looking across at Henry as if he wanted to establish contact with him. It wasn't Obradin and it didn't look like that policeman Jenssen either; *he* was broader in the shoulders and blond. Nor could it be that poor soul Fasch who was still in hospital. Henry waved to the figure, but it remained propped against the poplar and didn't wave back. Once again, Henry fetched his binoculars; once again the figure disappeared.

Now it was in the garden.

Henry opened the door to the broom cupboard, took out the short axe, left the house by the veranda door on the west side, which was still in shade at that time of day, and crept towards the back of the barn. Poncho followed him, panting. Keeping his head down, Henry stole along the wall of the house and sought cover behind the stack of arm-length pieces of oak wood.

Swarms of midges danced over half-empty water butts that were quietly stagnating against the back wall of the barn. Henry clambered onto a rusty threshing machine that was covered in bird drop-pings with a scattering of rotten straw like a strange kind of wig. He swung himself through an opening into the barn. Poncho stayed put, wagging his tail, then tore around the barn, seized with hunting fever.

An old lamp swayed on a wire. Swallows had left their nests and were circling agitatedly beneath the wooden rafters. Now, Poncho came running through the open door, stopped and panted, raised his muzzle and sniffed. Henry waited, the axe in his fist. Without much interest, Poncho began to run to and fro, but in the end he cocked a leg and marked a post. Henry lowered the axe.

'Hello?'

There was only the will-o'-the-wisp fluttering of the swallows. Henry stretched out his arm and stilled the swaying lamp. The beat of the birds' wings must have set it moving. To Henry's right was Martha's white Saab. The paw marks of a cat showed up in the fine dust on the bonnet. Henry noticed that the driver's door wasn't quite shut. Half of Martha's face and the fingers of her right hand were visible through the side window. Her pale fingers were moving. Henry dropped the axe and backed away a couple of steps. The half-face opened its mouth and shut it without any sound coming out. Henry could feel thousands of little muscles pushing up every hair on his skin.

He stood like that for an indefinite period. It is well known that situations of this kind feel immeasurably short and endlessly long at the same time. Shyly, Henry raised a hand in greeting. The face behind the side window remained expressionless. The fingers felt their way up and down the glass. It seemed to Henry as if there was a weightless pitch-black cloth covering the missing half of the face. After the shock of the first sight had subsided, Henry closed his eyes and opened them again. The face vanished and then reappeared, together with the groping, handless fingers.

It wasn't Martha. The apparition was not complete; it didn't even look like her. It was an illusion and yet seemed as real as the car it was sitting in. Henry steeled himself and walked slowly towards the face in the Saab; it did not shy away. With a jerk he pulled open the driver's door. The smell of damp plastic rose to meet him. The interior of the car was empty. Poncho pushed his hairy head past Henry's leg and sniffed. 'There's nothing there,' said Henry softly and shut the door. He looked through the glass again. The face did not reappear. Henry took the axe from the hay-strewn floor and closed the barn door behind him. Just to be sure, he searched the loose soil by the blackberry bushes for footprints, but only found tracks left by Poncho's big paws.

With only a towel wound round her hair in a turban, Sonja stepped out of the guest bathroom naked. She came up behind Henry, who was back at the kitchen counter boning a pheasant. Gleaming on her wrist was the Patek Philippe that Henry had bought as a parting gift for Betty before killing his wife. 'Don't be frightened,' she whispered and wrapped her arms round his hips, pressing her breasts against his back. They had spent a wonderful morning. Together with Obradin, they had gone on a short cruise along the coast on the *Drina*. Obradin had barely spoken.

'Does anyone know what love is?' Sonja purred. 'Is there research on it?'

He didn't reply—just kept on hacking away with the knife.

'I wonder whether you can measure how intense it is, how long it lasts and what comes afterwards?' She drew away when she felt the damp heat of his skin. The shirt on his back was completely drenched. 'Goodness, you're soaked.' His face was covered in sweat too and an unhealthy grey. 'What's happened?' She wiped his forehead with her hand which smelt of rose oil. He put the knife down, turned round to look at her.

'My wife's sitting in the car.'

Instinctively, Sonja reached for her saffron-yellow silk scarf that was hanging over a chair back, stood up on tiptoe and looked apprehensively over his shoulder out of the kitchen window.

'Where?'

'In the barn. She's sitting in the barn in her car.' Henry grasped her upper arm. 'You can't see her.' He could feel her well-developed triceps under the skin of her arm. She's far too young for all this, he thought. 'It's just half a face and fingers without a hand. It doesn't look like Martha, but I know it's her. She's getting in touch with me.'

'It's a hallucination, Henry.'

'Call it what you will. I can see her and she sees me.'

Sonja was a whole head shorter than Henry. She looked up at him anxiously. A drop of water fell from a strand of hair under the turban and ran down to her chin like a tear.

'You're grieving,' she said softly.

How could it have been otherwise? Perhaps grief wasn't the right word, but he missed Martha. He missed her love. He missed her presence and nothing could replace it. But in all seriousness can a man talk of grief when he feels the desire for forgiveness and longs only for peace of mind and relief from his guilty conscience? Does a murderer even have the right to grieve for his victim? Betty and the baby were also in a place from which no one returns, and Henry felt no sadness. Shouldn't he, if he was capable of true mourning, grieve for the two of them as well?

'Come with me.' Henry took Sonja by the hand. 'I'll show you something.'

He pulled aside the heavy chest of drawers that was blocking the stairs to the attic. It didn't seem to bother him that it left deep scratch marks in the parquet. Sonja had never set foot upstairs. She knew that Martha had lived up there, and didn't feel the slightest desire to see her room, particularly as there were two bathrooms with a Turkish bath and various spare rooms downstairs, the wood-panelled living room with the fireplace and the studio with the picture windows.

'Do I have to, Henry?'

He didn't reply.

'Wait. I'll just put something on.'

Henry waited on the stairs until she came out of the guest bathroom in a dressing-gown. He held out his hand. She took it and followed him up the stairs into the darkness of the first floor.

She clapped both hands to her mouth when she saw the devastation in the attic. The ceiling under the roof had been completely torn open. Strips of blue plastic rippled like seaweed. All the dividing walls had been knocked down or ripped open, powerlines and water pipes had been torn out, insulation fibre was bulging out all over the place. Rain had come in through the broken tiles and the cracks in the battens, leaving ugly white stains on the walls and floorboards. There were long lengths of rafter lying around sawn into pieces.

'The place isn't quite as stable as it was. Can you hear?' Henry bounced up and down, and the floorboards creaked. 'They didn't used to creak.'

'Was all this you? Did you . . .?'

Henry pointed to the remains of a wooden partition. 'This was Martha's room. He was here first of all. Then he gradually crawled through the roof to the back until . . . Come on, I'll show you where he's hiding now.'

Sonja withdrew her hand. 'Where *who* is hiding?'

'The marten. He's still there, but I'm going to get him. I'll skin him and grill him and eat him and shit him into a hole.'

Sonja took two steps backwards towards the landing.

'A marten? You're destroying the whole house because of a marten?'

'Shhh!' Henry held up his hand and listened.

'I can't hear anything,' she whispered. She saw his strangely altered look, his outstretched hand. The wind rustled a sheet of plastic. 'That's the wind, Henry.'

Henry nodded. 'He's stopped. He knows we're here.'

'Let's go back downstairs, shall we?'

Henry looked at her in silence for a while. 'I know what you're thinking. I sometimes think he doesn't exist, too, or else I'd have caught him long since.' He rolled up his shirtsleeves and showed her the bite wound on his wrist. 'I almost had him. He bit me.'

Henry pushed aside a timber batten with the tip of his shoe. There was a small pile of reddish brown droppings with fine tufts of hair. Henry squatted down. 'That's marten shit. Can you smell it, Sonja? Tell me I'm imagining things.'

Sonja saw his lower jaw grinding. 'You need help,' she whispered. 'You can't get over this by yourself. No one can. Come on, let's go back downstairs.'

'Are you scared of me?'

She turned round and walked down the stairs. He watched her go. Sonja slipped off her dressing-gown and hastily began to dress. When she came out of the bathroom, Henry pulled the chest of drawers back in front of the stairs. She wanted to help him, to save him, but he went into the kitchen without a word to finish boning the pheasant.

* * *

The phone woke Henry from his afternoon nap.

It was Fasch calling from his sickbed. 'A Herr Jenssen's been here. He was sounding me out about you ... Hello? Are you still there?' Fasch was suddenly unsure, because he hadn't heard an affirmative 'mmhmm' from Henry.

'Yes, I'm still here,' Henry replied.

'This detective is from the homicide squad,' Fasch continued. 'He wanted to know if it was pure chance that you were at the accident—and why we know each other. I'm afraid you're in trouble.'

*

After Henry had sat down at his bedside, Fasch resumed the conversation. 'You know I followed you.' The curtains were drawn; books and newspapers were piled up on the bedside table. 'You waited for me around the bend, didn't you?'

Henry's expression remained amiably vacant. 'Why didn't you brake?' he retorted.

Fasch laughed uncertainly. 'You've already asked me that. I don't know. Perhaps because everything has to come to an end at some point. Be that as it may, we'd met before. You won't remember.'

Fasch noticed Henry shift his weight and cross his legs.

'Saint Renata,' Henry said softly. 'You had the top bed.'

Touched, Fasch screwed up his eyes. 'Only until you came along. But let's not talk about those dark times.' He reached for the lifestyle magazine photo. 'I know you lost your wife.'

Henry nodded.

'I'm sorry. It must be hard for you. She looks so nice and intelligent. Your dog's well?'

Henry considered the portrait, made no comment on the circle drawn around his head and laid the picture back on the bed again. 'Poncho. He's in great shape.'

Fasch felt for the switch to raise the head end of his electric bed a little. 'I don't know how I can ever thank you for this room and all that you've done for me.' Henry wanted to reply, but Gisbert waved him aside. 'There was a woman killed recently who edited your novels, Jenssen tells me. He's trying to find a link between my accident, your wife's death and the death of this other woman.'

'There is no link.'

'I can well believe it. But he thinks there is. When the police start looking, they always find something. I had a brown briefcase in the car. In it was everything I'd collected to do with you. This picture'—Fasch placed his hand on the photo—'was in the brown briefcase with my documents. Jenssen returned it to me and claims not to have found any bag. It's my belief the police have everything.'

'What did you collect about me?'

'Your past. Legal documents concerning your parents, all the children's homes, and then everything about your career as a writer. Whatever I could find.'

'What for?' asked Henry without a trace of indignation in his voice.

Fasch bent his upper body even further forward. The splints on his legs cracked softly. 'To destroy you, Henry. Because I was envious. Because I was a pathetic little loser out for revenge. Because I'd done nothing with my life, because I wanted to be like you, because everyone wants to be *something*, has to *do* something. I was so lonely that I spent the last years living with

Miss Wong, a woman made of silicon.' Fasch coughed, laughing, and reached for the water. Henry got up and handed it to him. Fasch drained the glass.

'I was so terribly envious of your success. Envy is worse than cancer. I've suffered, if that's any consolation to you. I wanted to harm you and to prove'—he had trouble getting out the last grain of truth—'that you hadn't written the novels yourself. Can you forgive me?'

Fasch sank back onto the bed. Now it was out. He closed his eyes in exhaustion and counted silently to three. But he wasn't speeding into the bend towards Henry; he saw only soothing darkness. When he opened his eyes, Henry was standing at the window looking out over the park.

'Was Miss Wong pretty, at least?' he asked.

'Pretty? She was *fantastic*. And her IQ was off the graph! Not any more though—she got burnt.'

'I'm sorry about that.'

'Oh, forget it. We hadn't had anything to say to each other for a long time. Speaking of which, I still have to pay off a loan on her.' During the fit of laughter that followed, a plug of catarrh came loose in Gisbert's affected lung tissue and got into his wind pipe. He turned blue. Henry rang for the nurse. The young woman with the pageboy haircut rushed into the room, put an oxygen mask on Fasch and lowered the electric bed again.

'You're supposed to lie flat, Herr Fasch,' the woman scolded her private patient, and she smoothed his bedclothes. Henry looked at her shapely bottom as she bent over the bed. She must have noticed his gaze because she stood up and smoothed her overalls. 'Do you need anything else, Herr Fasch?' Before Fasch could reply, she cast a glance of curiosity at Henry and walked to the door.

The two men waited in silence until she had left. 'Every time she comes in, I have a near-death experience. Miss Wong was a country bumpkin compared with her,' said Fasch and sighed. 'But at least she listened.'

'Gisbert,' said Henry, sitting down again on the chair at his bedside. 'What do you know about me?'

21

The area of low pressure originated somewhere over the North Atlantic to the west of the Faroes. Unusually for the time of year, there were rising columns of warm air and, because of the falling atmospheric pressure, cooler air was being sucked in. The first gusts of wind were getting up. Millions of tonnes of superfine water droplets were rising, turning to ice crystals and beginning to rotate anti-clockwise. The low-pressure area drifted eastwards with increasing speed. Only an hour later, the meteorological service for shipping transmitted the first gale warning to the Scottish coastal radio stations.

In the garden of his property, Henry had positioned himself next to a sweeping branch of the cherry tree and was pointing the 85-millimetre lens of his Canon towards the open barn door. He swatted the midges out of his face and waited. The figure inside the barn wasn't moving; it seemed to be standing in its own shadow. Nor was the body transparent. There were even individual fields of light reflected on it. As usual, half the face was missing. Henry pressed the shutter release yet again. As expected, the camera display showed a shot of the barn door and nothing else.

Henry had been sure right from the start that figments of the imagination couldn't be photographed, not even with state-of-the-art digital cameras, for the very reason that they are just figments. Only recently, he had learnt in the *Forensic Journal* that amputees who suffer from phantom pains feel relief when they wear a prosthesis. The brain accepts the artificial limb and stops sending pain alerts; it seems content with makeshift solutions.

He had acted on this admittedly rather simple-minded train of thought by taking photographs of his hallucination in order to convince himself of its non-existence. If my brain will just grasp what I already know, he thought, maybe these hallucinations will stop.

Meanwhile, Poncho was dozing in the shade like a Mexican level-crossing attendant. Now and again he opened one eye, in case something happened to pass by after all, and then shut it again. In his world there was nothing makeshift—only pleasant and unpleasant things. Henry placed the camera on the tripod, set the delay to ten seconds and turned around. He closed his eyes and waited with his back to the barn until he heard the sound of the shutter releasing.

On board the *Drina*, Obradin heard the gale warning on his mobile radio transceiver as he started up the new diesel engine. The barometer showed a fall in pressure of three hectopascals in the past hour. The cold front was already moving over the Shetland Islands. The storm with hurricane-force gusts was heading for the southern North Sea. In the course of the coming night, it would smash into the coast. Shipping to and from Stavanger had already been suspended.

The diesel started up, emitting a grey cloud of soot, and began to run steadily. Obradin checked the oil pressure and laid his hand on the side of the boat. The Volvo engine barely made the wood vibrate. A fabulous engine, thought Obradin, but no way had his wife won it in the lottery.

Meanwhile, Jenssen was attaching a nylon rope to a concrete bollard and carefully lowering himself over the reinforced roadside. He rested on a rock ledge, from which he was able to climb down further until he reached the crevice that held the brown object he'd seen from the road. He lay down on his belly and looked into the dark hollow. On the gleaming leathery surface, he could make out a metal fitting that looked like tarnished brass, and on it a handle. Triumphantly Jenssen stuck his muscular arm into the crevice; he couldn't quite reach the handle. He sat up, took off a trainer and sock, and tried to get hold of the bag with his foot. That too failed, because his calf was too fat for the narrow crevice. Above him he could hear the sound of a car driving round the bend where Fasch had come to grief. Cursing, Jenssen began to look for a stick. The sparse vegetation around the crevice yielded nothing, but he could see a dried-up bush about five metres away whose withered boughs seemed to be the right length. He wound the rope around his belly, pulled on it to check the tension, then swung out along the rock face.

Henry's phone rang. Honor Eisendraht's voice was husky with excitement. 'We've found your manuscript, Herr Hayden, we've found it!'

Henry put the Canon on the ground. 'Where?'

'On this little memory stick in Betty's office. Imagine. The police only opened the office again this morning. The stick was in a glass dish on her desk. She digitalised your manuscript page by page. We're all over the moon—Moreany in particular. He's making a special trip into the office. *White Darkness*— is that the title?'

Henry bit his lip, and rubbed an earlobe. 'The working title. You've saved my life, Honor,' he exulted as best he could. 'That's marvellous news.' With a glance over his shoulder, he looked into the barn. The phantom had vanished.

'I'm so happy for you, Herr Hayden. I'll get it printed out straight away if that's all right with you.'

'No!' Henry yelled. 'Wait till I come.' He made a plan. 'I'll come round this evening. As soon as I've seen off my visitor here.'

Honor hesitated. 'You weren't thinking of driving in the storm, were you, Herr Hayden?'

'What storm?'

* * *

The bag was moving. Carefully, Jenssen pulled on the small branch whose bent tip was hooked into the brass fitting. Sweat was pouring into his eyes. He took no notice of an extremely rare lizard climbing over the stones. Then the branch snapped. 'Shit!' Jenssen bellowed. 'Shit, shit, shit!' The policeman threw the broken stick into the crevice and thumped his fist on the stone. It had taken him a quarter of an hour to tear off that gnarled old bough. Although it was long since dead, it had resisted with every last one of its withered fibres—only to snap now like candy floss.

Jenssen removed his shirt and felt the cold air coming off the sea. Dark mountains of cloud were gathering on the horizon. He pressed himself up against the sandy rock once more, pushed his hand into the crevice again, breathed out to gain another centimetre, grasped the handle and pulled the bag out. It was a lady's handbag made of artificial leather. The contents were entirely rotten. Dead insects spilt out and crumbled into dust in the wind.

Henry unscrewed the can and poured half a litre of Super 98 octane into the briefcase containing Gisbert Fasch's documents. He closed the can again, set it down, struck a match. The wind blew it out. The fourth match was the first to burn properly. With a dull bang the bag ignited and emitted thick black smoke. He watched until the leather darkened; gusts of wind made the fire hiss. The dog had awoken from its level-crossing attendant's sleep and was dashing about in agitation, barking at the wind.

Clouds were scudding over the roof and the blackberry bushes were being buffeted. Henry saw that the attic windows were open. The gale would complete the work of destruction that he had begun. *Can you guess how it ends?* Martha's last question was also a warning and more precisely a vision— that everything that is begun must somehow also come to a close.

* * *

After the devastating storm tide in January, fifteen years earlier, disaster control had been steadily improved. Back then the hurricane caught everybody off guard. It had lifted the fishing cutters out of the dock, swirling them up and piling them into grotesque rubbish heaps. It flattened the historic houses on the harbour and plucked chestnut trees like buttercups from outside the parish hall. Torrents of water had surged through the town like a winding sheet, ploughing the streets and sweeping away the gravestones from the little cemetery.

The last windows of the main street were being boarded up with chipboard as Henry drove into town. Two hours before sunset it was already dark. Heavy rain had set in with gusts that reached gale force seven to eight. Men were having to hold on tight as they threw sandbags from trucks onto front doorsteps. Henry stopped at the road block where Elenor Reens was standing, dressed in the uniform of the voluntary fire brigade. He let his window down a little. Rain sprayed into his face.

'Do you need any help?'

'We need all the help we can get.' Elenor pointed down the street. 'Help Obradin's wife board up the windows.'

'Where's Sonja?'

'She's too young for you.' Elenor knocked on the roof of the car and waved him through.

Helga was struggling all alone outside the fish-shop window. She was small, and her arms were too short and too weak to fasten the heavy sheets of chipboard into position. Henry got out of the car; the rain drenched him instantly. He took hold of the board, turning it out of the wind. '*Where's Obradin?*' he yelled. Helga shrugged and shouted something he didn't understand. After two unsuccessful attempts they pushed the board into the brackets together. Helga snapped the iron bolt shut. Then Henry dragged his barking dog out of the car into the shop. Scared, and small as a pup, it fled into a corner and cowered there.

Henry noticed that the fish counter was empty and clean.

'What's going on? Where's Obradin?'

'Where do you think? On his mistress!' Helga wiped her face with the back of her hand—hard to tell whether it was rain or tears. 'That maniac's started to drink again. He spends his entire time on that bloody cutter fiddling around with the new engine as if there was nothing else in the world. He's going to leave me, I can feel it.'

The *Drina* was dancing in a veil of white spray, the mast listing in the swell like a metronome. The masthead lights and sidelights were on, and the motor was running. Henry kept his head down as he ran over the pier, so as not to be blown into the sea. Only two ropes held the cutter to tall wooden posts. Jets of water gushed up between the side of the boat and the pier. Henry reached one of the posts, clung on to it and crawled on all fours over the wooden gangplank to board the pitching and tossing cutter.

Obradin was lying in full oils beside the engine. A lot of water had already got into the engine room. Henry turned him onto his back.

'Cast off, my friend, we're setting sail!' Obradin mumbled in a drunken stupor. His lunch with a good deal of onions and lettuce was sticking to his face and chest.

Henry sat Obradin up, who at once let loose a volcanic belch. He slapped him in the face a few times with the back of his hand. 'Don't be stupid, come ashore. Don't make your wife unhappy.'

'What does she know about unhappiness? Tell her I'll be back tomorrow.' More water surged in. Obradin's eyes closed again.

Henry shook him. 'There is no tomorrow, you boozer. The hurricane's coming. You won't get back!'

Henry tried to pull Obradin up. With an effortless arm movement the massive man shoved him away, so that Henry went crashing into the engine. Obradin came to for a second, got to his feet, and clenched his fists. 'We're quits, Henry! You've given and you've received. I don't owe you any more.' Then his eyes rolled up and he collapsed backwards, ending up with his head lying in the water.

Grand last words. Henry weighed things up. They were quits. Obradin's death would eliminate that blasted residual risk, the devil in the detail, the thoughtless word, the mere nothing you forget, the trifling mistake that wrecks everything. Obradin would drown and the human factor would drown with him. No one would ever see any link with Betty's disappearance. Henry only had to leave the boat and let fate do its work. It hadn't disappointed him yet. But, instead, Henry loosened his belt, tied it round Obradin's torso and hauled him off the cutter. We'll have to regard it as one of those sporadic acts of goodness that Henry thought of as mere interruptions to human wickedness, and that inescapably lead to punishment.

The hurricane raged for two hours. The shipping alert came over the radio transceiver every few minutes: + + *Violent storm 10 to 11 in north veering westerly, Skagerrak west 12 veering north-easterly, decreasing 11 + +.*

Henry lay down in exhaustion next to the snoring Obradin on a camp bed in the parish hall where a kind of emergency hospital had been improvised. The outer walls of the building were strengthened with reinforced concrete, and windows and doors secured with aluminium blinds. They could have survived an air raid without even noticing. Occasionally, the earth trembled. Otherwise it was as dull as the waiting room of a doctor's surgery. Women whispered, men murmured, children wailed, dogs panted, and in between times the monotonous voice blared out from the radio transceiver . . . *Skagerrak west 11 veering north-easterly, decreasing 10* . . . It would have been a good moment to die, but he, Henry the Great, did not die—only others did that.

Dressed in her fire brigade uniform, Elenor Reens was distributing coffee and butter biscuits. Henry thought of Sonja and his dog. His eyes were drooping. In a blur he saw Elenor with her coffee pot and her goddamned kindness and generosity, her striving for happiness and justice, and that desire for togetherness that he found so incomprehensible. His trousers were soaked and his face was numb. Then he closed his eyes and was entering his parents' house. He climbed the stairs slowly, the way his father used to. He saw light under the door of the bedroom. He heard a rustling in the room, opened the door, saw the drenched mattress. Little Henry had tried to hide the wet sheets again. Behind his closed eyelids he felt anger. He grabbed hold of the boy, pulled him out from under the bed. 'Why are you hiding from me? Why aren't you in school? Why do you wet the bed every night? Where's your bloody mother?'

22

Here and there splintered rafters still stood out against the cloudless sky, hung with shreds of insulating fibre. The entire roof truss had taken off in the wind. Countless pieces of debris lay strewn about the garden. Timber, branches, leaves, splinters of wood, bricks, uprooted plants and a great deal of glass. In amongst all the detritus, Henry found the dead marten. The animal was lying between the bricks with a broken neck. Henry buried it to stop the dog from eating it.

Apart from the odd broken window, the rest of the building was battered but unscathed. His goodbyes had been made in instalments. First to Martha, then Betty and now the marten. There was no more reason to stay here. He would sell the house, no doubt at a bad price, but at a profit nevertheless. It was time for a fresh start.

Poncho ran about sniffing, wagging his tail in great excitement. The creative destruction of the gale had released some new and interesting smells. A bombed-out city with its aroma of putrid devastation must be an El Dorado for dogs. The gable wall of the barn had been blown in by the wind; parts of it had fallen onto Martha's Saab and put dents in the bodywork. The windscreen was shattered, and the driver's door stood open.

'Come on, get in, come and sit with me.'

Henry turned his head to where the voice was coming from. It was Martha's voice, as clear and gentle as during all the years of their marriage. It had never been loud and it wasn't loud now. Martha wasn't sitting in the car, which didn't really surprise Henry. After all, incorporeal presences can go where they like.

'I'm fed up with playing at being a writer,' he said quietly, but firmly, for hallucinations should be treated with respect, but not mollycoddled. 'It was what *you* wanted. I did it for you, I enjoyed doing it, but you no longer exist. I don't want to be a writer any more.'

'What are your plans?'

'Nothing definite. Bring all this to an end.'

* * *

Henry gathered from the local paper that the hurricane had wreaked considerably less havoc than had been feared. Among the insurance companies, the news went down as a red-letter day in the history of natural disaster settlement. One can only congratulate the shareholders. For the most part the storm had affected ordinary people who couldn't afford expensive insurance policies. A lot of fishing boats, some docks, school buildings and bridges near the coast were destroyed or damaged. Nothing of any significance to a multinational concern.

Under *Local News*, Henry came across the following announcement: 'On the stretch of coastline that was particularly badly hit, voluntary coastguards yesterday discovered the wreck of a car with a dead woman at the wheel. The homicide squad has already begun conducting investigations.'

So they had found her. Henry tried to imagine what poor Jenssen would make of it when he found out who the corpse had once been, and in whose car it was now sitting. He would presumably be astonished. Martha's decomposition was no doubt quite a bit more advanced than that of the fat drowned female body that Henry had seen in forensics. The storm would be ruled out as a possible cause of the accident.

Henry wasn't counting on being informed about his wife's death any time soon. It is well known that the police begin by looking for the most plausible explanation to help them come up with a strategy for solving the crime. Every crime is based on a matrix of invisible connections, but only the culprit has the key to the motive and the sequence of events. The search for a perfectly plausible explanation would take a little while and was bound to lead nowhere, in as much as Martha's death in Betty's car had been a simple mishap, an unfortunate chain of circumstances. A 'mishap' like that is beyond all logical reasoning. Long hours would then be wasted on trying to puzzle things out, amid growing frustration and annoyance. Only then would the investigators come to Henry to ask him for the most precious thing needed to ascertain the truth: the culprit's knowledge. Henry alone could clear everything up, and he alone was not willing to do so. This gave him plenty of time to prepare himself. He resolved to employ a proven tactic for keeping out of trouble: he would play dumb in a clever way.

Henry spent the days that followed clearing up in his garden. As he had predicted, nothing happened. He received an estimate on the damage to his house, informed the insurance company and got in touch with an architect. Then Claus Moreany died.

He died in a hospital in Venice. First, though, he married his secretary Honor Eisendraht on his sickbed and bequeathed to her the publishing house and his entire private wealth. She had his body flown home and his grave prepared in the Moreany family mausoleum. The funeral was to take place a week after his death. In the meantime, Honor Moreany took provisional charge of the company, until everything to do with the will had been settled. She continued to work from her dragon-tree outer office, where the Bisley filing cabinet housed those confidential documents without which no one can run a publishing house. Honor spared no time in giving up her small flat and moving, together with her budgerigar, into her late husband's villa, where the first thing she did was to get a pest controller to decontaminate the larder. Being a methodical person, she immediately began to sort through the tower-high piles of unopened post that rose up like stalagmites in Moreany's study. First, she sorted it in order of date of receipt, and then she opened all the envelopes one after the other using an Aztec sacrificial knife she had found in one of the drawers of Moreany's antique bureau.

Two days before the funeral, Henry Hayden put in an appearance at the office. He was wearing a dark suit. He kissed Honor's hand in greeting and invited her to call him Henry. They drank gunpowder tea and talked for a while about the deceased man. Honor told him how they had spent his last days together in the city of lagoons until his liver failed and he proposed to her in the Ospedale Giovanni e Paolo. Henry sat in Moreany's Eames chair and listened to her, deeply moved. He was ashamed not to have seen his friend and patron Moreany one last time.

Honor laid her hand on his. 'It was so quick and so many awful things have happened, Henry. Things we can't comprehend. The greatest gift for him was finding your novel again.'

'Have you read it?'

Honor nodded, smiling. 'I know you didn't want me to. Claus printed it out and took it with him to Venice. We read it together. It's a great book, Henry. It's great literature.'

'And the end? What did you think of the end?'

There was a longer pause. 'That was amazing,' Honor finally replied. 'I found it quite by chance in the post.'

She got up and went over to Moreany's desk, opened a drawer and took out a brown envelope. She pulled out a pile of typescript, half a finger thick. Henry recognised the font of Martha's typewriter.

'It was a very odd feeling reading *this*, Henry.'

She handed Henry the pages. He sat glued to the seat of the Eames chair, his ears burning. It felt as if a hot, wet cloth had been pressed into his face. In Martha's handwriting on the front page was a—how shall we put it?—a note.

Dear Henry, my darling husband, I'm saving you and saving this ending, because I could never bear to

314

leave you without anything. I don't know what has happened or what is going to happen today, but the bright colours which shone out of you from the day we first met are now granite-black. I'm frightened for you.

At this point we must pause, because Henry was sobbing so much that with the best will in the world he couldn't carry on reading.

Whatever it is that drives you to destroy the things you love, I have always felt exempt from your rage. You protect me, you understand me, you let me be myself. You have thrown away this beautiful ending to your novel in order to follow your demon to a shady rendezvous. I shall make sure it gets to you. I shall keep it for you and send it to Moreany. With fondest love, Martha.

We often have the wrong idea about things we've never actually seen. When we do finally get to see them, they are often surprisingly familiar. Honor had never seen a grown man cry. Henry cried long and hard, like a child calling for its mother. If Honor hadn't gently taken the manuscript from him, his tears would have made a watercolour out of it. She left him alone and closed the door to Moreany's office behind her.

When she had found the last chapter amongst Moreany's unopened post, late in the evening of the night before last, her first thought had been that it was a mistake, especially as Martha's note was addressed to Henry. But on the envelope, in her exquisite handwriting, Martha had written Moreany's private address. It couldn't be a mistake. To Honor's esoterically broadened intellect, the connection between Martha's disappearance and this lovingly sinister farewell letter was irrefutable. Martha wrote of ruin and of Henry's shady rendezvous with his demon; there was something disturbing about her note. Honor would have informed the police if she hadn't been the director of a publishing house and Henry Hayden its golden idol. The closing chapter of the novel was a blank cheque and as such it took priority over moral reservations. For that reason, rather than consult the police, Honor Moreany, née Eisendraht, consulted the Arcana of Tarot. The eleventh card fell from the deck—Justice. Well, there you are then. Some doubts are dispelled all by themselves.

* * *

If it is true that there are funerals where the mourners make a show of false humility and shocked grief, then it is often the dead themselves who are to blame

316

for this hypocritical play-acting: maybe they didn't keep the best company when they were still alive, or just met the wrong people. Claus Moreany was buried as he had lived: with respect, with pathos and attended by honest tears. A lot of people had gathered in the little cemetery on this overcast day in early autumn. Some three hundred mourners lined the path from the chapel to the mausoleum, many of them without umbrellas. The coffin was carried past them and at that moment it began to rain.

Within eyeshot of Henry were Jenssen and a few other gentlemen from the police. They were the only ones not dressed in dark clothes, which suggested they had come on official business. Why not? thought Henry. Today's a good day to talk about death. Between a couple of old plane trees stood Gisbert Fasch. He waved shyly with a crutch when their eyes met. He had put on weight, and hair now covered the shaven side of his head. About an hour later the last mourners placed their flowers on the coffin, then the procession moved towards the cemetery exit, where the convoy of vehicles was waiting to shuttle the guests to the wake in the Moreany offices.

'We've found your wife,' Jenssen murmured to Henry as he passed him. The heartless nature of this greeting must have become clear to Jenssen the minute he'd spoken, for he fell silent—or perhaps it was Henry's glare.

317

'Are you sure you've got the right woman this time?' Henry asked.

Jenssen's superior, the aforementioned genius of case analysis, butted in: 'My name is Awner Blum. I'm in charge of the homicide squad and I'd like to apologise for the somewhat brusque manner of my colleague.'

Henry came to a halt. 'You really have found my wife?'

'Not a doubt about it. I'm . . . sorry, but that's how it is. She's been identified.'

'Not by me, she hasn't. Is she dead?'

'I'm afraid she is. My condolences.'

'Where? Where did you find her?'

'*We* didn't find her. She was found. But maybe, rather than discussing it here, we'd be better off talking in peace down at headquarters, if that's all right with you.'

'Where is she?'

'In forensics.'

Honor Moreany left the head of the funeral procession to join Henry and the policemen. 'What's happened?'

'They've found Martha.'

Honor stared at the policemen. 'And you come *here* to tell us that?'

'We'll explain everything calmly at headquarters, Herr Hayden. It won't take long.'

318

Honor put her arms round Henry and gave him a big hug.

'Go along with them, Henry. Claus would want you to.'

Henry kissed Honor's hand and looked at Jenssen. 'Which way?'

'Over here, please.' The man walked away from the funeral procession to the side exit of the cemetery.

Henry caught the mourners' speculative glances. 'It looks as if you're arresting me. Is that what you want?'

'Not at all. Our meeting here is purely for reasons of convenience, Herr Hayden. We need your help. This is not an arrest nor a formal interview.'

They had made a public spectacle of him. They could just as easily have waited for him at the exit. Experts on police interviewing tactics might like to note that neither Blum nor Jenssen had volunteered until asked by Henry the information that Martha was dead. They had not told him where, how or when she was found. They had obviously decided to extract every last scrap of guilty knowledge out of Henry. Be my guest, motherfuckers, thought Henry. He was extremely well prepared.

Jenssen stopped when he saw Gisbert Fasch limping along behind them as quickly as his stiff legs would allow. He went to meet him and they exchanged a few words while Henry, escorted by the three gentlemen from the police, left the cemetery grounds and got into a white Audi A6. Fasch remained behind. Henry never saw him again.

23

They had nothing.

The merest shimmer of a hunch or the tiniest scrap of evidence would have made that pathetic intimidation ritual in the cemetery unnecessary. They had nothing, knew nothing, were nothing. They were just doing their jobs and they wanted results. Solving crimes is as difficult and laborious as committing them, with the difference that the lunchbreaks are paid.

'When's your new novel coming out?' Jenssen asked as they drove along. He was clearly trying hard to make amends with Henry.

'In time for the Frankfurt Book Fair.'

'May one ask what it's about?'

'Yes, you may.' Henry watched the symmetrical grey façades go past. It would be a long, tough battle. They had come four strong in order to register every movement, every word and every contradiction right from the start. During the fifteen-kilometre drive not another word was exchanged.

The red-brick wall with its topping of barbed wire ran for a whole block around police headquarters. The compound had served as a military barracks before the outbreak of the First World War, and the ensemble of buildings, walls and razor-wire fences still had something of the charm of a doomed siege. 'Saint Renata,' Henry said softly, as the barrier went up.

The 'meeting room', as they called it, was a gas chamber with vents. Henry saw coffee stains like mould cultures on the lino floor. In the middle of the room was a large collapsible whiteboard covered with a mouse-grey cloth. Henry sat down on an upholstered swivel chair and eyed the concealed item. Jenssen brought him coffee. This no doubt was Phase One of the inquisition—being left alone in front of the shrouded board. There is documentary evidence going back to the Middle Ages that just showing an offender the instrument of torture will be enough to break down his resistance.

'We have many answers for which we are yet to find the right questions,' said Awner Blum by way of introduction. Pretty slick, thought Henry, sipping his coffee, which was hot but extremely weak. 'You must be wondering why we've asked you here to our headquarters, Herr Hayden.'

'That doesn't surprise me, Herr Blum, but it hurts me that you're keeping the truth from me like this. What happened to my wife?'

Blum and Jenssen exchanged brief glances. 'The fact is we've come up against a mystery such as I have never before encountered in my career. We need your help. You knew your wife better than anyone else.'

'So it *was* a crime.'

'Why do you think that, Herr Hayden?'

'Well, here we are in police headquarters and you're from the homicide squad—or am I mistaken?'

'Not altogether. What is certain is that your wife didn't die of natural causes. But it could have been suicide.'

Henry looked across at Jenssen who gave a friendly smile and, like Henry, sipped his weak coffee. Had he woken up next to a woman this morning? Had he read the paper, taken the wet laundry out of the washing machine and made himself a hard-boiled egg for breakfast? Or did he prefer his eggs runny? What distinguishes policemen from criminals or civilised people from barbarians apart from the brutality of their instincts and the consistency of their breakfast eggs?

'I've already told Herr Jenssen that suicide was not an option for my wife. She was happy. We were happy. She'd never have left me on my own.'

Again silence descended.

'Is this going to be a quiz?' Henry asked. 'Am I supposed to guess what my wife died of?'

Jenssen put down his cup. 'You found her bicycle and swimming things on the beach.'

'We've already had that. My memory of it is beginning to fade, but, yes, that's where I found them.'

'Your wife didn't drown on the beach. She drowned thirty kilometres further east,' Jenssen continued. The men watched Henry process this information. Henry pictured the campervan on the cliffs and the naked British children throwing pinecones at each other.

'How is that possible?'

'We're wondering that too. Your wife was sitting in a car. She was still strapped in. She crashed off a sheer cliff in the car into the sea.'

Henry jumped up. 'That's not possible!'

'Why not?'

'Her car's still in the barn.'

'It wasn't her car.' Blum went over to the board and pulled down the cover with a jerk. 'This car belonged to Frau Bettina Hansen, your editor.'

The photos were in colour and terrifyingly precise. The Subaru in profile and face on. Eaten away by fish, Martha's body sat in the driver's seat, held only by a seatbelt. Her exposed skull was barely covered by shreds of skin, the fleshless mouth was wide open, the teeth perfectly preserved. Henry closed his eyes. Once again, the pictures returned. He saw her screaming soundlessly as she hit the windscreen, saw her trying to open the door and the horribly cold water entering her lungs. He saw Martha die.

The men let him take his time. He contemplated the pictures in silence, then he turned his back on the men and looked out of the window onto the bleak yard.

Eventually, Jenssen cleared his throat. 'An earth slide on the cliffs produced a shock wave which washed the car up to the surface between the rocks, in case you're interested.'

'Who did you say the car belonged to?'

'It belonged to Frau Bettina Hansen, your editor.'

Henry turned round and looked into the men's faces. They looked like deaf and dumb men hearing the Queen of the Night's aria for the first time. 'That's the answer,' Henry said quietly, 'and what's the question?'

'The question is: Can you, Herr Hayden, explain why your dead wife is sitting in the car of your missing editor?'

'I don't see how it's possible, no. Would you be so kind as to cover the pictures up again? It's very painful.' Blum cast a glance at Jenssen, who pulled the cloth over the pictures again.

'Did your wife and your editor know one another?'

'They'd met. At a cocktail party in the garden of my publisher—now also deceased.' Out of the corner of his eye, Henry saw one of the police officers put his hand in his jacket pocket without taking it out again. He was presumably switching on a hidden recording device.

'They sometimes went swimming together.' Henry could feel the atmosphere in the room gradually becoming charged. 'I never went with them. Martha told me that Betty was not a good swimmer. You must know that Martha's passions were swimming and hiking.'

Jenssen whipped out a biro. 'Do you mind if I take notes?'

'Not at all. We led a very—how shall I put it?—regular life. I write at night. That's when the best ideas come to me. In the mornings I sleep in. My wife would go swimming or hiking.'

'Where? Did she have favourite hiking paths?'

'That wasn't her style. She always made quite spontaneous decisions. She liked to take out-of-the-way paths where you don't meet a soul. She loved nature, solitude . . . Do you have a map?'

The men looked at each other, then Jenssen shot out of the room and returned shortly afterwards with the dart-riddled map. Henry watched as the officers struggled to spread the map out on the floor. He could see all the lines and dots on it. 'Just ignore the holes in the map, Herr Hayden. Do you know where your wife liked to go hiking?'

'But of course,' replied Henry, crouching down. 'She told me a lot about it.' He pointed to various regions. 'Here, for example—this forest here where all the dots are, she often went walking there. It's supposed to be quite beautiful.'

The detectives were getting into holiday mood. 'And here?' Blum pointed to the area by the cliffs.

'Martha loved the sea and had an excellent head for heights. She loved walking high up above the sea, right by the edge as it were—you couldn't look at her. I always wanted to give her a phone so she could reach me in an emergency, but she didn't want one. She hated mobile phones.'

'There's our mystery caller!' crowed Blum in the gents'.

'And that,' Jenssen replied, concentrating on establishing a stream, 'would make Henry Hayden the baby's father, the man leading a double life who's a master of disguise and knows all about location technology?'

Blum was already drying his hands. 'A successful detective, Jenssen, must be capable of abandoning working hypotheses. Think abstract. We were barking up the wrong tree. Now there are new facts coming in.'

Jenssen washed his hands, which he wouldn't have done if his boss hadn't been standing next to him. 'Why,' he asked, 'does she ring the editor rather than, say, her husband? What does she have to discuss with her? And why in secret?'

Blum reached out for the door handle. 'That's what we were born to find out. But not you, eh, Jenssen?'

When the two men returned, Henry had pulled the cover off the board and was looking at the photos again. 'I can't believe my wife crashed into the sea in *that* car. Are you sure it's Betty's? She told me it was stolen.'

'It is her car, Herr Hayden, and that question is very much on our minds too. She reported the car stolen, but couldn't produce the key. Of course she couldn't, it's still in the ignition, as we now know. She told the insurance company'—Jenssen looked at a document—'that she didn't want any money for the car.'

'That's odd. She told me about this man, this . . .'

Blum waved him aside. 'If the car had been stolen, she would have had at least one key.'

Thank goodness for that key! More than once, Henry had blessed the helping hand of fate, whose interventions are indifferent to personal status, to make small corrections that transform hopeless situations into victory ceremonies. He, who otherwise thought of everything, had not expected a trifling object like a car key to assume such significance. Or to be as helpful as it was proving in this case.

For criminals of every kind, and doubtless also for insurance frauds, this can only mean that there is no such thing as a trifling matter when it comes to fabricating stories. There are only details of equal importance to one another.

'We don't believe, either, in the existence of this mystery man you mentioned.'

'But she was pregnant,' Henry replied. 'Who's the father then?'

Jenssen was going to say something, but Blum interrupted him again. 'We hope you might be able to help us answer that question.'

'Help you? She didn't tell me who it was. Did she tell anyone? I don't know.'

'Didn't you ask?'

'Oh, yes, I asked her. She only said he was a dangerous man.'

'She didn't mean you, did she?'

Henry laughed. 'You overestimate me, Herr Jenssen. I don't know whether to take that as an impertinence or a compliment.'

Henry thought it was time to let the gentlemen into the secret of what had *really* happened on the cliffs. Awner Blum spoke the magic words that paved the way for him.

'So your wife and your editor went swimming together quite a bit.'

'That's right and wrong at the same time. My wife was my editor.' Henry paused for effect. 'She read every word I wrote every day. She saw things I didn't see. Without her, I wouldn't have managed a single novel. I think that was tough for Betty.'

'And what'—pensively, Blum formed a globe with his fingers—'what, if you'll allow me the question, did your Moreany editor edit?'

'Nothing. She wasn't competent. She was too ambitious. I didn't trust her. When a novel was finished, I'd take it in to the office. Betty only ever read the finished manuscript.'

'And what was she paid for then?'

A question that only a police officer could have asked. Henry smiled sympathetically, for what do bureaucrats know about literature? 'Please don't get me wrong. I have a lot to thank Betty for, if not everything, because she was the one who discovered my first novel, *Frank Ellis*—I don't know whether you've read it.'

'I haven't,' Blum replied, 'but my colleague Herr Jenssen here has. He's our bookworm and he's still waxing lyrical about it. Isn't that so, Jenssen?'

Jenssen nodded, embarrassed. Henry could see that the poor fellow hated being paraded as Blum's isn't-that-so-Jenssen dancing bear. *There's* a motive for murder, thought Henry. Go on, Jenssen, shoot the bastard with your service pistol and chuck him into the yard. You have my blessing.

'Now and again,' Henry continued, 'Martha would talk to Frau Hansen about how my work was progressing. Probably when they were out swimming. Betty would convey the gist of it to her boss Moreany and pass it off as her own editing. When I realised this I was outraged. I was furious. How *can* you pass off someone else's creative efforts as your own? But my wife just laughed and said: "Leave her alone. Everyone does the best they can. Everyone is good at something." That was Martha for you. She only ever thought well of people.' Henry looked once again at the photos of his decomposed wife on the board. 'Now I think that was a mistake.'

'You said your novel had disappeared. Now it's turned up again.'

'The novel was finished. The date of publication was fixed. After my wife had disappeared, I gave Betty the manuscript. She was supposed to take it to Moreany. She didn't. The manuscript must have been burnt in the car with her. Have they found out what happened to her yet?'

You'll never find her and you know it, thought Henry. Even he didn't know where Obradin had dumped her.

At last, Jenssen found the right question for the

large number of answers lying around all over the place. 'And how did you find it again, your novel?'

'I didn't. Honor Eisendraht, who's now running the publishing house, discovered it by chance. On a USB stick. Frau Hansen had secretly scanned the manuscript. I don't know why.'

24

The coffin was made of rough-hewn pinewood and very small. Four iron mounts were fixed to the sides. Henry had decided that his wife's remains should be cremated. Martha would not have wanted anything else. That way, nothing would be left of her but a quick blast of fire and then ashes. The heavy steel plate of the cremation furnace rose, waves of heat poured out, an electric conveyor belt shunted the coffin inside, the wood combusted, white light dazzled Henry, and the steel plate descended again. The fan started up, the computer-controlled furnace performed its automated work. Henry thought there was a certain reverential air about the whole process with its lack of all human involvement.

Martha's funeral took place not far from Moreany's family mausoleum. In accordance with the cemetery regulations, the undertakers carried the urn to a hole that had already been neatly dug out, edged with a square wooden frame and covered with a green mat of artificial turf. On the black granite stone was just her name without a date. There had been no death notice and Henry had not invited anyone to the interment; only he would see the urn disappear into the earth. It was an almost anonymous funeral. As Henry had never been interested in God or life after death, there was no priest present, and no one delivered a eulogy. A strange woman holding a watering can paused, then kept going to her dead husband's grave.

As Henry stood in front of the hole that now contained the urn, he was overcome by immense weariness and wondered what to do with the rest of his life. His guest performance as an author had come to an end. Sonja hadn't been in touch since the storm. She must have realised that there's no such thing as a complete life with a man like him, that everything remains a mere fragment. Henry had carried off the perfect crime, but now he was alone again. There would be no more novels published, no woman to wait for him, no child to come out of school, no one to welcome him home except his dog. Even the police would lose interest in him sooner or later. Henry was aware that he would leave nothing behind but a highly entertaining story of imposture—but to whom was he to tell it? The only thing left was to make himself scarce. The undertakers began to fill in the little hole. Henry watched them.

At the cemetery gate, Jenssen was waiting next to Martha's little bike. He had saved it from destruction, for the chronically jam-packed police exhibit room was being enlarged, and exhibits with no legal relevance were being destroyed. Henry didn't ask Jenssen how he knew about Martha's funeral. After all, a policeman is paid to know about the movements and activities of a suspect. You pretty much expect him to know more than you think possible. Together they loaded the bike and Martha's swimming things into the boot of Henry's Maserati.

'Have you found new questions for your answers yet?' Henry asked sarcastically as he shut the boot.

Jenssen ran his hand through his hair, and his shirt-sleeves strained over his monumental biceps. 'I don't understand you, Hayden. I've tried, but it's no good.'

'What is there to understand?'

'You lose your wife. You see those appalling pictures and remain calmness itself. You don't even cry.'

'If I cry, I can't see anything.'

Jenssen waved this aside. 'You save the life of a man who's evidently following you and don't say a word about it, but you pay his hospital bills. You don't even know the bloke. What makes you do it?'

Henry took off his dark jacket and threw it into the car. He took two steps towards Jenssen. 'You're a hunter, Jenssen. You hunt people. Why the devil don't you shoot?'

Jenssen placed a leg behind him and pushed his shoulders forward. 'I don't hunt people. I search for the truth.'

'*In me?*' Henry yelled in his face. 'There's no truth in me. The truth has been eaten up by the fish, the truth has been burnt up in the furnace, the truth is ashes.' Henry calmed down again. 'You think I'm a murderer. You'd like to hunt me down—and what do you do? You try to understand me. If you want to hunt, then hunt. If you want to understand, then start with yourself. But I can tell you now: You won't find the truth.' Henry walked back to his car again. 'If you call the deer, you drive them away. They don't come until they feel safe.'

Henry got in and started up the engine. Jenssen laid his broad hand on the roof of the car and bent down to him.

'Where is your mother?'

* * *

The estate was in the waking coma of industrial decay, which had set in when the big corrugated-iron factory shut down in the seventies. The afternoon sun shone on the west-facing fronts of the remaining houses. Most of them were already abandoned. Only here and there were chest-high hedges still growing and only some of the front lawns were mown. Parallel to the street, a disused narrow-gauge railway formed a boundary to overgrown fields and heaps of rubble and slag. Sorrel grew between the sleepers, along with the occasional birch and Virginia creeper.

The iron gate at number 25 was secured with a padlock. Behind the fence, bushes ran wild. The path to the house was completely overgrown. 'If you were interested in botany, I expect you'd find quite a bit here,' Henry said as he unlocked the padlock. 'You don't happen to have a machete on you?'

Jenssen immediately noticed the new, gleaming padlock. The men fought their way through the garden. In the high grass an animal made a rustling noise. Jenssen was struck by grass-covered heaps of earth.

'The brute lives there at the back.' Henry pointed to a low shed set among hazel bushes. Jenssen stayed where he was and shaded his eyes with his hand. The sun was noticeably lower at this time of day than when they'd first met in May. 'I used to play in there when I was little. The shed was my palace. *Beauty and the Beast*—have you read it?'

'I've seen the film.'

Henry continued to forge ahead to the entrance of the house, which was boarded up with massive sheets of chipboard. Burrs caught on his mourning suit, but he ignored them. 'Guess who I was?'

'The Beast?'

Henry laughed and pulled a key on a chain out of his pocket. 'I had a feeling you were going to say that. Beauty—I was Beauty.'

Jenssen wanted to ask who the Beast had been, but refrained. The lock on the chipboard was new too. Henry unlocked it and lifted the chipboard from the door. Jenssen felt for the Heckler & Koch in the holster on his belt and released the belt-strap over the weapon. The front door showed clear signs of having taken a beating and was split lengthwise. Jenssen recognised the remains of a faded police seal still stuck on the old keyhole.

Henry pushed open the unlocked door. 'You're the first guest for a very long time. Make yourself at home.'

Sun fell through the open door into the hallway. The rest of the house was in darkness. Jenssen took his LED pen torch from the inside pocket of his jacket. At the door the cement floor was still intact, but three paces in it had been broken up with a crowbar. Instead, there were planks left resting on the foundations and on old iron girders.

'I bought the house seven years ago. It was municipal property, hadn't been lived in all that time and was, as you might expect, pretty cheap. Like everything round here.' Henry picked his way across the planks like a cat. 'Watch where you put your feet.'

Jenssen shone his torch into the darkness between the planks. 'Is that a cellar down there?'

Henry stood still. 'The boiler room. Not brick— just clay and earth.'

Jenssen pointed his torch into a small kitchen. Here too the floor was broken up, even under the stove and, at every step, small insect shells cracked under foot.

'Do you want to see the stairs?' Henry asked from behind. Jenssen followed him through a room full of nooks and crannies that might once have been the dining room to a narrow staircase with banisters, not much broader than his shoulders. An old synthetic carpet was still stuck to the stairs.

Jenssen looked up. The stairs were steep and not more than three metres long. 'Here?' he asked.

Henry climbed past and turned to face him. 'My father landed right where you're standing now.' Jenssen shone the torch on him from the bottom of the stairs. As soon as he moved the beam of light, Henry's outline disappeared.

'You saw it?'

'I was standing up here.'

Jenssen let the light play up and down the staircase. 'That was the same day your mother disappeared?'

'As I said, for a very long time I thought my mother had just gone to live somewhere else. I waited for her. Here in this house. But she never came back. There was never any sign of her. It's over thirty years ago now.'

Jenssen climbed the stairs. 'You said you were standing at the top of the staircase. Why the top?'

'My room's up here. Come and see.'

Henry opened a little door. Jenssen stood beside him and shone his torch in. The floor was intact. The child's bed stood under a boarded-up window. The bed was neatly made up and black with mould and mouse droppings.

'My father came up to look for me. But I was hiding.'

'Where?'

'Under the bed.'

'Why?'

'He was very angry and disappointed in me. So he pulled me out from under the bed and asked me if I knew what the son of a whore was.'

'The son of a whore?'

'Yes, the son of a whore.'

'What did you reply?'

Henry laughed. 'As I said, I was nine years old. At nine you don't know what that is. I could imagine it was something bad. My father explained it to me. Henry, he said, very quiet and friendly, you're the son of a whore, because your mother's a whore. You're not my child. That seemed instantly plausible.'

Jenssen scratched his head behind his ear. 'And what do you think now?'

'Now I understand that he was angry with me, because I wasn't his child, and the discovery must have been painful to him. But I didn't know that at the time.'

'Even so, you call him father.'

'I have no other.'

'Why did he come into your room that night?'

'He came to get me. He pulled me to the top of the stairs. I clung to the banisters. He yanked at me with all his strength. Then my pyjamas ripped. They were completely soaked because I'd wet the bed. He lost his balance and fell down the stairs. For ever.'

'What did you do?'

Henry laughed. 'I went back to bed. Do you want to see the cellar?'

As they were fighting their way through the garden to the street, Jenssen stopped again. He placed a foot on a grass-covered mound of earth. 'What's this?'

Henry wiped the dust and burrs from his sleeve. 'Holes. I dug everything up—looked for her all over the place. But I never found my mother.'

They reached the car park outside the cemetery after nightfall. For a while they sat beside each other in silence, then Jenssen opened the door. 'Herr Hayden, do you know where Betty Hansen is now?'

341

'If I knew that, I wouldn't be here.'
'And where would you be?'
'At home with my wife.'

* * *

Henry Hayden disappeared without trace before the novel was published. Contrary to all expectations, the book did not become a bestseller. Critics described the ending as strange and distressing. A year after Hayden's disappearance, Obradin Basarić received a postcard from a stranger, on which was written in exquisite handwriting and brown ink: 'Better always alone than never.'